SURVIVAL IN ANOTHER WORLD WITH MY MISTRESS

NOVEL 5

WRITTEN BY **Ryuto**

ILLUSTRATED BY **Yappen**

Airship

Seven Seas Entertainment

Goshuzinsama to yuku isekai survival Vol. 5
©Ryuto (Story) ©Yappen (Illustration)
This edition originally published in Japan in 2021 by
MICRO MAGAZINE, INC., Tokyo.
English translation rights arranged with
MICRO MAGAZINE, INC., Tokyo.

Seven Seas press and purchase enquiries can be sent to
Marketing Manager Lianne Sentar at press@gomanga.com.
Information regarding the distribution and purchase of
digital editions is available from Digital Manager CK Russell
at digital@gomanga.com.

Follow Seven Seas Entertainment online at
sevenseasentertainment.com.

TRANSLATION: Elliot Ryouga
ADAPTATION: Harry Catlin
COVER DESIGN H. Qi
INTERIOR LAYOUT: Jennifer Elgabrowny
INTERIOR DESIGN: Clay Gardner
COPY EDITOR: Meg van Huygen
PROOFREADER: Jade Gardner
LIGHT NOVEL EDITOR: Nicasio Reed
PREPRESS TECHNICIAN: Melanie Ujimori, Jules Valera
PRODUCTION MANAGER: Lissa Pattillo
EDITOR-IN-CHIEF: Julie Davis
ASSOCIATE PUBLISHER: Adam Arnold
PUBLISHER: Jason DeAngelis

ISBN: 978-1-63858-993-8
Printed in Canada
First Printing: May 2023
10 9 8 7 6 5 4 3 2 1

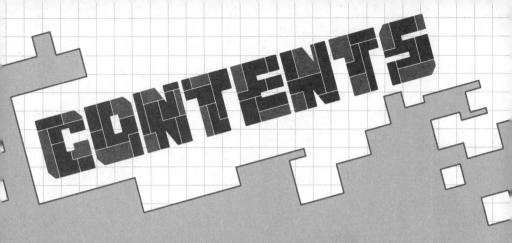

CONTENTS

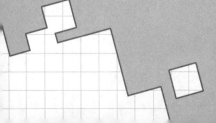

PROLOGUE

Survival in the Badland Ruins

9

HEYO, IT'S ME, KOUSUKE. Otherworld survivalist.

I've been through quite a lot lately: traveling with Melty through dangerous mountains, befriending the grand dragon Grande, relaxing back at the Black Forest with Sylphy, celebrating the surprise rebirth of Grande as a dragon girl thanks to her family acting out... But hey, I'm doing good today.

Man, though, talk about busy, right? It's just been nonstop trouble and commotion left and right. I guess I should be happy that I'm not bored. I mean, I do think things are moving in a good direction overall, y'know?

Play time is just about over. There's a lot we need to take back from the Holy Kingdom, and they're currently much more powerful than our Liberation Army. We need to come up with a strategy to take them down.

A logical, clearheaded, and effective plan.

"And so," I said, "I'm counting on the both of you, Professor Melty and Professor Ira."

"'And so' what now?" said Melty. "Well, fine. I understand."

I wasn't so foolish as to think I could come up with that plan on my own. Yeah, you don't have to say it. If it was left in my hands, the plan would just be me blowing everything to hell or something.

To be frank, if our negotiations ended poorly, the only plan I could come up with was to make an explosive block (out of magic jewels), target an area that would produce low civilian casualties, and threaten them like some sort of terrorist, telling them to heed our demands lest they suffer our wrath.

I knew myself better than anyone. Which is why I knew that outsourcing the planning to Melty and Ira was the right move. Effective, no?

"So, what are we talking about again?" Sylphy tilted her head in confusion.

We'd only just finished eating when I started talking nonsense to the girls. It was me, Sylphy, Melty, Ira, and Grande at the moment. The harpies all went to the public bath today, saying they'd sleep at the barracks for the night. Grande was buried under a ton of cushions in the corner of the room, sleeping.

"I spoke to Danan, Sir Leonard, and Madame Zamil earlier today," I said. "We're not doing so hot in negotiations with the Holy Kingdom, are we? The longer we take, the more time they have to develop a strategy to counter our harpy bombs. They have more territory than we do, too. If they decide to go all out and get reinforcements from the homeland, things are going to be difficult for us. That's why I've been thinking about what I can do to get us out of this situation."

"I see," said Sylphy. "So you want to talk things over with us?"

"Bingo. What do you three think about our current situation?"

"It's not very good, quite frankly," said Melty. "Just as you've said, they have more territory by far. The more time we take, the more at a disadvantage we'll be. Personally, I think we should strike while the iron's hot."

"I don't agree that taking more time puts us at a disadvantage," Ira put in. "Right now, Kousuke can produce new, mega-high-quality materials at a super low cost. That's drastically increased our technological abilities. We've also found a path forward to upgrade the quality of our equipment. It's true that we don't have many troops, but in terms of their quality, the quality of our equipment, and the breadth of tactical options available to us, we have the overwhelming advantage over the Holy Kingdom. On an open field where numbers mean everything, sure, we're at a disadvantage. But if we stick to defensive battles and surprise attacks, we can whittle down their forces, bit by bit. Of course, this all depends on having Kousuke at our disposal."

Ira wasn't against the idea of doing battle; she simply felt we could cut down our enemy by staying on the defensive instead of rushing things. It was clear she wanted to strike down the Holy Kingdom as much as Melty did.

"Sylphy, is it just me, or are they a little trigger happy?"

"Well, you know, Melty... Ira isn't the type to show any mercy to her enemies, either."

"Yeah."

Sylphy must've been referring to the fact that Melty was an overlord. At first glance, Melty looked like some ditzy, kindhearted older sister type. But in reality, she was a being with combat skills so incredible, she could make a dragon tremble in fear.

Ira was small and adorable, but her skills as a mage were formidable. She was also talented with alchemy, and she had once been a court mage. Basically, when it came to magic, she was an elite professional.

"If possible, I'd prefer we didn't just rush in and blow them away," I said. "I'd like to handle this politically and peacefully if possible."

The pair shook their heads simultaneously.

"Not happening."

"Nope."

"Whether or not the saint's Nostalgia-sect succeeds at strengthening their sphere of influence, we'll still have to fight if we hope to take back all of Merinard's former territory," Ira argued. "We might've strengthened our forces and successfully pushed back the Holy Kingdom, but from their perspective, we're still just a tiny, inconsequential force. They'll never agree to give our land back to us through negotiation. If the Nostalgia-sect gains influence, they'll help shrink the enemy we're up against, but that's it."

"...You said everything I was going to," Melty added with a frown. Ira snorted victoriously.

I opted to give Melty some head rubs, since she was tearing up.

Ira approached me. "Me too."

"Okay, okay."

I ended up giving her some head rubs as well. This, of course, meant that I had to do the same for Sylphy.

"...What is it?" she asked.

"Get over here!"

Sylphy let out a sigh but nonetheless came over to me for her head rubs. *Such a good girl. There you go.*

"So, uh, let's see," I said. "You're all saying we can't avoid combat?"

"Mm-hmm."

"Correct."

"Yep."

I decided to put everything out in the open. Being honest here felt like the right move, even if it meant me suffering somewhat. Healthier than keeping things secret, right?

"Quite frankly," I said, "I want to hurry up and meet with Elen ASAP."

"That sure was frank," Ira replied.

And Melty added, "You've got the wrong kind of courage, saying that to us."

Sylphy was quiet, but she pinched the side of my stomach. *Ow, ow, ow!*

"I also want to see Lime and the others," I admitted.

"Kousuke, you've got some odd kinks," Sylphy said. "Those three are way more dangerous than I am."

"For real?"

"If my father hadn't been forced to surrender after they took our citizens hostage, the three of them alone would have protected the castle themselves."

"I should've figured as much."

Those slime girls put me through the wringer, but they also saved my ass. I wanted to see them again and sleep in that amazing slime bed one more time. Once you got a taste of that comfort, all other beds felt inferior. What, was I being too honest about my desires? Better to be open about it than keep it secret and let it blow out of proportion. If I ended up going too far, someone could call me on it.

"Anyhow," I went on, "I wanted to talk to you ladies about what I can do to make those desires come true."

"We could always wring you dry until you don't have those desires anymore."

"You should really let your big sister dote on you more."

"Kousuke's mine. Mine!"

Melty had slid up to my right side and gently caressed my jaw with her hand, while Ira pulled up on my left and caressed my cheek. As for Sylphy, she knelt in front of me between my legs and looked up at me with tear-filled eyes.

"Okay, okay! Calm down, ladies. I know it's whack that I've come to you three about this. But if there's anyone I trust with every fiber of my being, it's the three of you. I'll take whatever punishment you want to dole out if it means getting your cooperation," I said, looking at all three of their faces.

Eventually, they looked at one another and nodded together.

"He said he'd take whatever punishment, right?" Melty grinned—or maybe it was a warm smile?

Ira nodded seriously. "He did."

"That's what I heard," Sylphy agreed, rubbing her tearful eyes.

Had I just dug my own grave? No. I was forcing everyone here to do something they clearly had trepidations about. The risk I was taking was nothing in the face of that.

"Then let's leave what we'll have you do for us for a later conversation," said Melty, "and agree to lend you our knowledge, since you seem serious about this."

"Er, I said I'd accept any punishment, not do whatever you..."

"Did you say something?" Melty interrupted me. "Accepting any punishment means exactly what it means. Don't tell me you're going back on your word after reducing Sylphy to tears?"

"Er, of course not."

How could I have possibly said no to Melty once she dragged Sylphy into the mix?

"Now, then, Kousuke, there's a limited amount you can do on your own. In truth, everything depends on how well the saint does on her end. There are two ways to support her. The first is to find old Adolist scriptures that support the Nostalgia-sect's stance. The second is to present you to the world as an apostle of God, then have you declare your support for the Nostalgia-sect."

"Huh."

"Revealing you to the world is very risky," Sylphy said. "If you're going to do that, I suggest it be a last resort. Doing it now would be far too dangerous."

"Really?" I asked

"Really," she affirmed. "Depending on how things go, the Holy Kingdom or the Adolists might send assassins your way. It would be best to do it after we free Merinesburg. That way, you can live in the castle."

"And let the slime girls protect me?"

"Precisely. Nobody's assassinating you with those three around," Sylphy said.

Ira nodded. She and Melty seemed to have absolute trust in the slime girls—not that I had any reason to doubt their combat skills either.

"All right, then let's start with searching for scriptures in the Badlands," I decided.

"Mm, that would be a good idea," Ira said. "I can help with that."

"Wait, what?" Melty protested. "That's not fair."

"Not fair at all," agreed Sylphy.

"You and Sylphy need to be around to run the Liberation Army from day to day. I'm part of R&D, so I have a lot more freedom. Plus, sticking close to Kousuke is good for R&D, and I can support his excavation work with my magic detection."

It was a perfect argument in Ira's favor. She was right that the R&D division in Arichburg could function without her, and while her healing and alchemy skills were useful, there were other alchemists and pharmacists in the division.

"We'd need a few harpies, Zamil or Leonard as a bodyguard, a few adventurers, and Grande."

"Grr..." Melty growled.

Sylphy held back tears. "Kousuke..."

"Sylphy, you just got back from a week-long vacation with Kousuke," Ira insisted. "Let me and the harpies have some time now."

"Ugh... You're right." Sylphy could say little to such a legitimate request.

"And Melty, you went to save Kousuke on your own and got plenty of time alone with him."

"Ugh... I guess you're right."

Ira pumped her fists in the air like she'd just won some kind of battle. Was this her victory pose?

"Then it's settled," she said. "We'll get things ready and head out in a few days."

"All right."

"But before you go, I think it's time for Kousuke to listen to our requests." Ira grabbed my arm.

"Um..."

"Give up and let it happen," Ira said with an alluring smile quite a bit different from her usual expressionless face.

I was screwed. Literally and figuratively.

I let the energy drain from my body in the hopes of saving some stamina. I would let myself become one with the waves... *Although I'd likely become one with someone else before that could happen! AAAH HAH HAH...hah...!*

CHAPTER 1

Off to the Omitt Badlands

THE NEXT DAY, I retreated into my shell. Spiritually, anyway.

"Here, Kousuke. Say *aaah*."

"..."

I stared at the impaled wiener that Sylphy had thrust at me, then looked up into her face.

"Now, now. Aren't you gonna listen to your big sister?"

"...Aaah."

Incapable of resisting Sylphy's smile, I opened my mouth, allowing her to happily thrust the wiener into it... Hahaha, it was real salty.

"I'm next, Kousuke."

With a smile on her face, Melty took a small piece of bread and brought it close to my lips. At this point, I understood all too well that resistance was futile, so I simply accepted the bread into my mouth. Heh, it was so fluffy and delicious.

"Thanks, Big Sis Melty."

"Hee hee hee..."

When I thanked her, Melty offered me her brightest smile. Amidst all of this was a single cyclops girl who watched us with a grin.

"Ira..." I called out to her.

"Big Sis Ira," she corrected me.

"Big Sis Ira..."

"Yes?"

"Can I get a little help?"

"Nope. Not until we're satisfied."

I groaned.

The night before, they'd doted on me to hell and back. Seriously. The three of them really went at me. On a physical level, it wasn't nearly as exhausting as one might expect. But emotionally? Psychologically? I suppose since they got me drunk, it was mostly an out-of-body experience, so it wasn't that bad.

The problems started to stack after I got up in the morning. The memories of the previous night came flooding back— countless shameful acts I couldn't possibly describe out loud! As time passed by, my soul took more and more damage. This was it. This was the end of Kousuke... And yet the three women were in such happy moods!

What about Grande, you ask? Grande was still sleeping under all those cushions... Dragons sure were something else! Once they got to sleep, they just didn't wake up! Honestly, the silver lining was that Grande wasn't awake to see any of last night's unmentionable activities.

Eventually, though, the harpies arrived and changed the course of history.

"Goooood morning!"

"G'morning!"

24

"Morning!"

"Heya."

Just like that, things became delightfully noisy, wiping away any weird brother and sister roleplay that had been happening up until then. Thank goodness! I knew I could count on the harpies! They were always there for me when I needed them most. I adored them!

"Good morning!" I greeted them. "Have you had breakfast yet? If not, I'll treat you to your favorites!"

"Oooh, ooh! Pancakes, please! With lots of cream and strawberry jam, too!"

The ever fearless, always joyful Pessa made her request with sparkling eyes. Right, pancakes. I'd feed her and the others as many as they wanted.

I whipped out a plate stacked with pancakes and cut them into bite-sized chunks so that the harpies could easily eat them. Harpies weren't particularly good with those kinds of things, but this way, even they'd be able to use forks to enjoy their pancakes.

And so the harpies excitedly began to eat their breakfast. Munching noises filled the room.

Without my noticing, Grande had mixed herself into the group. When did she even wake up? Wow, her sense of smell when it came to pancakes was something else.

After finishing breakfast, we took a bit of a post-meal break. The people of this world weren't particularly bothered by the flow of time. Farmers and merchants were a different story, of course, and people like Sylphy and Melty usually started working very early. But today? Well, today, we were all taking it easy.

"Kousuke's going to be heading out to the Omitt Badlands for a while. He'll be searching the ruins of Omitt Kingdom for old scriptures."

In response to Ira's explanation, the harpies went from loud excitement to complete silence.

Munch, munch... Grande, however, remained unmoved. Grand dragons were made of tougher stuff.

"As far as the traveling party is concerned, I'll be joining him, on account of my detection magic," Ira continued. "We'll also be bringing Grande, a number of harpies for sky recon purposes, Zamil as a bodyguard, and some experienced adventurers who can help us with our ruin diving."

An invisible shock wave coursed through the crowd of harpies and their feathers fluffed up. They exchanged glances with one another as if they were keeping each other in check.

"One harpy will report directly to Kousuke, then two to three harpies for recon. How does that sound?"

"Let me see... If you're going to be exploring the Badlands, that means Kousuke will be making raised floor temporary housing at night, right?" asked Pirna.

"Very likely."

"In that case, you won't have to be too on guard during the evenings. I'd say bringing at least one girl with good night vision would be a wise idea."

Pirna often managed the entire group of harpies, and now she was casting her gaze at two girls who had good night vision. One was a small, brown-feathered harpy named Flamme who had feathers on her head that kind of looked like beast ears. The other girl was Capri, who also had brown feathers but lacked the beast ear look.

"M-me or Capri then, huh?"

"So it's gonna be me or Flamme, eh?"

The two turned to look at one another and nodded simultaneously.

"Wh-what if we both went?" Flamme asked.

"We've got great night vision, but our vision's excellent during the day, too."

Ira made an "X" in front of her chest and shook her head. "Not happening. Depending on how things go, we might need someone for night recon right here, so we need at least one of you to stay behind.

"Normally you've worked in sets of three," she added, "but we have to make sure nothing happens to Kousuke, so the squad will consist of four harpies this time. One of them will be either of you two, which means we need three more girls."

How exactly were they going to decide?

"Wouldn't Ingrid be a good choice?" suggested Pirna. "She ain't never spent that long on the field with the master."

"M-me?"

Ingrid widened her eyes in hesitation. She had white feathers and was a beauty with a kind of elegant aura surrounding her. Compared to the other girls, she had a fairly large body. She kind of reminded me of a swan, actually.

"Good idea," said Rei, the black-feathered harpy. "Aja would also be a good choice for the same reason."

"...?"

The brown-feathered harpy named Aja simply looked puzzled. Much like Ingrid, she was a harpy of a large bird species. She was also very quiet. I could barely remember ever hearing her voice, to be honest. Aja had a sharp gaze and was quite the beauty.

"Who's gonna be the last one?"

"Hrmmm, if Orio, Aigis, or Dikle were here, I would've recommended them, but they're off on a mission," Pirna said.

"Then we'll decide the final girl in a contest."

"That's what I like to hear!"

Flamme and Capri were talking things over, and the rest of the harpies, besides Ingrid and Aja, began to exit the manor. What were they going to do? Out of pure curiosity, I decided to follow them outside.

"How are we doing this?"

"Battle royale."

"That'd be fairest."

"I'm not losing today!"

There was one spot left, and the harpies competing for it were the blue-feathered Pirna, the purple-feathered Fronte, the pink-feathered Bron, the orange-feathered Fich, the black-feathered Rei, the red-feathered Shou, the brown-feathered Pessa, and the green-feathered Toch. Seven harpies in total, all smaller bird types of a similar size.

"Harpies, fly!"

At Pirna's shout, a massive gust of wind exploded from the ground, and all seven harpies took off into the sky. After circling the manor a few times, they formed a ring in the sky. Suddenly, the ring fell apart and the harpies began chasing one another in different directions. It was hard to follow them, almost like watching a bunch of jets in a dogfight.

"How do they decide the winner?" I asked.

"If you manage to land a physical or magical attack from behind, you win," another harpy told me.

"Wow."

"Hrm... Not bad," Grande remarked, keeping her eyes on the battle happening above us.

Her tone was a wee bit condescending, but that was understandable. She was definitely faster when flying in a straight line. I didn't think she was capable of the kind of zigzagging the harpies were doing, though.

We watched for a while, until harpies began to descend to the ground; probably the losers. Eventually, the only one left was...

"I did it!"

Pirna posed proudly as she descended from the sky. I supposed her winning made sense, considering she was kind of the head honcho harpy.

"I couldn't beat the captain..."

"She's so strong."

"I was so close..."

The harpies who'd been defeated were on their knees looking distraught, but Ira stepped in.

"We won't be leaving immediately; we have prep to do. Use that time and spend it with Kousuke as much as you can."

"That's a good idea. You're okay with that, right Kousuke?"

"I don't mind," I told them. "Just be gentle, please."

The losing harpies' faces lit up. Ira really was excellent when it came to these sorts of things; she was so considerate. Was this what they called "damage control?"

"I'll also step back while preparations are being made, so be gentle with the girls staying here, okay?" Ira instructed me.

"A-all right," I said. "I'll do my absolute best."

"Mm, thank you."

Ira looked up at me with a smile. Argh, Ira had such a motherly vibe, it was like nobody else could take her place. She may have been small, but in terms of maturity, she was probably the most adult of all of us.

"What kind of prep should we be doing?" I asked.

Melty raised her hand. "I'll handle getting the supplies and contracting the adventurers."

Yeah, that'd be for the best.

"Kousuke will be the one carrying supplies, right? But that also means it'd be bad if he got separated from the group. Everyone should probably have their own supply of food and water."

"I'll prepare golem communicators for the harpies," I offered.

"That'll be very useful," Ira said.

"I could also make a Grande gondola that can carry more than two people."

"That would be wise," Grande agreed. "I can only carry two people with your current gone-do-lah."

"Let's see. It'd be me, Ira, Madame Zamil, and a few adventurers riding, yeah? Would eight people be doable?" I asked her.

"That should be more than fine. I still have strength to spare."

"Gotcha."

Grande had told me previously that the carriage-like gondola put up too much wind resistance, making it difficult to fly with... I thought about making something a bit more aerodynamic, maybe shaped like a bullet. Either way, I'd try all sorts of things out.

Our destination was the Omitt Badlands. Our objective, the procurement of Adolist scriptures from before the teachings were altered. I was accompanied by Ira, Madam Zamil, a few adventurers, Grande the grand dragon, and the harpies Pirna, Ingrid, Aja, and Capri.

Grande and the harpies had it easy, since they could fly, but me, Ira, Madame Zamil, and the adventurers didn't have that ability. As such, I had to build a gondola that could carry us all.

"What a bizarre shape," said Grande.

"This is how it turned out after I took wind resistance into consideration," I explained.

Sitting in front of the two of us was what looked like a thick missile, of sorts. It was extremely aerodynamic, equipped with round glass windows. I also attached four wings for stabilization. I wasn't actually sure how effective they'd be, but hcy. Seemed like a good idea at the time.

No, I had to be honest. It looked like a huge toy rocket. For materials, I went primarily with wood, so that I could make it as light as possible.

There was a door on the back that we could climb in and out of, and in the center of the rocket-shaped gondola were eight seats, each with suspension springs to help prevent motion sickness. I wasn't sure yet if they'd work or not, so all I could do was hope Grande would do her best not to rock too much.

"I'm going to hold this while I fly?"

"Is it too much?" I asked her.

"No. Let me give it a try."

"All right. I'm going to put in enough weight to represent us."

I loaded in 50 kilogram sets of weights, eight of them to be exact, for a total of 400 kg. I then locked them in with seat belts. I did what I could to shave weight off of the structure itself, but I also didn't want it falling apart in midair, leading to our untimely demise. Keeping sturdiness in mind, the rocket ended up fairly heavy on its own.

"Mm... This is quite heavy. But..."

Grande took off her protection bracelet and slipped it into her skirt pocket. She was wearing a halter top and miniskirt. She'd had new clothes made for her by a seamstress in Arichburg the other day, while I was talking to Danan and Sir Leonard at the manor.

The reason nobody was home when I woke up at the time was because they were taking the cloth I gave them to seamstresses to have clothes made. Until then, Grande had no proper clothes other than her bikini armor.

Grande had large claws for hands and feet, so she couldn't wear anything with cuffs. And since she had wings, she needed to wear open-backed tops. Because she couldn't wear pants, skirts naturally made the most sense. She could also only wear string panties, but because she couldn't tie the strings herself, someone else had to help her put them on. *I wonder who helped today?*

"Mmm."

Grande grabbed the handle of the rocket-shaped gondola, spread her wings wide, and began to float up into the air.

"Ah, yes. This should be fine. Let me go fly for a bit."

"Okay, just be careful!" I called.

Grande flew off holding the weighted rocket gondola in her claws. As far as I could tell, she was flying just fine with it. Oh, and by the way, her panties were white. Her skirt was so short that it was impossible not to see. Not that it actually meant anything; there was literally nothing sexy about this.

"So, we're good as far as the gondola goes..." I said.

All that was left were the supplies and adventurers. We were probably going to be in the Badlands ruins for a while, so it'd be a good idea to create a small farm while we were there. I decided to prepare some seeds and crops to bring along. I stuck around to watch Grande circle in the sky for a bit, zooming to and fro. Before long, she landed back on the ground, and the two of us headed for the Liberation Army's storage.

"So, how're you feeling?" I asked. "Think you could fly long-distance?"

"If I fly for too long, my arms will get tired."

"Then let's take breaks along the way. I don't want to push you too hard, not to mention we'd all be dead if your grip slipped and the gondola fell to the ground."

The rocket was actually equipped with an emergency parachute to slow our descent, should that happen. We could activate it from the inside or the outside. Actually, I'd have to properly test that. It'd be real bad if it didn't open in the case of a proper emergency. *"Oh, gosh, it's not opening! We're dooooomed!"*

We left Grande's nest outside of the city, passed through the gates, and entered Arichburg proper. Eventually, we arrived at the storage facility, where Melty happened to be working.

"Yo, Melty."

"Oh, hello, Kousuke." She turned her horned head and smiled at me. She looked like a kindhearted goat demi-human big sister type, but those horns were actually the devil's horns. Shocking, right? "Have you finished running your tests?"

"The flight tests, yeah. I haven't done any falling tests yet. I didn't wanna put Grande through so much all at once, so we're taking a break, and I came here to put in an order."

"Oh?" said Melty. "For what?"

"We might be out there for a while, so I figured I'd bring some seeds and stuff. Then we won't have to worry about our food situation."

"Oh, I see. All right then, let me get what you need." Melty promptly pulled a notepad from her bag and began to write something with her ballpoint pen. Needless to say, I was the one who made that pen. One day I heard Melty complaining about how quill pens were so annoying to use, so I gave her this as a present.

She was absolutely thrilled and ended up ordering a thousand of them, and ever since then, she'd been coming to me with orders in the hundreds at regular intervals. It was hard writing on the type of paper most common in this world, but most found these new pens very useful. The only problem was that I was the only one who could make them.

Well, that wasn't quite right. Other people could make them, but it'd cost so much to mass produce them that it'd probably be unsustainable. I used steel, wood, and slime-related materials to make them. The slime stuff apparently functioned as a plastic replacement and as materials for ink. Slimes really were amazing.

"Oh, before I forget, how did the adventurer hunting go?" I asked.

"That's all done," Melty replied. "To go along with prepping supplies, I put out a request for three days from now."

"Adventurers, aye? What sort of people are they?" Grande asked.

"Dependable and trustworthy," said Melty. "They're people both you and Ira are familiar with, Kousuke."

"Wait, are you talking about Shemel and her girls?"

"Yes. Is that an issue...?"

"Oh boy, I'd better redo the gondola..."

Shemel was a red ogre, and the other two ladies in her party were... Well, one of them was also a red ogre, and the other was a cyclops ogre. Since they were all ogres, they were all tall and ripped. In other words, there were just a lot of them to go around.

"Grande, would you be okay handling more weight?"

"Hrm? I believe so. Why?"

"Our three adventurers are all ogres."

"Huh...?"

"Each of them is about one and a half times taller than me, and they're all super jacked women," I clarified.

"They sound heavy."

"Yeah, which means I might have to make the gondola bigger."

"Would it not be better if I simply found a way to transform back into a dragon?"

"Is that possible in three days?"

"If I try really hard, maybe...?" she said, tilting her head ever so slightly.

God she was adorable... Wait, that wasn't the point!

"I'll work on redoing the gondola, and you work at transforming," I told her.

"Understood."

"Um, I'm sorry, Kousuke. I didn't think this through enough," Melty said apologetically, but I shook my head in response.

"Nah. In terms of pure power and dependability, they're definitely the best choice. If anything, I was naive for not considering this possibility. The gondola won't go to waste, anyway, so no worries. I might be able to just modify it."

The current gondola would be more than capable of carrying eight people of standard height. That wasn't an issue. I could just modify the next gondola so that it could hold three ogres and three humans. It'd be fine, I was sure of it.

Well, it might end up a wee bit tight.

CHAPTER 2
A Sightseeing Flight with the Ogre Girls

39

IT WAS THE DAY before Kousuke got to modifying his gondola.

"We're here!"

"'Scuse us!"

"Pardon us."

"Mm."

Three large women, Shemel and her party members, dropped by Sylphy's office. The owner of the adventurer's inn where they were staying informed them of a job request that was waiting for them.

"Long time, no see! So, you've got work for us?"

"Correct. I want you to protect Kousuke."

Although Sylphy was right next to her, it was Melty who spoke, with a smile on her face that the ogre women couldn't read. The three of them went on guard instinctually.

"Melty, don't threaten them," Sylphy scolded.

Melty put a hand to her cheek and gave a pained smile. "I wasn't trying to, I swear..."

"If the job is just as described, we ain't got no reason to say no, but... Just to be clear, don't expect any of that political business from us, okay?"

"I know," said Sylphy. "And, well, erm, I suppose I should tell you why I had you come here today."

Shemel tilted her head. "What's up, Princess? You're not one to mince words."

As far as she knew, Sylphy never stumbled over her words, which meant there must be something complicated going on with this job. It put her on edge.

"Well, what do the three of you think of Kousuke?" Sylphy asked.

"Hah?"

"Er, what?"

"Eh?"

The ogre women raised their voices in confusion, and understandably so. Sylphy's question seemed to come out of nowhere. Plus, they'd been called to her office to talk about the job, not about Kousuke. What was going on?

Melty cut in. "Sylphy, you need to explain things in order, or they won't understand."

"G-gah, right... Um, we might be requesting similar jobs from you more often, going forward."

"Okay...?"

So how did *that* relate to Kousuke? The ogre women were puzzled.

"I can't talk specifics, but... Kousuke's skills generally shine best on the front lines."

"...Yeah, that's true."

Shemel nodded in response. She had seen some of Kousuke's talents for herself, so Sylphy's words certainly made sense.

"It'd be great if myself, Melty, Ira, or Zamil could be by his side at all times," Sylphy went on, "but that's not always possible. Which means he needs people he can trust to protect him."

"And that's us? Just to be clear, if I planned on serving this country, I would've stayed with the Liberation Army."

Shemel had returned to adventuring because she wanted the freedom it provided. The red ogre and the cyclops ogre with her both seemed to feel the same way, since they nodded along.

"We've known each other for quite a while, so of course I know that," Sylphy said. "You have no intention of throwing your newfound freedom away, right? It's just..."

"Just what?"

"What about supporting Kousuke...as one of his wives?"

"...*Excuse me?*"

Shemel was at a loss for words. Of course she was. She'd seen Sylphy and Kousuke expressing their love for one another multiple times, and she was certainly interested in the man, but she'd given up on ever trying to make a place for herself by his side, especially as a big, un-cute ogre woman.

"Wh-where is this coming from?" she finally asked.

"I want to protect Kousuke. All his wives do, but we don't have the power to do that on our own, which is why we need you and your friends," Sylphy explained, staring straight into Shemel's eyes.

It was this very gaze that made Shemel hesitate.

"I-I mean, this is just so out of the blue," Shemel said. "How can I possibly give you an answer? And what does Kousuke think about all of this?"

"Needless to say, none of this is set in stone," replied Sylphy. "Part of this job's objective is to see how close the three of you can get to Kousuke. Almost like a test."

"A test?" the other red ogre cut in.

Sylphy nodded. "Yes. But I don't want you to overthink it. Just interact with him normally. Ira and the harpies will be there too, and I'll make sure they know about this. Just give it your all."

"Okay," said Shemel. "How, uh, *close* can we get?"

Sylphy leaned back in her chair and thought for a moment before forcing out her next words.

"...I-I'll allow you to bathe with him."

"Is touching fair play?"

"...J-just touching."

"Can we eat him?"

"...You'll have to take responsibility for your actions if you do."

"Gotcha. If we do that, we do that knowing we're dead," the red ogre said jokingly as Sylphy shot her a sharp glare.

Meanwhile, the cyclops ogre watched on in complete bewilderment. Of the three women in the party, she was the one with actual common sense, and she was horribly shaken when her red ogre compatriot started chatting so casually to the commander of the Liberation Army, and in a way that might offend her to boot.

"Part of this job is to judge how well you can live with Kousuke while on the road doing your adventuring," Sylphy summed up. "Please don't think too much about it."

"It's gonna be real hard not thinking about something like this..." Shemel said.

"So, we just gotta do what we usually do, right?" said the other red ogre. "And we can touch him as much as we want? No problemo!"

"I wish I could be as carefree as you..."

Shemel and the cyclops ogre looked at their friend with exasperated expressions, which she brushed off, easy-breezy.

"Right...! Well, that's everything. Will you take the job?" Sylphy asked.

Shemel looked at her two companions, and, having confirmed their feelings on the matter, she nodded.

To put it simply, I was able to figure out the gondola problem. It was going to be a bit tight, but we'd just about fit everyone. As for the supplies, that posed zero problem.

Oh, and what about Grande transforming into a dragon?

"I couldn't make it happen," she reported.

"Aw, really?"

"I feel like I'm close."

"Oh?"

"Mm," she replied while stuffing her cheeks with pancakes.

Who could condemn such a happy creature? Who would dare make her sad? Not me.

"I mean, if we can't fly, we could always use a carriage, and we can walk, too. It'll take time, but there's no reason we have to stick to one form of travel."

"That's true," said Ira. She and our party's harpies were sitting at the breakfast table munching on pancakes alongside Grande. "We can take it nice and leisurely."

"Indeed," Pirna agreed. "Why rush?"

"More time for playing around, if you get what I mean," added Capri.

"..." Aja silently nodded.

After talking it over with one another, Flamme and Capri had decided it would be Capri who'd come with us.

"...It'd be a huge help if you didn't take your time," Sylphy said.

"Exactly!" Melty jumped in. "The faster you do this, the faster we can break out of this situation! So please move quickly."

"Now that I think about it, we could get there pretty swiftly, so if this trip ends up being a long one, we could always swap places, no?"

"Yuuup."

Compared to the group of girls who were all about "safety first" even if it took time, Sylphy's side was complaining about speed. *Stop! Don't fight over me!*

"Jokes about taking our time notwithstanding, safety first," said Ira. "If things seem bad or look impossible, we'll consider traveling by land."

"Absolutely," Pirna agreed. "Us lot and Grande are fine if something were to happen, but if Kousuke or Ira fell from the sky, that'd be it."

"Well, I did attach a parachute to the gondola, just in case," I whispered in between sips of morning tea. I'd tested the parachute after fixing the gondola, and it worked as intended. "But either way, it's not like I want to experience free falling, so if things look bad, let's just hit the road."

"Mm, leave it to me," Grande snorted, cream all over her mouth.

Gosh, she was such a mess. I ended up cleaning her mouth with a napkin.

"When you interact with Grande, you're so... Well, you're different from how you deal with us," Ira commented.

"Yeah", agreed Melty. "For some reason it makes me feel all warm and fuzzy."

"It's less like he's interacting with a woman and more like he's interacting with a child. Or even his daughter?"

"He feels so fatherly."

"It's not that complicated," I said. "Out of all the women in my life, she's the only one I have to take care of. You all have your acts together, so there's no reason for me to be like that with you."

Sylphy and the others exchanged glances. Then they started spilling their food, drooling out their drinks, etc. Yeah, not gonna work. They were being far too obvious.

"All right, let's cool it, okay?"

Ira growled.

"Why do I feel like I've lost?" I asked.

"Our chance is coming."

"Right."

"Have none of you any shame?"

"I prefer spoiling the master..." Pirna chimed in.

Sylphy and Melty wore disappointed looks as Ira and the others had what could only be described as an unsettling conversation. Okay, so Aja was a cool beauty, but she was a lot like Grande in that she made me want to take care of her. I'd have to make it a point to watch out for her during our trip.

Shemel and her team were waiting for us at Arichburg's southern gate.

"Yo, Master. Long time no see."

"Long time!"

"Long, long time. I'm looking forward to working together."

"How are you ladies doing today?" I asked.

"Not bad. This little guy you made for me has been great, too."

Shemel grinned and flicked her metal club with her finger, making a satisfying metallic noise.

Next to Shemel were her party members: a red ogre and cyclops ogre. Now that I thought about it, I never did get their names.

"Been a while, ladies. So, uh, I completely missed getting your names last time."

"Hrm? For real?"

"Oh, you might be right," said the cyclops ogre holding the big mallet. "We knew of you, so we just assumed you knew of us. My name is Tozume. It's a pleasure."

"I'm Bela!" the red ogre with the giant axe chimed in.

So the cool cyclops ogre was Tozume, and the one that acted like a stereotypical underling was the red ogre Bela. Noted.

"By the way, where's the horse and carriage?" Shemel asked. "Don't tell me we're walkin'?"

She stuck the tip of her club into the ground and looked around. She was never going to find a carriage no matter how hard she tried.

"We're not using a carriage," I told her. "We're also not walking."

"Bzuh?"

"Let's just head outside the gate."

I led everyone through the southern gate and off to the side of the road.

Madame Zamil tilted her head, resting her trident on her shoulders. "Sir Kousuke, if we're not using a carriage or walking, then...?"

"We're riding in this."

I pulled out the six-seater gondola from my inventory and set it down. It really did look like a toy rocket.

"What is it...?"

"A vehicle of sorts. I've already tested it out and it's perfectly safe. Trust me."

I opened the entrance hatch, where the boosters would be if this were an actual rocket, revealing the vehicle's interior.

There were six seats visible. Since Madame Zamil had a tail, one of them was like a stool, but hopefully she'd forgive me for that.

"...Uh."

"Now, now, just climb on in. Oh, for balance's sake, I need the three of you to sit one seat apart from each other. Also, as you can see, it's pretty narrow in there, so I'll store your weapons."

"Gotcha!"

Madame Zamil didn't seem fond of the idea, but the ogre girls were fully cooperative and handed me their weapons. Eventually Madame Zamil caved.

"Everyone other than Madame Zamil got your seat belts on?"

"Mm, yeah."

"Y-yup. All snug."

"Snuggy-snug!"

"Hey, so, what kind of vehicle is this?"

"..."

Madame Zamil seemed to have caught on to something, because she was clearly losing her calm. Hahaha, I expected as much from her! But it was too late.

"Grande, close the hatch."

"Aye," she said.

"And once you're ready, let's rock," I told her.

"But of course."

Grande closed the back hatch, and soon we could hear her above us on the top of the gondola.

"W-wait, don't tell me..."

"All right. Lift off, Grande!"

Grande let out a huge roar, and I could hear the wooden frame creaking a bit, and then all of a sudden, my insides felt weird. We had successfully lifted off.

"Grande, how's the weight?" I called out to her.

"Mm, no problem," she replied. "Harpies, stay with me!"

"You got it!"

"You might be a dragon, but we're no slouches either!"

"Be gentle."

What a heartwarming conversation coming in from the outside. As for Shemel, she was next to me trembling in fear, the blood drained from her face.

"M-master, please don't t-tell me..."

"Yup. We're flying. Just sit back and enjoy our little stroll through the air."

I shot her a smile. She responded by sucking in air, then letting out a terrified squeal.

"Glad to see you're having a great time," I said, laughing.

With Shemel's terrified screams as our background music, the dragon express continued its journey through the sky. Unfortunately, we were long past the point of no return. My ogre companion would just have to give it up.

CHAPTER 3

Preparing at the Badlands Base

"AIN'T NEVER HEARD Boss Shemel scream like that before," said Bela.

"Maybe that's the real her," Tozume mused.

A few hours after departing Arichburg, we arrived at the rear base that once functioned as our primary stronghold. Each member of the party stepped out of the gondola and took a big breath of fresh air. The base was located on a vein hollow that supplied infinite magical power and also powered the anti-magic barrier surrounding it. There were all kinds of magical tools that utilized that energy, improving daily life for those who lived at the base.

There were water wheels and magically powered processing machines all over the place, collecting ore from the nearby Badlands and modifying wood carried from the Black Forest. Elsewhere, devices that could collect the overflowing magical energy and convert it into magicite had been developed, as well as devices that could artificially transform metals into magically infused metals. Unfortunately, production on the latter wasn't going particularly well.

And how was Shemel doing? Well...

Sniffle...

"Now, now. I know it was scary."

"I'm starting to feel sort of bad..."

She was a little way away, in tears. Ira and Grande were seeing to her at the moment, gently caressing her head and back while she sat and clutched her knees. Ironically, even though the two of them were standing, they only reached the top of her head. Talk about a height difference, huh?

Actually, was it safe for Grande to use her claws on Shemel's back like that? Hopefully she wouldn't leave any scars.

"I never knew Shemel had a fear of heights," Tozume said.

"For really real," agreed Bela.

"It honestly never occurred to me."

The two of them seemed to have had no idea.

"Hm... All right, you ladies watch over Shemel," I said.

"Huh?"

Tozume and Bela watched in confusion as I dashed off toward the interior of the rear base. Ira and Grande were with them, so it'd be fine. I'd had the harpies go in ahead of us to do some info gathering, so I wanted to meet up with them.

"You really can't just go running off like that out of nowhere." Madame Zamil had followed behind me, upset.

"Oops. Man, I'm sorry." I just couldn't stand to be there and watch Shemel cry like that, you know?

"So, what is your next move?" Madame Zamil asked.

"For now, we'll spend the night here, especially given Shemel's condition," I said. "We'll wrap up our prep work and info gathering in the next two days, set our destination tomorrow night, and head out early the morning after that."

"Understood," Madame Zamil responded as we went over the details of the plan and made our way to the base's entrance.

"Yoo-hoo, passing through!" I waved breezily at the gate guards and headed through.

"You got it!"

The folks who lived at the rear base had taken refuge there early on, when the Liberation Army first got moving. Most of them still remembered my face, so I didn't have to go through any checks at the gate. Of course, the only people who would come in were the Liberation Army's transport squad (with guards), us, or elves from the Dark Forest. The guards were basically guards in name only.

But from a security perspective, they still had to be there. Some unknown traveler could always pop up.

After passing through the gate, I headed toward the central area of the base. Pirna and the others should've already been doing recon. Where were they now? Either the cafeteria or the gathering spot— somewhere with lots of people.

"Ah, Master!" Ingrid called out as I peeked into the cafeteria.

"Heyo, Master," said Capri. "Didn't think you'd come here yourself."

The two harpies were talking to some of the residents, farmers who had finished their morning work early and were taking a break. From the position of the sun, it was still a bit early for lunch, so they were probably going to relax inside until then.

"Howdy," I replied. "Hear anything useful?"

The objective of our trip was to find materials that the friendly Nostalgia-sect of Adolism (the one the saint of truth Eleonore belonged to) could use to face off against the primary-sect of Adolism. In other words, we were trying to find old scriptures, written before their teachings were modified.

Pirna, Ingrid, Aja, and Capri had headed into the rear base ahead of us to ask around and find out if anyone knew anything about such scriptures or the ruins where they might be found.

"Quite a few ruins have been discovered, but none have been excavated," Ingrid said.

"Diggin' up all that dirt is tough, after all," said Capri. "Plus, there are still gizmas around these parts."

"I see... Then, can you get an exact location on those ruins?"

"Absolutely."

"You got it!"

"We're gonna head to the gathering spot for now."

Leaving the cafeteria to the pair of harpies, Madame Zamil and I made for the next spot. The cafeteria was aptly named because it was just that, but the gathering spot was a bit less clear. It was where the head smiths and farmers, the leaders of the explorers who went out around the base, and the head of the folks who looked after the kids all came together to exchange goods and work. It sounded like kind of a stuffy place, but it was basically a place for talented folks to come together and share those talents.

"Pardon us...! Ah, there's Pirna and Aja."

As we entered the gathering spot, I spotted Pirna talking to the goat beastman in charge of running the rear base. Aja was extremely quiet, so she wasn't really suited for these kinds of conversations. That was precisely why she was working in a pair with Pirna, the leader.

"Hiya, Master," said Pirna. "Did you check out the cafeteria already?"

"Sure did."

"Oh, all right. Well, they're going to copy a map of the area for us."

"Now that's good stuff. Our exploration'll go a lot better if we know the lay of the land."

Trying to explore an area with no guidance whatsoever was the pinnacle of foolishness, not to mention a huge pain. Just having a map would be a huge help.

"No books have been excavated or anything, huh?" I asked.

"None... There hasn't been much progress on that kind of thing in general, other than the ruins beneath this base," the white-furred goat beastman explained apologetically. "Crossbows might be effective against gizmas, but excavations require days and weeks of staying in one spot, digging up dirt..."

"Gotcha," I said. "You don't have the time or effort to spend on that sort of thing, I get it. The people, artisans, researchers, and farmers are the main focus here."

"Yes, exactly... Former adventurers who live here have been drawing up maps, digging up supplies, and guarding miners and the like, but we've yet to get around to any ruins..."

"Hey, no worries. I took a good, long look at the folks in town as we came in here, and they all looked happy as heck. I think you've been going about things the right way."

"Really...?" The goat beastman wiped tears from his eyes. "I can't tell you how much that means to me. Thank you so much."

Aw, what a softie!

"Um, so, let's see," I said. "We'll be staying here today and tomorrow, then we're gonna go do some exploring. Could you set us up with two empty houses?"

"Of course," said the goat beastman. "As far as your lodging is concerned, Lord Kousuke, we've left it as is since you last used it, when you made this base. We've kept it nice and clean, so you can continue to use it if it pleases you."

"In that case, we'll only need one house." I turned to the others. "Ira, Grande, and the harpies will be staying with me, while Shemel, her girls, and Madame Zamil will be staying at the house. Does that sound okay?"

"Sounds fine," Madame Zamil replied.

"Great idea," Pirna added.

"..."

Aja simply nodded quietly. Apparently, that was fine.

"Then there we have it. Could I ask you to prepare beds and such?"

"Of course. It will soon be lunchtime, as it happens. What were you planning on doing, Lord Kousuke?" the goat beastman asked.

"Hm, wanna eat in the cafeteria, since we're here and all?" I asked everyone.

"Sure," said Pirna. "I'm curious as to what they serve."

"It's important to know how the citizens live." Madame Zamil spoke as though she were giving advice to royalty.

"Just to be clear, I'm a normal citizen too," I said.

"Ha ha ha ha, surely you jest," laughed the goat beastman.

"Sir Kousuke's anything but normal," said Madame Zamil.

"I also don't think you're particularly normal, Master," Pirna agreed.

They all immediately called me out. *Why???*

"Oh, by the way, I have supplies and materials from Arichburg," I said. "Once we finish eating, I wanna drop this stuff off. Also, I'd like to get a read on where any possible ruins might be, so could you do some information gathering?"

The goat beastman nodded. "Of course. I'll get in touch with the manager of the storage facility. As for information on the ruins, I'll let the person in charge of doing the patrols outside know."

"Thanks. We'll be heading for the cafeteria, then."

"Right. I'll make sure your map is ready for you by tomorrow."

"You have our gratitude. Catch you later."

We parted ways with the goat beastman and left the gathering spot. Looking up at the sky, I noticed the sun was very nearly directly above us. Was it about noon?

"Pirna, sorry, but could you get Ira and the others and let them know to come to the cafeteria?" I asked.

"Absolutely. I'll be right back!" Pirna replied with a big smile.

She must've been happy that I was relying on her, because she looked thrilled when she flew off. Aja glanced in Pirna's direction, then back at me, unsure of what to do.

"Aja, you come with me to the cafeteria, okay?"

"..."

She nodded and smiled happily. She really was the quiet type, huh?

And so myself, the now-happy Aja, and the emotionless Madame Zamil (honestly, I could never tell how she was feeling because of her lizardman face) returned to the cafeteria, where we bumped into Ingrid and Capri.

"Welcome back! All done at the gathering spot?"

"Yeah. We're getting a map copied for us, which'll be ready tomorrow. Let's go over the info you two found and decide on our destination. Pirna's grabbing the other five right now, so I'll jot down what you ladies found in the meantime."

"Good idea! We might forget if we wait."

I set down some logs for seats and a wooden box near the entrance, away from foot traffic, and then asked the girls about locations where we might find ruins.

"So, there's something that looks like ruins in the middle of the northeastern Badlands, huh?" I said. "And some unnatural stone structures at the foot of a hill off to the east... And then to the west there's a large sunken area that could be a dried-up lake, with some building-like remains nearby that could be ruins from the past. Got it."

"Where should we even start?" said Capri, tilting her head.

The others were also pondering where to begin.

"It'd be amazing if we could excavate a library or a church or something," I said. "Sure would be nice if we had a map of what the place used to look like."

"If you're looking for the ruins of a library, I highly doubt we'll find one near water," Madame Zamil explained, very logically. "Humidity is no good for books or paper. Anywhere near the lake would suffer from frequent mist and fog."

She was totally right.

"I think you're on to something," I agreed. "Then should we hit the northeast or the east first? We might get our hands on more info in the meantime, so let's make our final decision tomorrow night."

Madame Zamil nodded. "That makes sense."

She was calm and logical. When I pictured her, I still first thought of her diving beautifully into crowds of soldiers with her spear, back when we were taking down the fortress. I'd assumed, back then, that she was more of the muscle-brained type, but I'd been wrong.

"I've brought everyone!"

It was Pirna, returning with Ira and the others. Shemel was... Yup. Maybe not back to normal, but at least doing somewhat better.

It was time to try out lunch in the cafeteria.

Our large group got in line and waited patiently until it was our turn to order.

"Looks like it's bread and some kind of soup on the menu today."

"Mm-hmm. Baked bread, and steamed potato and vegetable soup."

Pirna sniffed the air and tilted her head. "And it's not bread baked this morning. It's fresh."

"This base's facilities use the endless magical energy flowing from the vein hollow, so they don't have to worry about fuel," Ira explained. "In other words, they don't have to bake all of the day's bread in the morning, or multiple days' worth all at once."

"Oooh, right," Pirna said. "So basically, every time people eat, they get to have freshly baked bread."

"Getting to eat such soft, hot bread every day is a wonderful thing," said Bela, impressed.

"Can't say I'm too fond of how hard bread gets after a few days," Tozume agreed. "If you don't dunk it in soup, it's almost inedible."

Eventually it was our turn to order.

"Oh my, Sir Kousuke," said the server, an older monkey demi-human lady. "You'll be eating here today?"

"Yup. I figured it'd be good to see what everyone usually eats. Do you find yourself wanting for anything?"

She smiled. "Not at all. We can harvest lots of veggies, and every now and then gizmas come poking around, so we have lots of meat. As of late, we've been getting bantam birds and yams brought in from the Kingdom of Merinard, so I'd say the food situation here has been wonderful."

"Cool, very cool. If there's anything you feel you're lacking, get in touch with the gentleman in charge of everything and contact Arichburg, okay?"

"Of course. Thank you so much."

It would be mean to the folks behind us to chat for too long, so I loaded my bowl of soup and fresh bread onto my tray and headed for an open seat. Eventually, everyone else sat down around me, so we said grace and immediately dug into the soup.

"Let's see," Ira said. "We have dashin taro, skalion, carrol, dicon, cabbaj, and what's this… Gizma meat, I believe."

"Mm, probably," I agreed. "Dried gizma meat maybe?"

"Probably broiled. It's extremely aromatic."

"They modified the gizma meat so they could keep it for longer, huh?"

The soup was only lightly salted, but the stock from the vegetables and broiled gizma meat made it extra delicious. The dashin taro had the same mouthfeel as proper taro, the carrol had a similar flavor to carrots, the dicon was like black daikon, and the cabbaj was pretty much just red cabbage. The skalion was also, well, scallion. It was thicker and shorter than the kind I was familiar with, but the flavor and scent were the same. Aromatic vegetables were used in this world the same way they were used in the other.

"Mm, salted boiled potatoes."

"Yeah, delicious."

"All of these vegetables are filled with good nutrients."

"And there's tons of broth from the gizma meat."

The bread was fresh, but it was also just normal bread. That said, it paired wonderfully with the soup.

"This is all delicious, but how would you grade this meal in terms of food in this world?" I asked.

"Compared to the usual food in a farming village... It's like the feast you get during the harvest," Bela replied.

"Agreed," Tozume nodded. "Quite the meal, especially compared to what you'd get in Arichburg for five coppers."

"I've got a big body, but they went out of their way to make my bowl big and even gave me three pieces of bread!"

It was indeed true that the three ogres' bowls were larger than ours. Same with the bread.

"Being able to eat like this every meal would be paradise," said Bela.

"This is all possible because of Kousuke's powers," Ira put in. "Without them, these lands wouldn't produce any harvest at all, and nobody could live here."

"Mm-hmm," Madame Zamil agreed. "The defensive walls, the houses, the fields, and even the water system were created by Kousuke."

"The water and the fields are the biggest ones."

That made sense. The water source produced water infinitely, and the fields bore harvests rapidly. With steady food and water, people could live quite comfortably.

"Whazza plan after we finish eating?"

"Mm, checking our beds and equipment," I replied. We've still got time, so if we need to do maintenance on equipment, now's the time. If you've got something you need, I'll make it for you."

"Anything?" asked Madame Zamil.

"As long as I can make it, yeah."

Her eyes reflected a sharp light. Did I just make a fatal mistake?

"Then I'd like you to make me a short spear."

"Using *that*?" I asked.

"If possible. Shooting Star is too long, so it'd be difficult to use inside of a closed-in ruin."

By "that," she meant mithril. I could make as much of the stuff as I wanted, so it was no sweat off my back, but Sylphy told me not to make mithril weapons all willy-nilly.

"Would you be fine with mithril alloy?" I asked.

"Of course. It'll be heavier than using a pure metal, but it'll be much more destructive. That'd be perfect for a short spear."

"...Let me know by tonight what shape you want."

"But of course," Madame Zamil replied with a smile.

Yeah, her face was terrifying. It was rude to think that, but I couldn't help it.

"You're willing to make weapons?" asked Tozume.

"Armor, too," I said. "Though I'll have you work for 'em."

"What kind of materials are we talkin'?" Bela cut in.

"For metals, I have iron, pure gold, magisteel, and mithril alloy. I've also got a bunch of materials from the Black Forest, like wyvern and dragon scales."

As I explained what I had in my inventory, Bela and Tozume looked expressionless.

"Yeah, I understand that reaction, I really do. But this is what I have on me. It benefits me for you ladies to be as strong as possible, since that makes things safer for me. Don't hold back."

"Huh...? Um, for real? For seriously real?!"

"A-are you sure?"

"Yeah, absolutely. Actually, would you like me to remake that gold club of yours using magisteel? Or would mithril alloy be better?"

"...Mithril alloy is best known for its sharpness and viscosity, so it's not suited for clubs." Shemel had been quiet up until this point, but now she spoke up. "Magisteel would be best."

"Then I'll remake your club with magisteel," I said. I was glad she was finally in a better mood. "If there's anything specific you'd like for length and form, let me know."

"I'm fine with how it is now," said Shemel. "I'd be okay with it being a little heavier, actually."

"Got it. What about you two?"

"Mm, in terms of length and balance, I want it to be a lot like the axe I use now," Bela replied. "Er, for materials..."

"Mithril alloy would be good for sharpness, right?"

"A-are you sure you're okay with that, pal? I ain't sure I'm worthy of such high-level materials..."

"Then you'll have to work hard so that you are," Shemel scolded her. "Don't hold back."

Yeah, she was back to normal.

"U-um, I..." Tozume seemed unsure as well.

"So, about your weapon," I told her, "I have an idea. Since Shemel is in charge of dealing blunt force damage with her gold club, and Bela has slicing damage covered with her axe, I was thinking of making your weapon a piercing one. What do you think?"

"I... I don't know how to use spears," she said.

"I'll make it so you can thrust and stab with it, plus do blunt force damage."

So far, she'd been fighting with a large wooden mallet with a hammerhead, so I figured she'd be able to use a war hammer quite well. If I took the hammerhead section of her mallet and widened it, then made the opposite end sharp, she'd be able to use blunt force strikes as well as piercing strikes. It'd also be easier for her to use if I made sure its handle length and balance were the same as her current mallet.

"Mmm, I'm feeling it," I hummed. "Gonna rush through food and get cracking."

"I'll stay with you to make sure you don't do something crazy," said Ira.

"Then we'll do the rounds and keep gathering info," Pirna decided.

"We'll check each and every corner!" Capri agreed.

"I'll look over the security here while thinking up a design for my short spear," said Madame Zamil. So she was going to train the guards... Those poor guys.

"What should us folks do?" asked Shemel.

"I've gotta make adjustments on your weapons, so you're gonna be coming with me."

"Aye, aye!"

With today's business decided, we wrapped up our meal and went our separate ways.

◆ ⬡ ◆

"Now then, I'm gonna level up y'all's weapons."

"Level up?"

"Yup, yup. Come forth, workbench!"

Ira tilted her head as I whipped out my bestowing workbench, golem workbench, improved workbench, and smithing station, then set them down in front of the inn we'd be using today.

"That power of yours never fails to freak me out."

"Where'd all this stuff even come from?"

"You're better off not knowing," said Bela. "Your hair'll fall out from the stress."

I ignored her, pulled out a table, and put each of the ogres' weapons on top.

"Damn this thing is as heavy as ever. How the hell do you swing it around, Shemel?"

"I'm well trained, buddy."

"But it's not like your arms are that thick..."

Shemel was certainly larger and more muscular than me, but she was also perfectly feminine as well. She wasn't just some mega jacked woman. It was kind of mysterious, actually.

"Kousuke, you're looking pervy."

"I object. I'm innocent."

Of course, it *was* disrespectful to just stare at a woman's body, so I focused on my work.

"There's not much room for modifying your club, Shemel, which makes this simple. I just have to use magisteel for the materials... Hrm, that's boring. Want me to add something fun and interesting?"

"I don't need anything like that," she insisted. "I'm not dexterous enough to use extra features."

"Are you sure...? If you say so."

Using the golem workbench would make this fairly quick.

"What're you gonna do about your axe, Bela? Wanna widen the sharp bit a little?"

"Ah, that's a good idea. I'd love that."

"Then you want it like a bardiche... You don't want the handle too long, right?"

"Yeah. If it's too long, it'd be hard to use in the woods or ruins."

That settled it. Bela's axe was going to be a shortened mithril alloy bardiche. A short bardiche, to be specific.

"What are you thinking of doing with my weapon?" Tozume asked.

"Something like this, actually."

I drew a picture of the war hammer on the ground. One side of its head was wide and flat for blunt force damage, while the other side was sharp, like a pickaxe. A traditional war hammer, basically. The pommel was heavier than your ordinary war hammer, but a cyclops ogre like Tozume could handle it. Mithril alloy was quite a bit lighter than normal steel.

"I'm relieved it's not that weird," she said.

"Huh? Want me to make it all lyrical and magical?" I teased. "Is this the birth of the magical cyclops girl, Tozume? Hm? There's still time. I could make you a frilly pink magical girl costume. Eh? Hell, I could make matching costumes for all three of you, and you ladies can be Pretty Ogrecures. Hm?"

"I have no idea what you're talking about, and I don't like it," said Shemel.

"Leave us out of it," said Bela."

Tozume lowered her head apologetically. "I'm sorry. I was wrong. Please forgive me."

To be honest, I wanted to see the three of them dressed as magical girls. Were they really against the idea? Fine. I'd let them off for now.

"A magical girl costume... Was that what I wore before?" Ira asked.

"Yup! Want me to make a new one?"

Back when the girls did their fashion show thingy, Ira ended up wearing a magical girl-esque outfit.

"Want me to wear it tonight?"

"Oh ho ho... I like that idea."

Ira was going to cosplay for me. The last one I made was all frilly, so I'd have to do something different. Decisions, decisions.

"Anyhow, I'll get to work. I doubt there'll be problems, but if the balance seems wrong on any of the weapons or something, let me know. I'll make adjustments."

And so, work began on their weapons.

Now, then. I'd already put their orders into the queue, so all that was left was to wait for the weapons to be finished.

"I was thinking of dropping the supplies off at the storage facility while the workbenches do their stuff."

"Mm, I thought you'd forgotten for a second there," said Ira.

"Nah. We've got time before the workbenches run through their queues, so I figured I'd put in the requests first, then go drop this stuff off."

"Ah, okay."

I totally didn't forget until just now, so I really wished Ira wouldn't give me that look. It stung.

"Wait, you're all finished?" asked Bela. "Don't ya gotta start a fire and melt metals and clanky clank stuff?"

"With my skills, all I have to do is input what I want to make, and the facilities will take care of the rest for me automatically," I replied. "Amazing, right?"

"That skill of yours is picking a fight with every craftsperson in the world," Tozume said, turning her gaze in my direction.

Like Ira, she had one large eye. Where the two differed was that Tozume was a cool beauty, and because of her height, she was always looking down on me, which came with a helluva aura.

"Ha ha ha, right?" I laughed. "That's why you can't tell them about this. They might try to kill me in my sleep. Whenever

I need to create stuff en masse, I always hold back so that it won't become an issue for craftsmen all over. Or, well, I only go all out when it's an emergency, so it should be okay."

"What would happen if you didn't hold back?"

Bela tilted her head, unable to imagine such a scenario. I suppose without actual numbers, it wouldn't really set in.

"For example, right now I can make a steel sword or spear in under ninety seconds at one workbench. In other words, in an hour, I can create forty of them. With a single bench. Now imagine I had five workbenches. I'd be able to craft these weapons in a single hour. And the way this crafting skill works, I can have it running all day long. So in a single full day, I can create 4,800 steel swords or spears. If I added more workbenches, I could even make armor simultaneously."

"...That's legit terrifying. We wouldn't need smiths anymore."

"Right? And this is just talking about weapons. I can make bowls, frying pans, farming tools, food, clothes, and medicines the same way. If I didn't hold back, the people who make their livelihoods producing that stuff would economically die."

Plus the quality was stable to boot. No defective products. I had a real weapons blacksmith take a look at one of my steel swords, and they said that while it was far from being legend-tier, it was a high quality sword nonetheless, definitely above average.

What would happen if weapons of that level got mass produced? It wasn't hard to imagine.

"Kousuke is a considerate and compassionate man," Ira said. "He's a good boy."

"Hahaha, right? Praise me more!"

"Don't worry. Your big sis will show you lots of love tonight."

"Big sis...?" Tozume whispered.

"Ira's actually thirty-something or forty-something years old, y'know," Shemel informed her confused friend. "Twenty years ago, she was a court mage."

"For real?" Bela was stunned too.

Yeah, Ira seemed tiny, but she was a fully grown woman who was even older than me. She only looked and sounded young.

"I'm off, then!" I announced.

"I'll come with," said Ira.

"What'dya wanna do?" Bela asked Tozume.

"We'll come too since we've got nothing else to do."

"I'll wait here!" Shemel said. "Wouldn't want some rando fiddling with these behind our backs."

And so, Shemel volunteered to stay behind and keep an eye on things, leaving the four of us to head to the storage facility. Ira extended her small hand to me, so I held it, and we slowly made our way toward our destination.

Our hands were such different sizes that it was hard to hold hers like one would a lover's. Maybe that was why Ira typically just wrapped her hand around my index and middle fingers. This seemed to fit her best.

"It feels like they're showin' off to us, to be honest," grumbled Bela.

"Though you could say they almost resemble a father and his daughter... Eek!"

Tozume broke off with what sounded like a scream of fear the second Ira turned around to face her. Surely I was imagining things? Ha ha ha. Ira was a terrifying person when she was angry, so hopefully Tozume would be careful going forward.

This wonderfully peaceful atmosphere persisted until we arrived at our destination. A squirrel-like beastman, likely the manager of this facility, trotted toward us.

"Sir Kousuke, we've been waiting for your arrival."

"Sorry about that. We dropped in to check on the sleeping arrangements first. Here's the catalog."

I pulled out the supply catalog Melty gave me and handed it to the squirrel demi-human. This time around, I brought wood, refined metals, gemstones, spices, sugar, non-perishable snacks, alcohol, salted meats, and rock salts—all things that were difficult to get one's hands on at the rear base.

Metals could be mined back here, but the amount wasn't enough to satisfy demand, and there was always the danger of being attacked by gizma. And wood was literally impossible to acquire unless it was carried from the Black Forest; the Badlands were nothing but stone, sand, and dirt.

As far as nonessential groceries were concerned, food was prioritized, and even then, not in large quantities. They had just started raising cattle, but there still wasn't enough to meet demands. There were no places salt could be excavated nearby, so they were getting it transported here from the elves in the Black Forest or from the Kingdom of Merinard.

Refined metals, gems, and non-essentials could be used in trade with the elves of the Black Forest. I'd brought them with that specific purpose in mind, not that I knew how trade or commerce would work with them.

"You sure brought a lot this time!" said the squirrel demi-human. "I wonder if it'll fit..."

"We've got some pretty important and valuable goods to drop off, so if you want, I could always build another storage building for you?"

"If it doesn't trouble you too much, that'd be very helpful."

Ira, the squirrel manager, and I went over location and construction details, and we ultimately decided to expand the current storage facility rather than build a new one. Since it was a building I'd made in the first place, the process would be easy as pie. Usually, if you were constructing a building, you'd have to worry about the pillars supporting it and so on, but I didn't have to worry about any of that difficult stuff.

I knew from building in video games that used gravity as a mechanic that buildings could collapse if the weight became too much. But my skill wasn't like that. This was a comparably simple process.

"Thank you so much!" said the squirrel manager. "We should have no problems now."

"Order the shelving and stuff from craftsmen, okay?"

"Understood!"

The squirrel manager issued orders to a large bear demi-human, and I began to take out large quantities of goods from my inventory. The bear demi-human then carried said goods into the expanded storage facility.

"This is mad crazy," Bela said. "The storage building got bigger in less than thirty minutes."

"It's inconceivable," said Tozume. "You could probably be a hugely successful adventurer if you wanted to be."

Bela nodded. "You can carry as much stuff as you want, rebuild and fix weapons on-site if they break. You can even create safe shelter and good food on location. Any party would kill to have you."

"..."

Ira said nothing in response to the ogre pair's appraisal of me and my skills. I could heal folks, perform long-range attacks with firearms, and had other skills that were extremely useful for adventurers, but there was no point in telling the girls that. I wasn't planning on becoming an adventurer any time soon.

"Anyhow, all done for today?" asked Ira.

"Hrm, just about. All that's left is to head back and relax while we tinker with the new weapons. I suppose it's been a while since I made new outfits and stuff, too..."

"Magical girl clothes?"

"That included, yeah. I'll make something for Bela and Tozume, too. Dresses or whatever."

It looked like I'd shocked the ogres in question. That was exactly the reaction I was fishing for. Recently, folks in my circle had become used to my craziness, so they didn't react like that anymore.

"Say wha...? Dresses? For us?"

"Er, we're really not the dress types."

"You're beautiful," I told them. "And I'm sure you'd both look stunning. Just consider it a bonus for taking on this job."

"The bonuses from this gig could already pay for a new house," Bela replied with a grave look on her face.

I didn't know the market value, but weapons made from mithril alloy must've been worth a pretty penny given her reaction. There wasn't really that much mithril compared to iron in the alloy, but I digress.

"Now, now. Don't sweat the deets. You'll go bald."

"Seems kinda rude to tell a woman she might go bald, y'know." Despite how crude her tone was at times, Bela had a surprisingly serious personality. "I'm starting to understand the meaning behind what Shemel said..."

"Hm? What's that?"

"It gets exhausting commenting on everything, so it'd be better to just shut up and watch you do what you do."

"Ha ha ha, that damn Shemel. When she gets back, I'm going to make her wear a white, frilly wedding dress with lace and everything! And you two are gonna help me."

"Eeeeh?" said Bela. "...Fine, I guess."

"Sounds kinda scary to me, but also I kinda wanna see it," mused Tozume, "so I guess I'll help."

"Me too," Ira said.

Heh heh heh, even Shemel wouldn't be able to resist the four of us together. Time for our first fashion show in a good long while.

"Ain't magic kinda unfair...?"

"Nope."

Shemel had sent me flying, and so there I was, on the ground. Bela was knocked out with a punch, and Tozume had sand thrown in her large eye and was currently passed out from the pain.

Once we got back from the storage facility, I immediately made a frilly wedding dress and tried to put it on Shemel, but naturally she rejected the idea. That was when the battle gong rang and little ol' Kousuke was sent soaring! By the time I realized what had happened, I was flat on my back.

But even after all that—

All four of Shemel's limbs were bound by glowing bracelets of light. Her body was even floating slightly.

Ira's magic was *wild*.

"He was just trying to put you in a dress, and not a particularly embarrassing or humiliating one either," Ira scolded. "The fact that you responded with violence shows how narrow your heart is, Shemel. Quite frankly, you have a stick up your ass."

"So it doesn't mean anything that they tried to forcibly tear off my clothes and make me wear something I didn't want to?" Shemel protested.

"You really don't want to wear that dress?"

Ira stared at Shemel, who averted her gaze.

"Don't worry," said Ira. "Everyone's going to wear one, that way it won't be embarrassing."

I gave Ira a thumbs-up. This was perfectly fine with me, if it solved the problem.

And so, I did just that. Pure white, frilly, lace-covered dresses for everyone.

"Th-this really don't suit me..." Shemel had a tearful expression on her face.

"Nah, you look great, Boss," Bela assured her. "Less cute and more beautiful, really."

"I-I feel kind of uncomfortable..."

Tozume was fidgeting uneasily, but Bela seemed oddly fine. If anything, she was more concerned with how the other two were doing.

"Kousuke, how do I look?" she asked.

"Super good. Amazing, actually."

And then there was Ira. She was adorable. Insanely so. I could barely come up with words to describe her. Why didn't I have a screenshot function in my skill set?! No matter how hard I focused on pressing F2 or F12 or Print Screen, nothing happened. No shutter sound.

Dammit.

"I'll make some other outfits too."

"Mm, I want to try them on," said Ira.

"But what should I make next...? Ah, let's go with something that Shemel and her crew will look good in."

I whipped up some denim short shorts and cropped tank tops—outfits that exposed quite a bit of skin.

"This is way better than that dress," said Shemel.

"Ain't this tank top kinda short? Can you see anything from below?" asked Bela.

"This might be perfect for casual use at home," Tozume said. "Though I wish it was just a little longer."

"Kousuke."

"Let's just say this is incredibly easy on the eyes."

Swoosh, boom, yowee! The ogres looked incredible. The tank tops seriously emphasized their chests, and they had incredible six-pack abs. Goddamn.

How was Ira? Well, her smaller body was pretty enticing in a pair of short shorts. Her white skin was a sight for sore eyes, too.

"A normal length tank top looks like this," I said.

"Ah, I like it! I'd love a few, actually."

"Sure. You got it."

"Ah, me too!"

"I'd also like some."

"All right, five for each of you. Just make sure you wear the next set of clothes I make too."

Since the ogres were all generally the same size, I could make 15 of the same tank top. This was super easy for me at this point.

Next—

"It feels kinda tight once you tie the neck ribbon and button up the shirt."

"Could I undo two or three of 'em?"

"It really does feel kind of tight."

"Am I cute?"

"Adorbs!"

I had them wearing short-sleeved dress shirts with short pleated skirts. The high school girl style. This honestly felt like I was breaking some kind of law, but I kept that to myself.

Shemel and Bela immediately loosened their ribbons and undid some buttons like a couple of bad girls. Yeah, this was exactly what I'd hoped for. Much to my own surprise, Tozume didn't seem to hate the uniform as is and was wearing it like a champ. Yeah, she really was a cool beauty. She was like the cliché head of the disciplinary committee in a manga or anime.

As for Ira, well... Yeah, this felt illegal. This was supposed to be a high school girl uniform, but she looked like she was going to a rich girl elementary school.

No, this was bad. But it was also good. Help!

"Oh, I like this style. The fabric is tough and everything."

"You could blend into the forest with this."

"But you'd stand out like crazy in the Badlands."

"How do I look?"

"Cute outfits suit you best," I told Ira, "but you look adorable in this, too."

"Really?"

This next outfit was camo made from tough fabric. Yeah, the three ogre girls looked especially good in this. When Ira wore it, she mostly looked like a little kid in a costume.

"Um, this is kinda..."

"I-it's a little embarrassing."

"This ain't it..."

"How do I look?"

"You look so amazing that I'm wondering if I've died and gone to heaven."

Next I had the girls wear miniskirt outfits reminiscent of a certain lyrical magical girl. Today was the birth of the Triple Ogrecure magical girls!

Shemel was pink, Bela was red, and Tozume was light blue. I made Ira black. Sadly, Shemel and her girls seemed averse to these kinds of frilly outfits. Honestly, they looked adorable, but oh well.

"Y'know, I noticed you girls don't really wear much in the way of armor," I remarked.

"Hah?" said Shemel. "Ah, well, it's expensive to get armor made in our size, and if the stuff we wear is too heavy, it slows us down. Unlike soldiers, adventurers have to do a ton of long-distance walking, and we gotta carry our own food and drinks, too. Armor'd just weigh us down."

"Gotcha. Then all you need are clothes with protective effects on them!"

"Er, I'd prefer if you made something without so many frills. If I went into the woods wearing this thing, it'd catch on everything, I'd be torn apart."

"That camo stuff from earlier would be great. With all the bugs and leeches, it'd be good to wear something that covered skin."

"That's *boring!*" I sighed.

"Being an adventurer is full of excitement, but the jobs themselves can be pretty basic and harsh. We don't need the added excitement."

"'Tis a hard world out there... Ah, I know!"

I pulled a single piece of leather from my inventory. Well, it was technically one piece, but it was a massive one.

"Want me to craft you ladies some defensive gear with this?"

"Sure is big. What kind of leather is it?"

"Wyvern," said Ira.

"Huh, cool... Wait, wha–?!" Tozume yelped.

"We got attacked by them like crazy on the Sorel Mountains where we met Grande," I explained. "They were a real pain in the butt."

"Wait, did you take them down yourself?"

"Yup."

"Does someone who can take down wyverns really need our protection?" asked Tozume.

"This guy here is a real softy, so he's easy to trick and kidnap," Shemel told her

Tozume nodded. "He does seem naively kind. Stupidly so."

Meanwhile, I looked around us.

"...Actually, where is Grande?"

She was nowhere to be found. When had I lost track of her?

"...Now that you mention it, I think she was already gone when we were eating."

"Wait, really? Well, she's not a child. She's a sensible girl, so I think she'll be fine."

The people here were peaceful, so I doubted anything crazy would happen. But I was still worried.

"Um, what should we do? We should probably go looking for her, right?"

I fancied myself her guardian of sorts, so I felt like I should go look for her, but she really wasn't a kid. And even if she got lost in the base, it wasn't dangerous, but...I still had to search for her.

"Hey, we'll go look for her, so you stay put," Shemel told me. "She might be going around with the harpies, so we wouldn't wanna miss each other 'cause we all left."

"Right," agreed Tozume. "Bela, you stay with him. It'd be bad to leave him unguarded."

"For real? All righty then. I'll be waitin'!"

"You better be. But first, time to get changed."

Shemel entered the house so she could change out of the magical girl outfit into her usual attire. Aw, she could've gone as is! She would've been the center of attention like that!

"What should we do?" said Bela. "I'm antsy!"

"There's no reason to panic," Ira told her. "Like Kousuke said, Grande is no child. She's a grand dragon. She's not going to get herself killed or hurt anytime soon."

"Yeah, you're right. I'm worryin' too much! I wouldn't be surprised if she was playin' with kids somewhere or somethin'."

Somehow that picture didn't seem remotely unrealistic to me.

"I guess there's no reason to panic... Oh, I know. I'll use the time to make armor from the wyvern leather."

"I want some too."

"You don't need leather armor, Ira... Ah, but I could make you a cape from the wing membrane I have in my inventory."

"Can't wait to get my wyvern cape!"

Bela stared. "Um, do you realize that wyvern equipment is worth dozens of gold coins?"

"No biggie," I told her. "It's basically free to me, since I produce it all myself."

She let out a deep sigh. "I ain't sure that's the problem here..."

Ignoring her, I went to my golem workbench and opened the crafting menu. The weapons were done, so I'd have the girls test them out once they got back.

"Booo. I want clothes from Kousuke too!"

"Yeah, unfair! We want clothes you make too!"

"M-me too."

"I'm super jealous!"

"..."

"Okay, I get it already!"

After I inputted the wyvern armor and wyvern wing cape into the crafting menu, my winged companions descended and surrounded me. Yup, Grande and the harpies. Apparently, they'd been together the whole time. They got back before Shemel and Tozume did, just as predicted. Was it really that big a deal that I made clothes?

"You know, I'd happily make you girls clothes if you just asked me... But hm, what can I actually make...?"

"What do you mean?"

"In order to use my crafting skill properly, I have to be able to actually imagine what I want to make, to a relatively accurate extent."

"And?"

"...?"

Grande tilted her head, and Aja did the same next to her. Gosh, they were so cute.

"In other words, my crappy imagination limits me to producing slight alterations on what you're wearing right now," I explained. "If you're okay with that, I'd gladly make you all new clothes."

"I don't mind! I want clothes you made!" said Grande excitedly.

"R-really? Um, then before I make your clothes, Grande, I'll put out the weapons I made for the ogre girls, since they're done. Bela, when the other two get back, check to see if they feel all right."

"Aye! Whoa, is this how mithril alloy shines?"

I pulled three weapons from the golem workbench and handed them to Bela.

"All right, time to get crackin'."

"I want something exquisitely cute," Grande demanded.

"You're sure making this tough for me..."

I could combine the halterneck top and skirt she was wearing now into a halterneck dress, then apply a fastener to the back of the skirt area... No, I could use a hook instead and leave it open, maybe?

Grande had big claws on her feet, so putting this on from the bottom up would be difficult. Those claws were so sharp that if they got caught on the outfit, they'd rip it apart.

Lots of frills, lots of lace. And I decided to make it white and red.

"It's done!"

"*Whoa!* I'm trying it on right now!"

"Ira, I doubt she'll be able to put it on herself, so can you help her out?"

"Mm, okay. You can't take your clothes off here."

Grande had immediately tried to strip naked on the spot, but Ira quickly stopped her and dragged her into the house. I wasn't particularly surprised she had attempted this given her nature as a dragon; clothes were just accessories to her.

"Then next is..."

"..."

The harpies were staring holes into me with their sparkling eyes. What was I gonna do about these girls? Frilly stuff would get in the way when they flew around, so they weren't huge fans of that particular flourish.

That said, unlike Grande, they didn't have nearly as many body parts that could get in the way of clothes. From their knees down, their legs were birdlike, but if they closed them, they could hide away their talons, and their ankles were about the same size as your average human's. Their arms were wings from the shoulders down, so they couldn't wear tops with sleeves.

"I'm gonna try out a bunch of stuff. As long as we avoid long sleeves, you girls can wear pretty much anything."

They could wear one-piece dresses, if they were sleeveless. They could also wear sleeveless tops with short shorts, or miniskirts, too.

All I needed to do was take each of their sizes and change the color and design accordingly.

I quietly continued to work on their outfits, and as I finished them, the harpies or Ira would carry them into the house, then come out in their new looks.

Oh, right. I'd forgotten that Pirna and the other harpies had just about the same body size as Ira, so they could all wear the same clothes.

As my girls entered and exited the house with new outfits on, like a fashion show, multiple passersby from the base started to gather to watch—mostly women. This was bad!

"Kousuke," said Ira.

"Yeah?"

"It's important to know when to give up."

"...Yeah."

Beastwomen, lamia, dwarf women who I initially thought were children, a lizard woman... Wait, Madame Zamil?

Please don't just get in line like that. O-okay, yeah. I'll make you clothes. I personally think a military uniform would suit you perfectly, Madame Zamil. Huh? You want something white with frills...?

Well, I suppose I had no choice. And while it would've been rude to say so out loud, she actually looked great in her new outfit.

"I'm dead."

"Good work today."

It wasn't until the evening that I was freed from the crowd of women, and I was currently resting my head on Ira's lap. She had a smile on her face, and she was gently brushing my hair with her tiny hand. This was the best.

Fortunately for me, the ogre girls' weapons and wyvern leather armor didn't need any adjusting, so it didn't take much out of me. Dealing with the crowd of women was another story entirely.

"I think it was a good way for people to let off steam. There's not much entertainment out here."

"We really have to do something about that."

"Yes, but that's something for them to work out, since they're the ones who live here. Don't worry, the longer they live here, the more they'll start to figure this stuff out. Right now, they're still focused on living from day to day."

"Is that how this works?"

Ira nodded. "It is," she answered definitively.

If she said so, it was probably true. But I still wanted to do something for them.

"By the way, how's development on the golem communicator relay station going?"

"It'll be done soon. Why?"

"I was just thinking it might be a cool idea to start a radio broadcast sort of thing once it's done. It'd be a perfect form of entertainment."

"Radio broadcast...? If I remember correctly, you said that was for relaying information to various areas and playing music and such, right?"

"Yeah, that's it. When it comes to news, even the littlest things count. For example, this town had a festival, or some new dish at so and so's was delicious, or a monster was spotted on the road between this town and that town, but the Liberation Army took care of it so it's safe now. Stuff like that. Just being able to hear about things happening in another place is entertaining."

"I see... That does sound interesting."

"I know, right? When the research wraps up, I'd really like to make it happen."

Well, radio broadcasts weren't just effective as entertainment; they had military value as well. Y'know, propaganda and stuff. As far as I'd heard, the literacy rate in this world wasn't particularly high. In other words, education wasn't exactly available to everyone. Imagine if you were to run propaganda broadcasts in a place like that...? It struck me as dangerous... But if used correctly, it could be useful. I could just explain the dangers once we actually got the communicators up and running.

"Prepare yourselves!"

"Oof!"

Grande collided with my stomach while I was lying on my side. If she had actually gone full force, both me and the couch would've been split in two. Thank goodness that protective bracelet was working as advertised.

"Aye, Kousuke? So... I've gotten myself a human form and become one of your wives, yes?"

"Mm-hmm."

"So how come you never seem to want to touch me?"

"That's not true, it's just..."

I raised myself from Ira's lap and sat up, while Grande stood straight up in front of me. We were pretty much eye to eye; she was quite the mini dragon girl.

"No, you absolutely are avoiding touching me," she said. "You're always all over Sylphy, Ira, the harpies, and that overlord. But all you ever do is give me head rubs."

"Really...?"

Actually, maybe she was right. I might not have been all that touchy feely with her.

"Plus, you, um, have m-mated... Er, been intimate with everyone but me, no?!"

"Yes, well, you're right."

"I'm not so different in size from Ira or Pirna! Why am I the only one, um, left out?!"

"I'm not sure how to answer that..."

I mean, this was Grande we were talking about. Don't get me wrong; she was adorable. But she was more like a pet or a source of emotional healing for me... I just couldn't get myself to want to do those sorts of things with her.

"Just the other day while I was pretending to sleep, you and the other girls brought food and drinks to the bedroom and had a grand old time... Why am I the only one left out?"

Grande stared at me, tears in her eyes. I had to say something, but before I could—

"Don't worry." Ira suddenly said something incomprehensible from off to my side: "That's one of the goals of this trip."

Excuse me?

"Now that we've come this far, there won't be much need for flying, which means it will be fine if your body isn't at 100 percent."

"Wait, wait. What are you talking about?"

"I don't know if it will work on dragons, but I've brought medicine as well."

"What medicine?!"

"We're gonna help too!"

"Absolutely!"

"We know all of Master's weak spots, so don't worry!"

"..."

"Whoa! Where'd you girls come from?!"

Pirna and the other harpies were at another table a little way from us, but had suddenly leapt into our conversation. Ira proceeded to pull something out from inside of her cape: a medicine bottle filled with a colorful liquid of some kind, which she was explaining to Grande.

Wait, what was that? It was rainbow colored, and quite frankly had bad vibes.

Was this the kind of bad stuff that'd send me flying to the moon?

"Um, we haven't even had dinner yet, so let's cool our jets, okay?" I said.

"If we get hungry, you can just bust out some food for us," said Pirna. "No problem."

"Now then, you've made Grande wait long enough!" Ira told me. "It's time."

"Wait, seriously. Hold on! Let's talk this over!"

"Not happening."

Ira slapped a pair of magic handcuffs on me as I tried to resist. Hmph, foolish woman! Status effect magic didn't work on—er, uh???

"Kousuke, you have no magical power, so any magic that utilizes magical energies or magic circuits in the body doesn't work on you. But that doesn't apply to magic that has physical restraint abilities."

"Y-you planned this!"

"You're the one at fault for making Grande feel left out this whole time. Don't you feel bad for her? Ladies, bring him to the bedroom."

"Aye, aye!"

"Don't worry, this won't hurt."

"It'll all be over by the time you finish counting the stains on the ceiling."

"..."

With my hands restrained, Pirna and the others led me into the bedroom.

I won't give in! I won't lose to Ira's suspicious medicines!

One could not overcome medicine with willpower alone. Among Ira's various medicines were some that didn't have any effects, but whenever that happened Ira would just whisper, "I knew it."

Ira, were you using me for your experiments?

Curse you!!!

As for my current situation—

"Mmm. Munch..."

Grande was sleeping while clinging to my body. And for some reason, she was nibbling on my left shoulder. Upon further inspection, the spot she was going at had grown red and had teeth marks imprinted into it.

Please don't eat me?

What happened to Ira? I wasn't sure, but she sure as heck wasn't in the bedroom anymore. She either got up early or didn't sleep in here to begin with. I did remember her being present at least part of the way through the previous night's activities.

I tried to lift myself up, but Grande's tail was wrapped around my right leg, and she was lying on top of me, munching on my left shoulder, so all I could move was my head and right arm.

"Grande, honey, wake up. Also, please don't eat me."

"Mm...?"

As I called out to her, I gently caressed her head, causing her to finally open her eyes. Her gaze was clearly groggy. She looked at my face, and then back at my saliva and bite mark-filled shoulder. Then she began to lick it.

"Hey, that tickles."

But she wouldn't stop licking. She must've been half-awake— Or so I thought when she suddenly stopped.

"Mm."

And then for some reason, she directed her own left shoulder at my mouth. Um, what was she getting at?

"Do the same to me," she demanded.

"Huh???"

"Hurry."

Her tail wrapped itself tighter around my leg.

Ow, ow!

Her tail was crazy strong, so I opted not to put up much resistance. I drew my mouth close to her slender white shoulder and bit down on it gently like she had, but not hard enough to leave a mark.

"Do it harder."

"Seriously...?"

"..."

"Ow, *ow*! Fine. Like this?"

I bit down on her shoulder hard enough to leave a mark, then began to lick the tender red spot. She kind of tasted like sweat.

"Mmph! ♪"

Grande glanced between her shoulder and mine. Something about this was strangely embarrassing.

"Shall we get up?"

"Yup."

Grande released her grip on my leg and got up from on top of me. Yeah, my everything hurt. Either I hadn't been able to roll over last night, or I'd been womanhandled. Probably both. Strangely enough, I still had a mostly full stamina gauge. Was this thanks to all of Ira's medicine?

"I want to clean myself with water," said Grande.

"Shall we hit the bath, then?"

"Bath?"

"It's basically what you described."

I made sure to put on at least a pair of underwear before entering the living room, where I was met by Ira and the harpies.

Apparently, they'd been working on breakfast for us all.

Everyone zeroed in on our shoulders.

"...Hm," said Ira.

"Ah," said Pirna. "It all makes sense now."

"Not bad at all," nodded Ingrid.

"Aww, how nice!" Capri cooed. "I'm gonna copy her tonight!"

"..."

This was all a bit embarrassing; I wished they'd stop. Grande, on the other hand, looked like she was on top of the world.

I pulled at her hand and took her to the bath.

It was quick and easy.

What? No, all we did was wash off our sweat and uh, other juices, so it didn't take very long. It was morning, and breakfast was waiting for us, after all.

Once we exited the bathroom, I found clothes ready for me, but for some reason it was just underwear and a pair of pants. Were they telling me to spend the day topless?

"No hiding it."

"Nope."

"Don't even try."

"You mustn't hide it."

"Ain't happening."

"..."

What was with this insane peer pressure? I wasn't going to lose to—er, actually, I totally lost. Every time I tried to wear something that would hide my shoulder, Grande looked like she was going to start bawling. How could I possibly make her cry? And so, the next morning, I used my golem workbench to make a running shirt.

"Heh heh heh..."

Grande looked pleased as punch while eating the porridge the harpies and Ira made. There was dried gizma meat and vegetables mixed into it, so it was more like a Chinese porridge of sorts. The gizma meat's juices really made it delicious.

After breakfast, we were set to meet back up with Madame Zamil, and Shemel and her girls. We'd be resting and continuing our information gathering today. At night, we'd share our findings and decide on where to start searching. Oh, and the new short spear I was supposed to have made for Madame Zamil last night would get done now instead.

"It would've been unthinkable to have entered the room at the time," she said.

"Yeah, I get it."

Just as Madame Zamil had requested, I made her a short spear made from mithril alloy. I thought the blade would end up being long again, but it ended up being within acceptable short spear range.

"If it were too long, it'd just end up difficult to use. If I'm going to be wielding it in narrow areas, I likely won't be twirling it around much."

"Gotcha."

The new short spear had a wide and thick blade. Honestly, I couldn't tell if it was designed more for its sturdiness or for its blunt force damage. It appeared as though Madame Zamil was fond of unique bladed spears.

"All right, then. So, about today's info gathering..."

"We're going to be flying around the area and taking a look at things," said Pirna. "We'll be checking the three spots we know of now, plus the roads."

"We're gonna catch up with some hunters and patrolmen and ask them if there are any other points of interest to look for," Shemel said.

"I shall guard Sir Kousuke."

So Shemel and her team were going to gather info from within the base, and Madame Zamil was with me.

"I'm going to go check in with Ovis and see if there's anything that's been troubling him here," said Ira.

"Ovis?"

"The sheep beastman. He's the one in charge here."

"Ah, gotcha. Guess I'll come with you then," I said.

"I shall also accompany you."

Grande was seemingly back to normal and wanted to tag along. She was personally cooperating with me, though; she wasn't an official member of the Liberation Army.

After confirming the details of the day, we all went our separate ways. I held Ira's hand with my right hand and Grande's with my left, and Madame Zamil followed behind me. Quite the formation. Like yesterday, Ira was holding my index and middle fingers, and I was holding one of Grande's claws. I had flowers on both arms, baby.

And so, we made our way over to Ovis, but —

"Anything troubling me, you ask?" he said.

"Yes," said Ira. "If there is, we'd love to give you a helping hand."

"Since I'm here, there's plenty of issues I can solve quite easily," I added. "Anything involving buildings, farming, expanding the base, etc."

"Kousuke."

"Ira, I use my powers the way I want to use them."

"...Yeah, I know."

Both Ira and Sylphy didn't feel right relying on my powers so hard. It was true that an organization relying on the skills of a single person wasn't exactly in a healthy position. But I personally felt that we should use what we had available to us. I didn't hate self-imposed limitations and handicaps, but that sort of play was for the handful of pervs out there.

After thinking for a moment, Ovis spoke aloud.

"Farming, you say?"

A sheep that walks on two legs sure is a cute image, even if this guy does sound like a grizzled older man...

"It's quite difficult getting timber here, you see," he said. "Having it transported from the Black Forest is no simple task, but there are no trees growing naturally in this area. We've gotten seeds from the forest and tried planting trees here multiple times, but even if we water them properly, they wither outside of the base. They do grow around the fields, but..."

"Ah, I see, I see," I said. "Making the Badlands green, eh? That sounds like quite the struggle—"

"It's actually not," said Ira. "The land you cultivate, even in the Badlands, grows produce and plants at a normal rate. Even if it's not a farming block. We tested that out when we were first building the base."

"Oh, that's right. I totally forgot. Plus, we have this now."

I reached into my inventory and whipped out a single hoe.

Mithril Hoe +9 (Auto Repair, Effect Strengthening III, Area Strengthening III)

"Er, what's with the extremely fancy-looking shining hoe?" said Ovis.

"It's a hoe made from magic mithril," Ira explained. "When Kousuke swings it, about one tenth of a hectare gets cultivated."

"Um... You're joking, right?"

"Unfortunately not. It'll be faster to show you."

Together with Ovis and a few other onlookers, we went outside of the base, mithril hoe in hand.

"If we're going to restore this land, where would you wanna start?" I asked. "Too close to the base walls would be bad, right?"

"Considering future expansion of the base, somewhere a little ways away would be good," said Ira.

"Indeed," Ovis agreed. "Let's walk for a bit. Thanks to the anti-monster barrier, gizmas don't really get too close."

We walked for about thirty minutes, listening to any potential problems Ovis might be having. There didn't seem to be anything pressing at the moment, but there was someone who got sick rather often and an elderly person who had thrown out their back, so I said I'd take a look at them later. Other than that, things were going well.

"If we can expand the greenery, our farming efforts will be even more fruitful. And if we can raise livestock better too, our food situation will greatly improve."

"Ha ha ha, just leave this to me."

The ground we were on seemed fine enough, so I immediately swung my mithril hoe + 9.

"Let's go!"

Swoop!

My hoe stabbed into the ground, and the next moment, a massive impact-wave washed over the area, instantly cultivating a plot of land 20 meters wide and 50 meters long. Ovis and the others' jaws dropped.

"All he has to do is repeat this process," Ira explained. "The soil he cultivates can be used to raise crops. Normal weeds and so on, too."

"But it doesn't rain much around here, right?" I pointed out. "What should we do about water?"

Even if the dirt had been improved, crops couldn't grow without water. Irrigation was necessary.

"We've got a few options," said Ira. "We can create a waterway from the base leading here, we could make a magic tool that produces water magic... We can make as many magic crystals as we need, so the running cost would essentially be zero."

"I see..."

The base's water supply came from multiple unlimited water sources, so we could draw water from there. In the center of the rear base was a water tower taller than the base walls, and it used an unlimited water source, so... And like Ira suggested, we could even utilize magic tools.

"There are magic tools that sprinkle water, eh?" said Ovis.

"Normally, nobody would think to use magic tools just to sprinkle water on a field," Ira replied. "It's only possible because of the way this base operates."

"Then, to the drawing board?" I suggested. "I have an idea, in that case."

"Really? Let's hear it."

If we had a magical tool that worked like a sprinkler, we'd be set. If we were going to magically produce water, it wouldn't need a canister to hold the fluid, either. I could make it shaped like a stake and jab it into the ground, then modify the head so that magic crystals could be swapped in and out... No, having to swap out crystals for each one of them would be a drag. Instead, we could link tens of them together and connect them with wiring to pass magical energy through, connecting them to the main unit with a slot for magic crystals...

No, we didn't have to do anything that complex. I could just make uniformly spaced unlimited water source towers.

I decided to talk it over with Ira.

"But first, time to cultivate!"

"Mm-hmm. Good luck."

I ended up cultivating the shit out of the Badlands. To be honest, getting around to each spot of uncultivated land ended up being more tiring than the cultivating itself.

"Well? How's it feel? Great, right?"

"Mmph, real good..."

It was the night of the second day of our time at the rear base in our quest to locate ancient scriptures.

I was lying on my side on the bed, and the red ogre Bela was giving me a massage. Since I'd cultivated a huge chunk of the land around the base, I'd done a ton of running around and swinging my hoe.

Needless to say, I was tremendously exhausted after getting home. When Shemel and the ogres returned, they found me lounging about.

"It would be rude of us not to do somethin' for you after all you've done for us."

"Bela, how about you give him one of your massages?"

"Me? I ain't mind, I suppose."

Things rapidly came together, and before long, I was brought to the bedroom and on the receiving end of a Bela massage.

She was using just the right amount of power, and it felt incredible. I felt like everything in my mind was melting away.

Where had Ira and Grande gotten off to? What was everyone else up to? Ah, this was all too amazing for me to be thinking about any of that. Bela's big hands gripped my not-at-all slender calves and thighs, putting the perfect amount of pressure on them. My whole body felt warm; my blood flow must've been improving. I could fall asleep.

"You can sleep if ya want!" Bela assured me. "I might roll ya around a bit if need be, but don't even worry 'bout that."

"Aye..."

I let myself lean into the good feelings and allowed my consciousness to fade.

"Good morning, sleepy head."

I woke up to someone shaking me lightly and found a large eye gazing down at me in the darkness. It was Ira.

"Huh? Um..."

It took a moment for me to remember why I had fallen asleep. Bela had given me an amazing massage that put me to sleep. I could see light creeping in from the living room, but it was already pitch black outside.

"Sorry, we were supposed to discuss our findings, right? I totally fell asleep."

"Mm, it's fine. We're all done."

"Wait, what?"

"Yup. The meeting's done. We decided to investigate the ruins in the northeast that we heard about yesterday."

"For real...?"

"You seemed tired, after all. Should we have waited to talk things over with you?"

Ira looked concerned, but I shook my head.

"Nah, it's no problem. I'll just have to apologize to everyone tomorrow."

They were probably being considerate, but it wasn't a good look that the guy who organized the meeting couldn't even be bothered to show up because he was asleep. I'd have to apologize to Madame Zamil, Shemel, and the other girls tomorrow.

"Sorry, Ira. And thanks for looking out for me."

"...It was nothing."

Ira didn't seem all that happy. Was she thinking that it was her fault I felt like I needed to apologize to everyone?

I gently rubbed her head, hopped out of bed, and stretched out.

"I'm feeling a lot more energized, but I am hungry," I said. "Time to get some grub, hit the bath, and then get some more shut-eye."

"Mm, I'll make your dinner," Ira announced, clenching both fists triumphantly.

I dragged the little lady to the living room, where the harpies and Grande were excitedly chatting away. As soon as they noticed me, they all greeted me and waved their hands (wings?).

"Morning!" I said. "Er, even though it's already night. Sorry for missing the meeting, ladies."

"No worries, Kousuke. We know you were hard at work during the day."

"Exactly. Even from up in the sky, I couldn't believe what I was seeing. You cultivated a crazy big area of land."

Apparently, Grande and the harpies forgave me. I felt terrible, quite frankly.

After that, I took a bath with the girls, then ate the dinner Ira made for me and immediately went to sleep. Dinner was on the light side: slightly sweet porridge, fruits, and lukewarm milk. Ira felt it wouldn't be wise for me to eat something too heavy before sleeping.

And so, with everyone huddled up against me in bed, I went to sleep. The harpies' feathers made for tremendously comfy sleepage.

When I woke up the next day, I immediately apologized to Madame Zamil and Shemel's crew, but they didn't hesitate to forgive me.

"I'm really sorry about yesterday," I said.

"No, it's no biggie. The only new info we got was that there was an unnatural rocky area off to the south-southwest."

"Indeed. And it's quite far away, so it would be wise to start with the ruins to the northeast."

"Man, my bad too. He was so fast asleep that I couldn't help but let him be."

"Seems like things worked out for the best, no? You look recharged."

It was true that I'd recharged; I slept with everyone clinging to me, so that was probably why I looked so good. I was quite fond of those kinds of peaceful nights. I'd love to get that kind of thing into the rotation after getting back to Arichburg.

"So, um, it'll take about half a day of walking to get to our destination, yeah?" I said.

"Mm-hmm!" Ira nodded. "We leave now, camp out for the night, and then get there around noon tomorrow."

"Then shall we get going? Shemel's squad will take point, Ira and I will be in the center, and we can leave the rear to Madame Zamil. How's that sound?"

"I'm fine with that! What about you, Zamil?"

"I also do not mind. I am, however, somewhat surprised. I didn't think you were aware of the tactics used for moving in a group like this, Sir Kousuke."

"Let's just say I picked up a thing or two in my old world."

When it came to party tactics in SRPGs, putting your most powerful characters in the front and the back was a staple of the genre.

Apparently, when wolves moved in a pack, the point would be led by the strongest, youngest wolves, the middle would be the weaker wolves, then the rear would be protected by other young and strong wolves, with the one in the absolute back being the leader, the strongest wolf in the pack. To be more specific, the older but more experienced wolf would follow up the rear and make decisions for the whole group.

Adhering to the harpies' aerial guidance, we took small breaks every hour and a half to two hours to rehydrate and get some calories in us. Because Ira was so small, her strides were short, and she didn't have much in the way of stamina, so I ended up carrying her for a bit. She said she wasn't having any problems, but that was true for me, too; I had zero issue carrying her.

"I can't help but feel uncomfortable when I look at the way you...move, Sir Kousuke," said Madame Zamil from behind me.

"He barely shakes, which means you can't get sick," said Ira. "It's extremely nice."

I was imagining the command action W in my head, which allowed me to move forward while barely using my legs. It was basically the same as just standing still, so even though I was moving at a normal walking speed, I didn't get tired at all. Hell, I could probably even do the moonwalk if I wanted to.

Moving like this slowly carved away at Madame Zamil's sanity, but we nonetheless continued walking until we reached our destination around noon.

Barren badlands covered in rocks and gravel stretched out in front of us. But among that nothingness were rocks that clearly had been altered by human hands, along with the remnants of busted stone buildings.

"Is this it? Are these the ruins?" I asked.

"It's all collapsed... It's hard to imagine what this all looked like from what's left," Ira said. "Other than there was a large building here at one point."

Ira descended from my back and immediately started touching one of the altered rocks nearby. Madame Zamil was standing near us on guard, and Shemel's squad began exploring the upper area of the ruins to make sure there wasn't anything dangerous waiting for us.

"Suppose we should make a base of operations to start with."

Fortunately, there were plenty of materials on the ground here. It only made sense to use what was on-site.

SINCE WE'D ARRIVED at our destination, I immediately got to making a base of operations so we could stay here for the time being. In terms of safety, a raised floor made the most sense. Even if an enemy decided to pick a fight with us, we'd be too high for them to reach us, so we wouldn't even have to be concerned about it. There was nothing safer than that.

With that in mind, I could also go with an underground base where the enemies wouldn't be able to detect us at all. The problem with that idea was that they typically felt really claustrophobic no matter what you did to make them comfortable... For that very reason, I preferred raised floor bases. There was something freeing about them.

I collected the busted materials in the area using my pickaxe, then used them to build the pillars for the base. While I was doing that—

"Kousuke, didn't you say you were going to make a field?" asked Ira.

"I did."

"Are you sure a raised floor base is the right move?"

"Shouldn't be an issue."

Ira tilted her head in response to my confident answer. Once I had the pillars in place, I built the platform.

"It's so spacious."

"Well, it's gotta hold me, you, the harpies, Grande, and Shemel's squad, right? If I'm gonna make space for everyone to sleep, it's gotta be big. Plus, a bit of spaciousness is good."

The platform was 80 meters by 80 meters, making it a little narrower than a soccer field; the perfect size for us to live in.

First, I planted a cafeteria in the middle of the platform so that we could all eat together. Then, on the west side of that building I built one large house where me, Ira, the harpies, and Grande could stay. On the east side I built one house each for Madame Zamil, Shemel, and her girls. I say house, but really each one was only big enough for a bed, a table, a chair, and a little bit of storage.

The large cafeteria in the center had tables, chairs, and cushions, plus a space for lounging around and a space with a rattan couch and a low table. It was more like a living and dining room, to be honest.

"All that's left are the watering holes and the bath."

"The watering holes can be in the east and the west, and the bath can be to the north."

"With the field to the south, aye?"

"Mm-hmm."

I was used to this kind of work, so things proceeded quickly. The stone materials I collected here weren't enough, so I used the bricks I brought from Arichburg as well. I built three toilets on both the east and west sides. They were all flushable thanks to using unlimited water resources, and underneath the platform, I installed tanks. I'd simply swap them out at certain intervals and get rid of them in my inventory. I could take the whole thing apart that way!

On the south side I placed some farming blocks, then closed it in with brick blocks. Once we planted seeds, the base would be complete. As far as what we were going to grow, it'd primarily be a tomato-esque crop that we went through quickly, and a lettuce-like crop. Grande ate hamburgers a whole lot, so we would go through tomatoes and lettuce at a high speed... But tomatoes had plenty of uses, and we could use lettuce for salads, so everything would be fine. We'd just plant other vegetables when we happened to need them.

Apart from myself and Ira, everyone else was currently investigating the ruins, figuring out whether there was anything we could use, if there was an entrance to any underground areas, and if there was an underground at all.

"We probably have some time until everyone gets back, so I think it's time for some development," I said.

Sitting on one of the couches in the cafeteria, Ira tilted her head. "What were you thinking?"

"A way to move at high speeds without relying on Grande. I want to try making something that can travel over difficult terrain that carriages can't get through."

"That sounds fun! Do you have any ideas?"

"I don't *not* have any ideas, but..."

I whipped out a notebook from my inventory and showed her my sketch of a two-wheeled automobile.

Well, I called it a sketch, but I wasn't much of an artist.

"We had these kinds of vehicles in my world," I explained. "When you twist the handles, the engine here produces power and spins the wheels."

"Hm... If we replaced this engine-thing with a golem, it sounds doable," mused Ira. "It looks like it has a lot of parts, though, which might make construction difficult."

"That's the issue, right? In my world, this sort of vehicle was developed after the bullets used in bolt action rifles became mass producible. In this world, I'm probably the only one who can make these parts. And even if I did make them, using them normally would be difficult, just like the weapons from my world that I've made."

"Mm, but the idea is fascinating," Ira said. "Normally when one says 'vehicle,' they're referring to carriages or horses. Otherwise, there are other ridable animals. The sort of vehicle you speak of doesn't require an animal at all and uses generated power to move itself. This is revolutionary."

"With animal-drawn vehicles, you have to worry about feeding the animals and keeping them hydrated."

Ira nodded. "Exactly. But if you don't rely on animals to power transportation, you have more room for storage. This would be incredibly useful from an economical and military perspective."

"Let's leave aside the issue of cost for now. I guess if we're talking about power sources other than animals, golems are all we've got. Which means the cost to move these things is going to be magical energy, yeah?"

"I would say so. And if we're going to power these vehicles with magic, that requires magic stones from monsters, magicite made from those stones, and magic crystals developed in the rear base. None of these are particularly hard to get, as of right now."

We were getting a steady supply of magic stones and magicite from adventurers and Liberation Army soldiers slaying monsters, and magic crystals were in production at the rear base. The magic crystals were produced by taking the endless supply of magical power at the base and giving it physical form. Honestly, it was cheating.

"Then shall we think about the specifics?" I said. "Like what sort of performance are we looking for?"

"Mm, first we need to consider its ability to traverse over harsh terrain," said Ira.

"Good point. That's basically our primary objective. The next point is that it should be faster than a carriage."

"How many people can ride one of these?" she asked.

"Let's say two at the least, six at the most."

"So let's aim for it to be able to carry the same number of passengers as a two-horse carriage."

"Then that means it needs to be about as long and wide as a two-horse carriage."

"Yeah. If it's too wide, it won't be able to travel down roads well."

And so Ira and I brainstormed over the concept and eventually came up with a list of requirements for the vehicle.

★ Possess the ability to traverse difficult terrain.

★ Run on magical energy.

★ Can hold two to six passengers.

★ Carrying capacity and size about the same as a carriage.

"That seems about it," I said.

"Mm-hmm," Ira agreed. "So first up is its mobility, then."

"Actually, why can't carriages travel over difficult terrain? We should start there."

"Well, wheels easily get caught in unstable terrain or break on large rocks. The wheels even come off sometimes."

"The wheels are vulnerable, then? To solve that problem... How about we use tougher materials?"

"Like steel? That'd make them way too heavy. The wheels would sink into the ground. What did they do in your world, Kousuke?"

"Erm, well, the wheels in my world are covered in a thick, soft, elastic material. The wheels themselves are made of metal, then on top of that they're designed to cause low amounts of friction and... Crap. If we go in that direction, then we'll have the same issues as the sketch I showed you."

"Agreed. That's why we need to completely change how we're thinking about this."

"Hm, in that case... What if the vehicle itself didn't actually touch the ground?" I suggested.

"You mean like...flying?"

"No, it wouldn't have to be that crazy. I'm talking *floating* twenty to thirty centimeters off the ground, that way bad terrain wouldn't matter. Imagine a large board the same size as a carriage, then floating it above the ground with wind magic or something. It'd be kind of like a boat on land."

At this point, I was imagining a hovercraft. Something like that would be able to travel over flat lands, badlands, swamps, and rivers. It wouldn't be fit for especially jagged terrain, but that was a problem for later. Was it doable in a world of magic?

"There is levitation magic in this world, but there aren't too many ways to effectively use it. The object in question floats, but it doesn't move any more than that. It's basically useful when you're trying to move heavy objects."

"Say wha—?!" I gasped. "That's mega useful. Couldn't we attach a wind magic tool to it and give it propulsion?"

"Hm... But I don't know if it will be able to keep its balance if turned into a magical tool," said Ira. "When used as a type of magic, the balance is controlled by the caster, you see."

"Hm... What about the height? Can we adjust the hovering height?"

"By adjusting the magical energy we pour into the spell, yes. Up and down movement is fairly simple, actually."

"Then how about we attach levitation magic tools and golem eyes on each corner of the board, then have the golem core control the distance from the ground in each corner? If the board is too far from the ground, the generator can supply less energy to the tools, and if it's too close, it can supply more. That way it'd be able to maintain a proper distance from the ground, no?"

If levitation magic couldn't detect and correct tilting, then a golem would do the trick. The problem was the brakes. The only solution I could think of was blowing wind in the opposite direction or forcing contact with the ground... But at the end of the day this was a vehicle for harsh terrain, so I didn't think heavy brakes were going to be necessary.

"I can't say one way or the other until we try," Ira said.

"Then first I'll whip up a small prototype for experimentation."

"Yep, experiments are important."

Ira and I used a wood board about the size of a Japanese sitting mat and started experimenting. Developing this between the two of us would be difficult, but that didn't mean we couldn't try out lots of ideas.

I'd love to make an airbike sort of thing. Airbikes, airboards— the stuff of dreams!

Can't succeed without failing first, right? If we fail, we reflect on why, then try to correct those mistakes. That then connects to success. What am I trying to say? You get it, right?

"Urgh... Blegh."

"You've got this, Kousuke!"

"I-I can handle this... *Bleeeeeeggggh.*"

"Fight on, Kousuke!"

I was getting the feeling that me and vehicles didn't go together very well... But maybe this was the norm for vehicle development.

Put simply, by attaching levitation tools to each corner of the board, we were able to keep it from tilting one way or the other. Unfortunately, using golem eyes on each corner to measure the distance between the board and the ground and keep the whole thing stable wasn't going to work. It wouldn't be a problem for flat roads, but as soon as it moved to more jagged terrain, it started rocking like a ship in the middle of a storm. I was reduced to a queasy mess in five minutes.

Despite these failures, Ira and I kept at it. What if we lowered the golem eyes' sensitivity? What if we put the sensors in the front, back, left, and right instead? What if we simply put a sensor in the middle? Did we even need sensors?

It took us way too long to realize that last point.

Indeed: we didn't actually need sensors in the first place. This levitation magic manipulated height based on the area it was activated in. The spell itself was programmed so that it recorded that initial distance to the ground, so there was never any need to use sensors to adjust height in real-time.

In other words, to maintain balance for the floating object, we could set four levitation tools at each corner, then set a sensor in the center of the board at the bottom for measuring the standard height. We could then set the amount of magical energy sent to the tools and install a system for controlling it all.

Basically, we took the long way getting there.

"I've never really used levitation before..." Ira sighed. "I'm sorry."

"Don't apologize," I told her. "We succeeded in the end, right? Plus, we were able to confirm the principles of levitation magic.

That's a win, as far as I'm concerned. So, uh, what would happen if we used this thing on a tall mountain?"

"Beats me. It's not like I've ever tried it before."

If we turned this thing on at the top of a tall mountain and then walked off a cliff, would we stay levitated at the same height without dropping? If that turned out to be the case... This would need testing. I got the feeling things wouldn't work out so easily.

"Anyway, we've created a platform that can move along the ground without shaking or being affected by inconsistencies in the terrain. This alone would be useful as a tool for transporting heavy goods, right?"

"Mm-hmm. Simply having no friction changes things massively."

We actually tried placing a heavy object on the test board, and it had no issues moving with Ira on it too. The only problem was that the heavier the weight, the more magical energy was required, so if the energy flow was cut off during transportation, it could cause a serious incident. We'd have to apply safety measures, just in case.

"Next is the propulsion device," I said. "I actually have an idea for this, but I'm gonna need your help."

Ira nodded. "You have it."

"I know, and I'm grateful. Your help as a court mage is an absolute necessity to making this work. Okay, so hear me out. Wind magic is a thing, yeah?"

"Yup."

"I'm guessing there's a type of wind magic that literally just produces wind, right?"

"Mm-hmm. It's the simplest wind spell. Look."

Ira pointed her finger at me and blew some wind into my face.

"Yeah, that's it. How are you producing that wind?"

"...?"

Ira tilted her head in confusion.

"Like, wind is basically the flow of air, right?" I said. "I doubt you're actually producing air from your finger. You're probably gathering the air around you to your finger tip and then shooting it out. Could you fire wind like that continuously?"

"Hm, all right."

After using smoke and flour to test things out, I confirmed that this wind magic was indeed gathering air from the surrounding area and then firing it from Ira's fingertip of the tip of a staff.

"So that's how it actually works..." Ira murmured. "I thought I knew how wind magic worked, but I really didn't know anything."

"Well, at the end of the day, for people like you who can use magic, none of this really matters, right? But, hm..."

We now knew that some wind magic gathered air from the surrounding area then fired it in a single direction. What about the other types of wind magic? Stuff like invisible blades of wind, pressurized wind bullets, that kind of thing—well, it was beyond my understanding. Seriously, how did any of that stuff work? I had no clue.

Anyway, I was focused on the simpler stuff. Logically speaking, this was a lot like a jet engine. But there was one point in which they were totally different.

"Something's not right, though."

"What isn't?"

"You know how there's super strong wind magic, stuff that would just blow me away, yeah?"

"Mm-hmm. Wind pressure magic."

"That shit hurt like hell... But that's not the point. If you're using magic that can blow away another person, why don't you get blown away too?"

"...?"

If she was collecting air from her surroundings and turning it into a jet, then that had to be producing a counter-reaction. I had already confirmed that the three laws of physics applied in this world. So if Ira wasn't being shot backwards, something wasn't working right. I explained this to Ira.

"...Maybe because it's magic?" she concluded.

"Don't give up so easily, Ira!"

"I'm not sure what to tell you."

If we allowed ourselves to be content with *that's just the way it is*, there'd be no turning back. Sure, we had a way to create forward movement at this rate. If we attached a sail to the airboard (I'd named it just then), then used magic to blow wind into it, we'd have a boat that could run over the ground. But if we could solve the mysteries of wind magic, we'd be able to give this thing better and faster forward thrust.

"Basically, I'm thinking there might be some kind of equation built into the magic that cancels out the recoil. Y'know how the harpies and Grande fly using wind magic, right? But if you think about that in terms of normal wind magic, it doesn't make much sense."

"Mm, you're right. The magic efficiency is... Oh, is that it?"

"I'm guessing you figured it out, huh?"

This was probably the key to how Grande and the harpies used magic to fly: they expended extremely low amounts of magical energy in order to fly for long periods of time. It was clear they used wind magic, but how?

By conventional logic, the fact that they could fly at all was a mystery. If they were using wind magic to make their bodies soar through the air, the amount of magical energy they would have to expend would be absurd. They wouldn't be able to fly for long periods of time. Hell, dragons had massive bodies. As a species, they must have had far more magical energy than a human, but they still wouldn't be able to maintain long-term flight. This was the answer to that mystery.

"...Are you okay?" I asked.

"That was way more powerful than I expected," said Ira, who'd gotten dizzy from thinking about it.

After some more thought, Ira said she'd try hitting me with some powerful modified wind magic. I placed a soft straw block behind us, then stood behind her in a supporting position before having her test out the magic.

As a result, the two of us were blown backwards into the straw block.

"I love how being with you leads me to understand all kinds of new things," she said.

"I'm happy to hear that, but please be careful," I told her. "We were able to take precautions because we knew ahead of time there might be blowback. Please don't go adjusting other types of magic on your own and causing something to blow up."

"Mm, I know. I may be far from understanding the truth of all magic, but I'm still a former court mage. Plus, I'm older than you, Kousuke. You don't need to worry about me."

She pumped her small chest out, straw still mixed into her hair. Ira was typically pretty mindful of things, so... Actually, sometimes she could get a bit too passionate and lose track of her surroundings. This was concerning.

"Anyway, we've got a solid idea for propulsion," I said. "All that's left is the actual design... I suppose a simple tubular form would be best."

There might've been a better form for it, but this would do for the time being.

"So, we just need to activate wind magic in this tube with the recoil equation stripped from it?" Ira asked.

"Yup. That should work. Can we reverse the direction of the wind blast?"

If we could do that, we might be able to use it as a type of brake system. We could also physically have the vehicle make contact with the ground, but... Would air brakes using air resistance work? How would that even work?

We should probably stick with standard grounded brakes first.

"It's possible," she said. "Like the levitation tool, we can make it so its output is adjustable."

"It might be good to adjust the right and left separately. We'll be able to turn it around by adjusting the difference."

"Mm, okay."

A rudder on the back was a good idea as well. If we made it work together with the right and left output adjustments, that'd be for the best. I was planning on just leaving this in the hands of R&D.

While Ira was making a magic tool for propulsion, I was working on a basic set of grounded brakes and a vehicle body to attach them to. I'd taken the original prototype and updated it so it was about the size of two tatami mats, still made of wood, then fit a levitation tool to each corner.

"Done," Ira announced.

"Then I'll make a golem core that can adjust output, plus a control system."

The control system wouldn't be that complex. A right and left set of levers for two wind magic tools set to the left and right of the vehicle.

I should probably name this thing, huh? Eh, "the propulsion device" works just fine.

I made the left and right levers so that they adjusted the output on the left and right propulsion devices. If you pushed the levers forward, you'd move forward. The more you pushed it that way, the higher the output. Pulling the levers backward would cause the vehicle to move in reverse. Pulling the levers outward would raise the vehicle further off the ground. Pushing them inward would cause it to descend. When it made contact with the ground, it would slow down and stop.

"...It's kind of fugly," I remarked.

"Not much we can do about that. It is a prototype, after all."

The prototype ended up resembling a certain blue cat robot's time machine. I didn't plan it that way. If this thing was going to be moving at high speeds, it needed to have defenses that would protect the pilot from wind or flying objects, which led to this highly refined design. And hey, it was just a prototype, okay?

"All right, time for a test drive."

"Be careful," Ira reminded me.

"I always am."

As long as I didn't die immediately, I'd be fine. I'd become oddly tough since coming to this world, after all.

First, I pressed the activation switch and began pumping magical power into the various magic tools. Next, I pulled the levers outward, causing the vehicle to float off the ground.

"All good so far."

"Mm, it's floating properly."

"Let's try moving up and down first."

I pushed the levers inward and outward, causing the proto-type airboard to rise and fall. Everything seemed a-okay.

"All right, perfect. Next, we're going to test out the wind magic propulsion system."

"'Kay."

We'd already succeeded with this part. Well, actually, the propulsion was originally so strong that it blew prototype #01 off into the horizon. Going to find it was a pain, so we just pre-tended it had never existed. It flew off in the direction of the

Black Forest, so I doubted our secrets would fall into the hands of the Holy Kingdom...

Look, my bad, okay? Putting that aside...

I pushed the levers forward; I designed this thing so that there were four stages of power output based on the angle of the levers.

"Oooh, this is good."

"It's moving properly."

At its lowest output, the airboard hovered forward slowly over the badlands. This was about the same speed as walking on foot. By adjusting the output to each side, you could turn the vehicle as well.

"All right, let's raise the speed."

"Mm, be careful."

I pushed the levers forward some more, and soon the airboard was moving at a brisk pace. This thing was prone to skidding due to inertia when making turns, so it was going to take precise piloting. That'd take some getting used to.

I raised the altitude of the airboard to test out high speed movement. It'd suck if I collided with a boulder or something because I kept it low to the ground.

"Whoa! This thing's fast! *Ow!*"

Raising the speed to its max level, I was stunned to find the airboard was even faster than I expected. It was easily doing 50 km per hour. The strong winds were slapping against my face, and the sand in the Badlands was smacking me too. It hurt.

The pilot was definitely going to need goggles, a mask, or a full-face helmet.

After experiencing max speed, I slowed down and returned to Ira.

"I'm going next," she insisted.

"That's fine, but only go as high as the third level. The wind against your face can be rough. Same with small stones and sand in the air."

"Don't worry, I'll block them with magic."

"Crap, I forgot that was an option!"

If you had access to wind magic, you could just protect yourself with that. I could always just build that into the vehicle itself, though... I really hadn't considered that possibility.

Ira rode the airboard through the Badlands like a pro. Guess she wasn't the type of person whose personality changed the second they had their hands on the steering wheel.

After a bit, she returned to me with a pleased expression on her face.

"This is great," she said. "If we can mass produce these, the world will experience a travel revolution."

"We'll have to be careful of traffic accidents," I pointed out. "This thing's way faster than a carriage, so it could lead to some real tragedies."

"That's true. And if the Holy Kingdom got their hands on one, they could potentially reproduce it. It's been made using technology that exists in our world already, so..."

"Right, right... Well, if these do end up being used all over, it is what it is."

"Mm, but this..."

"Prototype airboard."

"The tech used in this prototype airboard has military applications as well, so it can easily be used as is. We have to be careful."

"Good point."

The wind magic propulsion system, for one. You could attach it to a spear, and just like that you'd have something with the same power as a ballista. You'd have to adjust it for speed and stability, of course, but still...

And then there were powder and explosives. If you built a magic tool with explosive magic, you'd have a devastatingly powerful weapon. I made an anti-tank rocket launcher myself, but when it came to propulsive power, it would be way more cost-effective to use wind magic, a technology that exists in this world already.

"And then there's the equation that erases wind magic recoil," Ira mused. "It might be bad if this gets out to the public."

"How so?"

"I'm not 100 percent sure yet, but I might be able to make a new type of magic," she said, thinking deeply.

Magic that erases recoil... I didn't understand it myself, but I did get the feeling it could be used for something.

"What the heck's this?!" said Bela. "Seriously!"

"A new vehicle that Ira and I built together. It's called the prototype airboard."

Bela lost her mind when she saw the new vehicle, but Shemel and Tozume were a bit harder to read. Madame Zamil, on the other hand, looked at the airboard with great curiosity.

The harpies observed it from a good distance away.

"This is a vehicle?"

"There is a seat-like thing attached to it."

"How does it even move?"

"...?"

The four of them knew all too well that, as a prototype, it wouldn't have been necessarily built with safety in mind.

As for Grande, she wore a look of utter despair.

"A vehicle...?" she wailed. "My purpose in life is being stolen from me..."

You don't have to worry, Grande. I'm not replacing you, I promise. You're more than just a vehicle.

Ira had suddenly stopped moving while thinking about a brand-new type of magic, so I decided to develop some goggles on my own. Eventually, everyone returned from scouting out the ruins and saw the prototype airboard, leading us to the present.

"Here, lemme show you guys how it works," I said.

I slipped on my goggles and mask, booted up the airboard, and slowly began to float around the area.

"Whooooa! This is kinda amazing! It's floating and moving around and stuff!"

Thank you for the passionate explanation.

Thanks to the lack of friction with the ground, once this thing got moving, inertia would really get it going. If we installed a magic wind wall into this thing to lower air resistance, it'd probably be able to travel a long distance without much magical energy consumption.

Actually, levitation was different from hovering, so how did any of this work? Was it fudging the amount of material being levitated? Was it working on an anti-gravity system? Was it lending buoyancy to physical objects...?

It was all a mystery. And since it was magic, was I foolish for thinking too deeply about it? Don't think, just feel? I suddenly felt like I understood how Ira felt whenever she called my powers unfair or absurd. Magic was *really* unfair and absurd. I figured that if I told Ira so, she'd punch me in the gut.

After getting back to everyone, I used the reverse wind blast to lower my speed and make contact with the ground to brake. Yeah, the brakes were gonna be a problem.

"See? We made this so we could travel at high speeds over uneven terrain. This is just the starting point. We'll be modifying and loading this thing with features as we develop it further."

Bela raised her hand excitedly. "I wanna try driving it!"

Mm, this thing wasn't exactly safe yet, and it'd be bad if it was destroyed.

"..."

She was staring at me with sparkling eyes. How could I say no to such an expectant gaze?

"...Just don't crash it."

"I won't, Boss!"

"Seriously," I said. "It's a prototype."

"No worries, Boss!"

Bela excitedly got on the prototype airboard, and I proceeded to explain its control system to her. She seemed to be listening, but was she actually understanding? I suddenly found myself very concerned... But hey, there were only two levers and only a few directions you could push them. It'd be fine.

"Just to be clear: Do not hit anything," I said. "I mean it. No matter what! Drive safely!"

"No worries, buddy! Time to put the pedal to the metal!"

"You idiot! You can't just go full throttle like that! Raise your altitude!"

The propulsion devices on both sides of the airboard were blasting out wind, causing the vehicle to zoom forward with Bela on top of it.

And then—

"UWAAAAH!"

"AAAAAAAH?!"

She collided expertly with a boulder in front of her. It all went down in less than ten seconds.

"Ugggh, please forgive me," Bela groaned.

"What?"

"Ugggh…"

I hung a board around her neck that read "I destroyed an important prototype," and dressed her in a miniskirt maid outfit as punishment for her deeds. Bela was currently sitting on her knees on the ground. Next to her I was repairing the annihilated prototype airboard.

I rarely ever got angry, but even I had my limits. I was furious, in fact. I'd warned her three times, and yet here we were. Like hell was I just going to forgive her as if it were no big deal. But was I taking it easy on her by dressing her up in a miniskirt maid outfit and making her sit on her knees? What if I put some gravel on the ground where she was sitting and then put some heavy stones on her knees?

Pirna and Shemel were observing the situation from a little way off.

"I think this might be the first time I've ever seen him so angry," said Pirna,

"I mean, I get where he's coming from, aye…?"

As for the prototype airboard's condition, well, the board itself was fine. It was just made of wood, after all. But the propulsion device on the left side was broken, which sucked, and so was the circuit that provided it with magic power.

I'd be able to use my smithing station to repair it, but it'd take time.

"Look, I'm really damn angry that you broke our prototype," I told Bela. "But more than that, I'm angry because what you did was stupidly dangerous. Things turned out fine because it was *you*

who collided with that boulder, but what if it'd been Ira or the harpies? They could have been killed. And you were in danger too! If you'd been thrown off the board into a boulder, you could've been injured. If you were unlucky, you might've even died."

"You're right..."

Ira and the harpies were comparably tiny, so they really might've died on impact. Man, how many times had I warned Bela? *Ugh*.

Maybe I was wrong to try and develop a high-speed vehicle in this world? I could already envision a future filled with horrific traffic accidents. It'd be fine if folks treated these new vehicles the same way as carriages, but the reality was that they could go much faster... If I was going to mass produce these and make them available to the Liberation Army, we'd need training schools and license tests.

"Well, at least I'll be able to repair the thing, but you're gonna have to sit here for a while. So, aerial squad, how'd the searching go?"

"From up in the sky, we didn't find anything that looked like an entrance to the underground."

"We're probably gonna have to dig, eh?"

"I see... How about you ladies who were on the ground?"

"We confirmed some remains, and they look to have belonged to a fairly large facility," Madame Zamil replied. "The location of the rear base is supposed to be where the castle once was, so if this place is about a day and a half to two days away on foot, these might be the remains of a satellite city or an inn town."

"So probably not a facility within the capital itself, huh…?"

"It's a bit too far for that. I thought it might be some kind of defense facility, but if it was, it would've been wiped out by the elves long ago. The fact that there are remains to be found suggests that's not the case. For the same reason, it likely isn't a lord's manor or a facility of any political value."

I nodded in response to Madame Zamil's concise explanation. "Gotcha."

The elven elders definitely would've annihilated any defensive facilities or manors belonging to the powerful. On the flip side, I suspected they'd have shown some restraint when it came to orphanages, hospitals, or educational institutions. In that case, it was still possible we might be able to find what we were looking for.

Grande was next to report her findings.

"I searched underground for a little bit and discovered a few open spaces that were likely man-made." She puffed her chest out proudly. "As a grand dragon, finding those sorts of things is child's play."

Apparently, grand dragons were equipped with something like sonar, which allowed her to detect open spaces underground.

"That being said, many of them seemed quite weak and prone to collapse, likely due to their old age," she added. "I'm not good with delicate tasks, so I didn't dig any of them up. But I do think this will serve as a lead."

"Whoa, awesome!" I exclaimed. "Helluva job, Grande."

"Hee hee, right? Right? Feel free to praise me more for being so reliable!"

Grande trotted over to me, so I gently caressed her horned head. She clearly enjoyed this, as she started smacking her tail against the ground. Grande was extremely easy to read, and that was part of why she was so adorable.

"You'll be getting a cheeseburger for dinner tonight," I told her. "And for dessert, pancakes loaded with cream and jam."

"Really?!"

"Yup."

"Yay!"

Grande spun in place to express her joy, which caused her tail to collide with me and send me flying.

Ouch.

"I'm sorry..."

I thought I heard my rib cage make an awful sound, but surely it was just my mind playing tricks on me.

"Hah... Hah, hah... I'm totally fine. Just be careful next time, okay?"

It didn't hurt to breathe, after all. Since coming to this world, my level had gone up, which meant my body itself had become somewhat inhuman. It was entirely possible that I simply healed faster than I could feel the pain. My healing speed had increased thanks to my survivor skill.

I should make sure to drink a life potion later just to be careful.

"I'm pretty much done getting our base together," I told everyone. "As you can all see, it's a large high-floored base. There's a ladder leading to the living areas, so use that to get up."

Gizma couldn't climb ladders, after all. It'd be bad for each pillar to have a ladder attached to it if we had human attackers, but I doubted there'd be any, so I focused primarily on ease of access.

I guided everyone up top, including Bela because I felt bad leaving her behind. Of course, I had her go up first.

"Heh, he's got you wearing a pretty cute outfit."

"Are you a cat?"

"Ugh... How shameful."

"It's not like I want to look like this..." Bela whined.

Everyone in the exploration party had seen her cute cat panties, so the stupid ogre girl was off sulking in a corner of the cafeteria. All right, that was enough punishment. I wasn't planning on denying her a hot meal, I wasn't that cruel. I was going to have her spend the whole day in that miniskirt maid outfit, though!

Now that everyone had been shown around the facilities, today's work came to an end. I had everyone unequip their gear, get comfy, and rest. We were still in the middle of the Badlands, though, so everyone kept their weapons nearby, just in case.

As for Ira, I didn't really understand what she was up to, but she was muttering to herself while thinking up some new magic. She told me she was on the verge of coming up with some revolutionary new spell... I wondered what it could be.

After we all enjoyed Grande's favorite foods for dinner, we got some sleep, woke up the next day, and began our excavation work early in the morning.

What happened last night? I slept soundly. Mm-hmm. Ira was focused on thinking, the harpies were all tired, and Grande was sleepy from eating so much. I put Ira to bed, since she showed no signs of doing it herself, and then we all slept soundly together.

"Now then, time to get diggin'!" I announced.

"You've got this!"

"We're countin' on ya!"

"Good luck."

"We're relying on you."

"You can do it."

"I'll help!" declared Grande.

She was a real angel for volunteering to help out, so I rubbed her head and gave her a candy as thanks. The problem was that Grande wasn't good at holding back, so it'd be better to have her on standby, enjoying her treat.

First, I dug out a huge section of dirt with my mithril shovel +9. This shovel could dig up a chunk of dirt one meter deep, twenty meters wide, and fifty meters long in one stroke and drop that chunk straight into my inventory. It was absurd, quite frankly, and there was no holding back with it. Moving that much ground in one go meant that any displaced boulders and such could drop down, crushing anything below them. I had to be very careful about when and how I used this thing.

Which was why I used a variety of materials to make a modified set of shovels.

Applying effects to a mithril shovel using a magic jewel resulted in a mithril shovel +9, but by using magicite, a magic stone, or a magic crystal instead, with a magic steel, magic iron, or regular steel shovel, I got a host of different shovels for different occasions.

Grande and Ira kept tabs on where I dug, directing me toward the man-made open spaces.

"I feel like I'm bearin' witness to somethin' extraordinary," said Bela.

Tozume stared. "How is he doing this...?"

I placed the shovels on different shortcut keys, so I quickly switched between them as I dug into the ground. Bela and Tozume were completely baffled by the sight, but I wasn't sure why.

"If he used that skill in combat, he could switch to different ranged weapons anytime," said Bela.

"From a sword to a spear to an axe. Then to a short sword to a two-handed sword with no time delay whatsoever..." Tozume mused. "That'd be a handful to deal with."

"If Sir Kousuke devoted himself to the combat arts, he'd become an amazing warrior," Madame Zamil agreed.

Not in the cards, folks. I've got guns, so why would I go out of my way to swing around metal?

I wasn't going to start wielding a bayonet in the twenty-first century. As long as nobody got close, I wouldn't be whipping out any close-range weapons. I had a machine pistol, a shotgun, a submachine gun, and an assault rifle, after all.

It was a secret to those around me that I actually had a mithril short sword equipped on one of my shortcuts, though. It was just part of my survival instincts to have something like that on me, even though I was loaded with firepower.

"Oh, looks like I hit the jackpot."

In front of me was a stone material that was obviously man-made. I carefully dug up the dirt around me, creating a path for us.

"That stone wall sure is tough," said Bela. "What's the plan, Boss?"

"Ain't it obvious? Kousuke!" Shemel barked.

"Aye, aye!"

I swung my mithril pickaxe +9 at the wall, digging a hole into it. A stone wall like this only took a single swing. The path inside was dark, so we'd need lighting.

"Ira?"

"Mm. I'll use my illumination magic."

Ira whispered something, producing a softball-sized ball of light that floated into the path ahead. The path revealed itself to be a stone passageway. It looked like we'd dug our way into an actual corridor.

"Time to see if they got what you're lookin' for."

"That sure would be nice."

"We can't go in yet. I need to make sure it's not filled with poison," Ira said, bringing up a glowing magic circle and a ball of light before her.

I had no idea how she was able to figure out things like that, but according to her, this allowed her to deduce whether there was poisonous gas, or poisonous dust or molecules in the area. Magic sure was something else!

Thinking about it, maybe it would be wise to make a poison detector of my own. If it was compact enough, I imagine adventurers would go crazy for it. Or maybe it'd be faster to just make gas masks? I bet if I utilized magic, I could make an anti-poison breathing mask that was functional in all environments, even under the water.

"Done… But I've detected multiple magical responses within," said Ira.

"Oh yeah? Treasure then?"

"It's possible they're magic tools from when this was still the Omitt Kingdom. But I also confirmed that they're moving. These relics should've been completely closed in from the outside world, which means if they're monsters…"

"They're the undead sort," hissed Madam Zamil, baring her sharp fangs as she gripped her new, mithril alloy short spear.

Um, Madame Zamil? You're scaring me. I'm sure you're actually smiling, but still!

"That seems likely," Ira said. "Either that, golems, or dragon fang soldiers. You know, magical beings."

"Hrm, dragon fang soldiers, eh? If I recall, they're puppets made from dragon fangs, correct?"

Grande removed her protection bracelet and opened and closed her terrifying claws. She'd gotten a bit better at controlling her power, so now she could participate in close-range combat with no problems. Any magical attacks were still a struggle for her, so she wasn't allowed to use them in closed spaces.

I really wanted to have her wait with the harpies up on the surface, but she'd be bored out of her mind, so she ended up tagging along. Our exploration party currently consisted of myself, Ira, Madame Zamil, the three ogres, and Grande. We couldn't use explosives in such a tight area, nor could we fly, so the harpies were keeping tabs up top. They were going to take care of the fields while we were gone.

"Before we go in, let's check our equipment," Shemel said. "After that, it's game time."

"Roger that."

With that, everyone responded and began their last equipment check.

This time around I was equipped with wyvern leather armor that I'd made when I prepared the ogre trio's equipment. I also had a submachine gun with a suppressor, and a pump action shotgun. Of course, I also had my mithril short sword as well.

The submachine gun I brought along for the ride was the "Greaser," as it was known in a certain hamburger-loving country. It was .45 caliber and could hold thirty rounds. Its thin metal stock was iconic, and its long magazine could be used as a grip.

The low velocity .45 caliber rounds paired well with a suppressor; the noise canceling was excellent. We weren't exactly on a stealth op this time, but since we were surrounded by stone walls, constant gunshots would hurt my ears and ultimately cause problems for everyone else. That's why I went with a suppressor.

I actually wanted to use a more advanced gun that utilized 8 mm rounds, but in terms of cost, this was way cheaper... There was a reason this thing got mass produced, after all. .45 caliber was more than powerful enough, so when it came to supporting and protecting Ira and myself, there wasn't really a better option than this.

As for the pump action shotgun, it was just in case of an emergency. Firing this thing down here would be loud as hell, so I wanted to avoid that scenario unless it was absolutely necessary. Our party had four talented warriors leading the charge, so I doubted I'd end up using the thing.

The fact that I brought it anyway was just a habit as a survivalist. Hopefully, folks would forgive me. It felt terrible not preparing for a worst-case scenario when it was within my means... I'd also prepared a powerful assault rifle, rocket launcher, and a shotgun, but I didn't expect to have to use them.

I could make a suppressor for my shotgun, but the cost wasn't worth it. Compared to the price of an assault rifle suppressor, submachine gun suppressor, and pistol suppressor, it was over five times more expensive.

Seriously, why???

Tozume cast her gaze down at my suppressed submachine gun and tilted her head. "What is that?" She was clearly interested in a type of weapon she had never seen before.

"It's like a bow that can fire metal arrowheads at high velocity. A weapon from my world."

"Ah, so that's one of those gun things, then? I've always been curious about them."

"I'd also like to get used to how this thing feels, so if I get the chance, I'll fire it," I told her.

I'd made some adjustments to the rounds as well, so they'd be effective against undead enemies, which were known for their resistance to physical attacks. These were full metal jacket rounds covered in mithril alloy. Mithril alloy was extremely hard and less extensile, making it better than silver when it came to jacket material. Much more practical.

The problem was that I'd only prepared five magazines of mithril jacket bullets, for a total of 150 rounds. I was really hoping we'd encounter magical beings and not the undead. Seriously.

"Are there that many underground facilities out there with magical beings patrolling them?" Madame Zamil asked.

"The Omitt Kingdom was at war during the time, and when that came to an end, it was recorded that things were quite turbulent," Ira replied. "There were many facilities that utilized magical creatures as anti-bandit security."

"The elves attacked whenever they pleased, plus society itself was in chaos... Sounds like hell," I said.

"But it's not for sure that there are magical creatures here," added Ira. "It's more likely that the beings roaming this site are undead former citizens who were buried alive, died of hunger or dehydration, and became undead beings out of rage. That would be more natural."

"Bleh... I'm not great with the undead," Shemel grumbled. "Plus some of those jerks are resistant to physical attacks, right?"

"The weapons Kousuke made for us should work just fine," Ira reassured her. "They're all made of magic steel or mithril alloy."

Magic iron and steel, mithril, and mithril alloy weapons were effective against enemies that standard weapons were not. In that sense, the weapons I made for our party were indispensable to anyone doing battle against the undead.

"We have my magic, too. It will be fine."

Ira made a tiny magical firework go off for us. I often forgot, because she rarely showed that side of her, but Ira was a former court mage who was more than capable of wielding powerful destructive magic. In terms of pure attack power, she might've been number one in this group, and that included me.

"Hmph, I can easily handle any undead or magical creatures myself!" Grande proclaimed.

Indeed, she could take down any undead or magical creature with one punch. A dragon's claws could rip any kind of astral being apart, regardless of their ability to resist physical attacks. Dragons were insane that way.

"We're all set then? Let's get a move on," Shemel declared and led the way into the ruins.

We followed behind her, beginning our little operation in earnest.

It was time to conquer a dungeon.

CHAPTER 5

Attacking the Dungeon Beneath the Badlands

ZOMBIES.

They were well-worn territory for any survival game player. They were an enemy type that functioned well within the genre framework.

Many of them walked slowly, but lately it wasn't uncommon to see sprinting zombies too. Those honestly sucked, as far as I was concerned. To me, what made zombies scary was their overwhelming numbers, and the fact that all it took was one bite to do you in.

Running zombies were scary because they upended the common knowledge that zombies were shambling slowpokes. Basically, the only reason running zombies were scary was because the slow-walking ones existed first.

What was I going on about? C'mon, surely you could imagine.

"Running zombies freaking suck! GO TO HELL!!!"

RATATATATATAT! The dry sounds of gunfire filled the air as bullets smashed into the running corpses.

"Kousuke, these aren't zombies. They're ghouls," Ira corrected me as the zombies—er, ghouls—were showered in her lightning magic.

Sorry, Ira. But this old man won't be fooled.

You could call them infected, runners, abnormal, ghouls, whatever, but at the end of the day they were goddamn *zombies*.

"Is it just me, or is that weapon of yours crazy powerful?" said Bela, cutting down the ghouls with her axe.

Meanwhile, Madame Zamil did the same with her short spear, impaling them as they came. "It's like firing a longbow rapidly and at close range," she said. "Extremely strong."

I fired off my suppressed submachine gun, which was apparently a real hit with the ladies. Was now really the time to be talking about this?

Shemel and Tozume were smashing ghouls left and right with their metal club and war hammer respectively.

"Talk about numbers..." Shemel grunted.

"I really don't want to think about how this happened," said Tozume.

Most of the ghouls down here were humanoids that had starved to death... Close to thirty of them, to be precise. Like Tozume, I really didn't want to think too hard about how they all ended up down here.

"So then what kind of facility was this...?" I said as I swapped in a new magazine and got ready to start firing again. This particular firearm utilized magazines of 30 bullets, but if you let loose willy-nilly, you'd quickly run out of ammunition. Since it could only be fired at full auto, it was important to hold the trigger down in short bursts. Firing on full auto often resulted in wasted rounds.

"It's quite a vast underground facility, that's for sure, with lots of people to boot," Ira replied. "This many people getting buried alive is a pretty unique situation. It might've been some kind of shelter, perhaps. The only problem is that I can't even begin to imagine what the ruins above used to be."

"They must have been terribly feeble, to have so many people and still not be able to escape," Grande muttered, sounding exasperated. She tore through the ghouls effortlessly with her terrifying claws and powerful tail.

She wasn't wrong, though. With such numbers, if they had worked together, they should've been able to dig their way out.

"Wouldn't it have been easy to just use earth magic?" I asked.

"Probably," said Ira. "But it's possible that while they were hiding from the elves, something unforeseen happened. The truth is lost to us."

"Someone might've left behind a journal or something."

After taking down the last ghoul, Madame Zamil sharply swung her spear to flick the blood from its blade. Then she wiped off the rest with the old, torn cloth that the ghoul had been wearing, as if just grabbing something off a zombie was no big deal. She really must be used to this sort of thing.

"Anyone hurt?" she asked.

Everyone responded: nobody was harmed. According to Ira, ghouls had poison on their claws and fangs, and if you didn't detox, you'd become paralyzed. Once that happened, they would eat you alive... This was apparently what happened if you lost to a horde of ghouls.

"Talk about creepy," I said.

"They're only slightly more capable than an average person, and any trained soldier or adventurer can take them down easily," replied Madame Zamil. "Nonetheless, one must never underestimate them."

I quietly wondered if their poison would have an effect on me. If this many of the bastards were going to come our way, maybe I would've been better off switching to a mafia-style submachine gun with a drum magazine. Because of how narrow the place was, I'd opted not to use it before we charged in. I'd have to make one later.

"Anyway, can we use their bodies?" I asked.

"We can use the poison from their fangs and claws," Ira said. "We could even turn it into an anesthetic. Also, on occasion they carry things of value on their person."

"Gotcha. Then I suppose I'll collect them."

It'd be bad to leave a bunch of corpses in an enclosed space, especially when we might be able to use the facility for something one day. Nothing wrong with trying to keep the place as clean as possible.

I couldn't think of a use-case on the spot, sadly. It was rather far from the rear base. But I didn't need to figure it out right that moment.

"This place is a mess... Do you think there was a battle here?"

As we explored, we passed through a bunch of different rooms and found that the place was really busted up. Signs of combat were all over.

"Did they turn against each other?" I wondered.

"Stuck in an enclosed space like this as food and water grew scarce... It's entirely possible," said Madame Zamil.

"Sounds like true hell to me..." Ira said.

And in the end, they all died of hunger anyway and became ghouls cursed to wander the halls for hundreds of years. It was all so tragic...

"Kousuke."

"Yeah."

I grabbed the junk lying around and dumped it all into my inventory. What was I up to? Well, by doing this, we could finish surveying a room pretty much instantly. Once I put something in my inventory, I'd immediately be able to identify it, which cut down on the time we had to spend in each area.

I put everything in the room into my inventory, then decided to look through it all after we left. The most time-consuming element of the whole trip was going to be digging through each room. I could just get rid of all the garbage in one go later, and anything worth fixing I could handle with my smithing station. As long as I put something in the queue, I could have it repaired while we slept or were exploring, so there was no need to be concerned about numbers or time.

As we continued to explore—

"GUAAAGH!!!"

—ghouls and other such undead would pop up.

"Hi-yah!"

"Take *this*!"

"Hah!"

"Rmph!"

"Grah!"

Grande, Madame Zamil, and the three ogres all made short work of such obstacles; as soon as they appeared, they were removed from this world. Ever since that first massive battle when we entered the facility, Ira and I hadn't had to do a thing.

"Lady Grande, you're incredible," said Madame Zamil.

"Right? Right?" chirped Grande.

She had just rushed into a room alone and immediately reduced four ghouls to piles of useless flesh. Apparently, to lizardmen and lizardwomen, dragons were beings to be respected, so Madame Zamil ended up praising Grande a lot.

"A lot of these rooms are the same size," I observed.

"Mm, it kind of resembles a fortress in that respect," said Ira. "Maybe it was a military installation?"

"An underground military installation, eh? Would the elves really overlook something like that?"

"The elves can be kind of sloppy. Especially the older generation."

"...Makes sense."

Ira wasn't wrong. It wasn't totally certain that this was a military facility, but it was highly possible that it was at least something similar. If nothing else, it was hard to imagine that citizens would need to use a vast underground space like this.

"A place as big as this has to have a library," I said. "Or there must have been some hotshot who kept books in their room."

"It's definitely possible," said Ira. "The problem is, not only do we not know where it is, there are multiple areas closed off by rubble."

"Sir Kousuke can easily take care of anything like that."

"Leave the rubble clearing to me!" I agreed.

"No, I can handle it," Grande said, volunteering for the spot.

It was true that, without her protection bracelet, she was incredibly powerful. She was practically a living construction machine.

We continued to talk things over as we proceeded deeper, until we were met with a large door in front of us. After Tozume checked for traps, Ira used her magic to search beyond the door.

"I'm sensing a powerful magical reaction beyond here. There could be an undead beast far stronger than any of the ghouls we've encountered waiting just beyond here."

"Hrm, is that so?" Shemel put her mace over her shoulders and grinned savagely. "Then it's time to get ourselves pumped up, eh?"

Madame Zamil pulled up to her side with her short spear in hand; the two of them were planning on charging in together.

We'd already won.

Bela and Tozume kicked the door open from both sides, and Shemel and Madame Zamil entered the room swiftly. Me, Ira, and Grande followed behind them, entering the large room on the other side.

Was this some kind of waiting room for the manager of the facility?

"Welcome! You have done well to— wait, *AAAGH?!*"

Shemel immediately swung her mace at the foreboding robed figure in front of the table, smashing them into the ground. Madame Zamil followed up by piercing the figure's body with her short spear over and over again.

"Ow, ow, owie! Wait, time out! Please stop! I submit! I surrender! Please, spare me!"

"Er..." Shemel paused. "They're begging for mercy."

"Don't care," I said. "Finish them."

"Aye, aye!"

If this thing was a friendly creature, it had plenty of opportunities to get in touch with or warn us before we were attacked by ghouls.

Instead, he sat here and waited for us. There was no way this thing was friendly.

"Aaaaah! Wait, wait, wait!" The black-robed figure screamed as he looked up at the mace above him. "You're looking for something, right?! I can help!"

Hearing this, Shemel and Madame Zamil ceased their attacks and shot glances at me.

What to do, what to do...

"What do you think, Ira?" I asked.

"You can never trust the words of a lich. It'd be best to annihilate him."

"Ah, so it's a lich? From what I know, lich are typically ancient, powerful mages who've turned into undead. Is that right?"

"It is. Did you have them in your world too?"

"Nah. Only in fiction."

I couldn't definitively state that they didn't exist, but since magic wasn't a thing, I was fairly confident they weren't real either.

"Don't worry, seriously! I'm a lich, but I became one thanks to the Ring of the Dead! I'm just a shitty, off-brand lich! Totally safe!"

"So he says..." Madame Zamil muttered.

"The Ring of the Dead is said to be an ancient relic that automatically turns its wearer into a lich upon death," Ira said. "However, its existence has never been confirmed."

"This is it! Right here! I'm not lying!"

The robed bastard—er, lich thrust his right hand's middle finger (bone) at us, showing off the golden ring.

"Fascinating," I said. "Let's take it."

"Please don't! I'll disappear if you do! Forgive me! I'll do anything!"

"Hm? Did you just say something?"

"Er, yes?"

The lich looked up at me. Yup, he sure was a skeleton. A skeleton with blue flames deep in his eye sockets. Could we really trust this thing?

"Then tell us why you used the Ring of the Dead to become a lich and why you're holed up in here," I told him.

The lich sat on his knees on the stone floor and began to talk. Was that how folks in the old Omitt Kingdom sat?

"Um, those shitty elves attacked the Omitt Kingdom," he said

"We're aware. So, what?"

"This was a shelter built into a dead dungeon. Citizens of higher standing in the area were evacuated here, myself included."

A dead dungeon? I was curious about the terminology, but I generally got what the lich was implying, so I let him continue.

"A shelter for hotshots, huh? Then why has it become a dungeon filled with ghouls, and you, a lich?"

"The entrance was destroyed by an explosion caused by the elves," he explained. "We waited for help to come, but it never did. Soon our food stocks were exhausted, and we began to fight amongst ourselves. I was kind of the person in charge, but I was murdered pretty early on."

"And then you became a lich?"

The lich nodded, still on his knees.

"Correct. But when I became a lich, I was still filled with rage from being murdered."

"What did you do?"

"I went mad and cast curses on the remaining food and water, forcing the survivors to fight to the death."

"That's as evil as evil gets, pal," I turned to the others. "Maybe we should get rid of this dude ASAP?"

Ira nodded. "Agreed."

The rest of the girls seemed to be on the same page as well. Not terribly surprising.

"Wait, wait, wait! Just a moment! Yes, the folks who killed me ended up becoming ghouls, but as the long years went by, my rage toward them was quelled."

"Don't undead like this one vanish when that happens?"

"Normally, yes," said Grande, ready to leap out at the lich at any point. "But this thing is not normal."

The lich nodded.

"Indeed. Because of the Ring of the Dead, I didn't vanish, and I even got my sense of self back. But...I just don't have the courage to take the ring off and end things myself..."

"So you've been pretending to be a dungeon master down here?"

"Yes. But there obviously hasn't been much to do, so..."

"Hmm, what do you think?" I asked the rest of the party.

"Sense of self or not, he's still a lich," said Ira, "a dangerous undead. We should eliminate him immediately."

"I agree with Ira on this," Shemel said.

"Undead go against the rules of this world," said Grande. "Eliminating them fixes that."

"I don't really get difficult stuff like this," I said, "but it's not like we got a reason to keep him alive. Or dead, I guess."

"Mm, I dunno. What I do know is that we can't trust this guy."

"He might've been playing dungeon master, but one wrong move and we might've been torn apart by those ghouls. I don't have the mental resolve to sympathize with someone who tried to murder us."

My team was quite harsh in regards to this lich, but he was an undead, so. There was no telling if he'd suddenly reveal his true colors and try to stab us in the back. There really was no reason to keep him alive (undead?) without a way to safely control him.

"There's no way we could keep him on a leash, right?" I asked.

"He's a lich, at the end of the day," replied Ira. "We can't force him into obeying us."

"So, a slave collar wouldn't work?"

"Nope. And anyway, someone with a Ring of the Dead couldn't possibly be a good person. All necromancers are garbage people."

"Prejudice!" yelped the lich.

"You necromancers created that stereotype yourselves," Ira snapped, looking down at the lich with an impossibly cold gaze. "You attacked us with ghouls, did you not? You have no solid ground to stand on here."

Mm, saw that coming.

"Then it's decided."

"Urgh, in that case...!"

The lich stared at me, his eyes suddenly shining suspiciously.

What's this now?

"Bwa ha ha! You let your guard down, fools! I've taken control of that man's consciousness! If you care for him at all —"

"Er, did you do something just now?" I asked.

"...Huh?"

The lich looked baffled. His eyes shone for a second, but did he actually do something to me? He said he took over my consciousness, so was it some sort of brainwashing or mind control?

"Probably some kind of psychological attack," Ira explained. "Forced brainwashing or mind control. But since you have no magical power, it doesn't affect you."

"Gotcha... So, this thing attacked me, then?"

I cast my gaze onto the lich, who tried to smile at me. Huh. Didn't know skeletons could manage that.

"P-please, forgive me..."

"I forgive you," I replied with a smile.

The lich looked relieved. It sure was emotive, for a skeleton.

"But do you think this baby right here will?"

I pointed my submachine gun loaded with mithril-coated rounds at the lich, then pulled the trigger.

"GYAAA?! I SWEAR I'LL HAUNT YOU IN DEATH!!!"

The lich was torn to pieces by the hail of mithril-coated bullets. Maybe I really should've gone with a mafia-styled machine gun.

I pulled the Ring of the Dead off the middle finger of the lich, then dumped the bones into my inventory.

"Don't think he's gonna be haunting anyone when he was undead to begin with," I commented.

"Yup," Ira said.

"What a waste of time," Shemel grunted.

"Agreed..."

Shemel shrugged her shoulders. She wasn't wrong; we didn't get any new info out of him, so this really was pointless. I just wanted to dig through this stuff and bid this dank place goodbye.

"Welcome back, everyone!"

"Glad you're all okay."

"You all must be super-duper exhausted."

SURVIVAL IN ANOTHER WORLD WITH MY MISTRESS

"…"

The harpies welcomed us as we returned to the surface. After they took care of the fields for us, they'd been guarding the area, waiting patiently for our return.

"How was it inside there?" asked Pirna.

"Ghouls for days," I replied. "And then a lich deep inside."

"Kousuke tore it apart with his submachine gun."

"I'd expect nothing less from Master."

We all made our way back to base, and I began lining up our findings one by one.

"Lots of busted stuff," Ira observed.

"We are talking about relics that are hundreds of years old, y'know," I said. "Plus, the folks in there turned on each other at some point."

"Lots of valuables too. Gems and precious metals."

"I guess that lich wasn't lying when he said it was a shelter for the powerful," I said.

Lots of the accessories and goods were made of precious metals that had either broken down due to the passage of time or because of the actions of the ghouls. I could fix the busted stuff with my smithing station and raise their value easily enough.

I decided to have Ira make a record of all the relics we found.

"Lots of accessories and furnishings."

"Plus some weapons and magic tools. Tons of trash, as well."

There were plenty of busted beds, trunks, and other pieces of furniture. Also some damaged illustrations and clothes that I wouldn't be able to fix.

"There's a whole lot here," said Ira, "but no ancient scriptures."

As far as written texts went, we found some journals, fictional tales, and travel diaries, as well as a few magical tomes and engineering books. Unfortunately, we didn't find any ancient Adolist scriptures. Didn't seem like there were any faithful believers among the evacuees.

"What is that?" I asked, watching Ira flip through an ominous-looking book.

"A necromancy tome," Ira replied.

No wonder it seemed so creepy. It had this whole skeleton design thing going on and what looked like the shape of a person's face. I wouldn't have been surprised if it was made from human skin.

"Are you gonna read it?"

"Yes, it seems fascinating," she said. "I don't plan on ever using necromancy, but this would be a good way to learn how to do battle against a necromancer."

"Ah, makes sense."

One must know their enemy in order to do battle with them, I suppose.

"Well," said Ira, "we found a lot of valuables, so I'd call this a success."

"Mm-hmm. By adventuring standards, absolutely."

"If you ever became an adventurer, you'd rake in the cash, Kousuke."

"Hell, just bringing home this much stuff would make you a big deal."

Being able to carry as much as I wanted at any time really was cheating. The fact I had no weight limits or anything was a major advantage, too. There were limitations on these kinds of things in most survival games, so this was basically real-life easy mode. That said, being thrust into another world with no prep was closer to playing on hard mode, as far as I was concerned.

"But when it comes to our actual mission, this could hardly be called a success," I sighed.

"Not much we can do about it. This is only our first stop; we've got other locations to search," Ira said, placing the necromancy tome down off to the side so she could start making a record of everything I'd collected.

We'd be using these records to calculate the bonus the three ogres would get after the fact. Myself, Ira, Madame Zamil, and the harpies all belonged to the Liberation Army, so that wasn't a concern for us.

Grande also wasn't an official member of our forces, so she was being treated like the ogres.

"Tonight, we're gonna have a little banquet to celebrate our success," I announced.

"Oooh, I like the sound of that! Kousuke, you're the man!" Bela happily proclaimed.

Heh heh heh. Time to bust out some high-quality booze and food for the occasion!

And so, our first ruin dive ended as a reasonable success. Hopefully the next one would go just as well.

After our first day of exploration, the team took a bath and gathered back in the cafeteria. The baths to the north were divided into two. They were both the same size: quite big.

The reason I split it into two was because I couldn't possibly take a bath with the ogres or Madame Zamil. Ira, the harpies, and Grande were of course a different story.

When I was first building this place out, I proposed either making a single bath and having us go in at different times, or making one bath for me and one for the women, but Ira wasn't into the idea.

"Grande, the harpies, and I all want to bathe with you, so no. Besides, if we decide to leave this facility as is while we move on, we could use it as a men's and women's bathhouse. You should make them both the same size."

She wasn't wrong that it would be handy to keep this place around and split it into two, so I did just that.

"Ruins filled with ghouls and a lich hiding in wait, huh...?" mused Pirna.

"Talk about cliché," said Ingrid.

"Things started tough for the first day," said Capri, "but I'm glad nobody was hurt!"

"..."

C'mon, Aja. You gotta speak up at some point. I'm pretty sure I'd barely ever heard her voice.

Judging by her expression, she was at least listening with great interest.

"Are you sure it was a good idea to put down that lich, though?" one of the harpies asked. "You could've gotten info from him about when he was still alive. We could've found lots of ways of using him."

"Nope," said Ira firmly. "He couldn't be trusted. The only reason Kousuke avoided his control is that he's a Fabled Visitor. Grande or I might've been able to resist, but any of the other four girls would have been taken over. And if that lich meant for a peaceful resolution, he had plenty of opportunities to move toward one. Instead, he sicced his ghouls on us and pretended to be a dungeon master. If we made the wrong moves, we could have been torn apart."

"That's true... Well, I suppose it's fine! Grande's already located a bunch of other underground ruins, after all."

"Hundreds of years have passed since he turned into a lich, and he spent that whole time in the darkness with a bunch of ghouls, right? Personally, I find it dubious that he managed to hold on to his sanity through all of that."

"That is pretty suspicious," I agreed. "I don't think I could've handled it. But, uh, I guess there's no point worrying about it now."

I already killed him with my submachine gun. Probably. No point crying over spilled milk.

Also, even though he was a skeleton trying to take control of my mind, I was surprised by how easily I pulled the trigger... I guess I was getting used to life in this world.

I slipped Grande into the bath once she'd received a full body wash by the harpies, then all of us got out, dried off, and got dressed before heading to the cafeteria. I felt awesome.

"That took a while, aye?" Shemel remarked.

"W-were you having sexy times in there?!" asked Bela.

"No!" I yelled.

She was strangely excited. Was she actually super lewd under the surface? Actually, the fact that she asked me so directly meant it probably wasn't under the surface. But whatever. It didn't really matter.

"Sorry to keep you girls waiting," I said. "We were just talking about how we dealt with that lich."

"Ah, that guy?" said Tozume. "Well, it's fine, right? Not to be mean, but it'd be way too hard to adventure with that thing around."

"He might have looked like he was self-aware, but an undead is an undead," said Shemel. "We weren't meant to share the same space."

"Yeah, I agree," I said.

"Yup!" Bela chimed in. "He did seem pretty interesting, but I doubt we could trust him!"

She was the only one of the group who found the lich "interesting," but even *she* wouldn't trust him.

"And anyway, he was hostile toward the elves," Grande pointed out. "Considering we're friends with Sylphy and the elves in the Black Forest, we'd never get along."

"That is indeed true. More importantly, I'm famished. Who cares about that bag of bones?"

"Hear, hear. Let's feast and get ready for tomorrow."

With that, I whipped out a whole bunch of dishes from my inventory and placed them on the table. Grande and the harpies had their favorite hamburgers and pancakes, Shemel had her favorite wieners, and then there were various steaks and salads and whatnot for everyone else.

"It's like some kinda fairy-tale magic, huh?" Bela wondered.

"Yeah, yeah," said Tozume. "I've heard stories about mages and stuff using magic to make big feasts."

Stuff like pumpkin carriages, candy houses, and genie lamps and the like? So did tall tales like that exist in this world too? Maybe there were stories about past Fabled Visitors?

I pulled some bottles of liquor out and continued to prepare for the feast.

"Good work, everyone. Let's all celebrate today's successes! Cheers!"

"Cheers!"

We all raised our glasses and took our first sips.

"Not that we did much of anything," said Pirna.

"We just tended to the fields," Capri agreed.

"Hey, don't sweat the deets!" said Bela, passing them dishes of food. This dumb ogre could be surprisingly feminine when she wanted to be.

"What sort of stuff did you recover?" asked Shemel.

"Mm, here are the records."

I had read out the contents of my inventory and Ira jotted it all down, so I had a good idea of what we recovered, but I nonetheless peered at Ira's records with Shemel.

There were a lot of silver candlesticks and silverware, as well as accessories with gems. It'd be cool if the silverware were recognized as works of art, but if not, they were still worth as much as any other clump of silver. A lot of the gem accessories were in garbage condition, so they were currently being repaired at my smithing station. If none of them were cursed, they could be sold.

We also found a few short swords for self-defense, but a lot of them were also in crappy condition. There were even ones that had rusted so badly within their sheaths that they couldn't be pulled out anymore. Many of the short swords were decorated lavishly, though, so if they could be repaired, they'd likely fetch a high price. Hence, they were under repair with the accessories.

There were remnants of other weapons, too, but nothing worth repairing. After the folks down there started going at each other, the weapons probably ended up tossed aside and weren't maintained properly. None of this stuff was made of mithril or mithril alloy; it'd have been preserved if it had been.

Additionally, we found what looked like currency from the Omitt Kingdom. We weren't entirely certain about all of it, though—the gold and silver pieces were fine, but the copper ones had rusted so bad that they'd just clumped together. We could probably sell the good stuff to collectors, so I held on to it all. As for the clumps of copper, well, I had no choice but to melt it all down so we could reuse it.

We stumbled upon some magic tools as well, but none of them seemed all that valuable. Torches, water sources, various tools to support day to day life. These days, there were far higher spec magic tools being made that served similar purposes.

There was something kind of cool and fascinating on a historical level about magic tools from an ancient time, but practically speaking, they were treated like old gen tech... The world was a tough place. Because some of these had been premium items, though, some of the parts were made from high-purity mithril, so they'd still be valuable.

And then there were all kinds of gems, mysterious magic tomes, and various journals and books from the era.

"Wow, lots of valuables," I said.

Shemel nodded. "Yeah. All of it together makes for quite the bundle of cash."

"Except we're not really here for valuables; we're looking for religious texts," I pointed out. "Still, seeing a list of treasures like this does get the blood pumping."

"Oh? Heh, you totally get it, Kousuke," she chuckled. "You sure you ain't ready to become an adventurer?"

"I know I've got the chops for it, but I have Sylphy, so."

"Whew, it's gettin' hot in here." Shemel raised her hands up as if to signal that she was giving up.

My answer couldn't have come as much of a surprise, though. The only reason I was out in the Omitt Badlands digging around looking for ancient Adolist texts in the first place was for Sylphy's sake.

While me, Shemel, and Ira were looking at the records, Grande slammed into me with a hamburger in hand. "Kousuke, Kousuke? Got anything sweet?"

Her horn jabbed into my side. It kind of hurt, actually.

"It's too early for dessert," I said.

"Hamburgers are tasty and all, but I want something sweet!"

"Okay, I get it already."

I went through my inventory and pulled out a giant plate of pudding and a bunch of mixed fruits. This giant pudding was one of the Grande desserts I made for her back when she was a huge dragon.

"Pudding!" she exclaimed.

"Don't use your hands!" I grabbed Grande before she could dive into the pudding face first. "I'll grab you a spoon and dish, so use those, okay?"

I pulled out plates and utensils for multiple people. It wasn't long before everyone started to crowd around it.

"What the heck's this?!" said Bela. "Seriously?!"

"It's sweet and jiggly... Delicious," said Tozume.

The two ogres were bewitched by the pudding; it was their first time seeing it, after all. Meanwhile, Madame Zamil and Aja...

"..."

"..."

...They were eating at hyper speed.

Excuse me, customers? Please refrain from eating directly from the pudding plate!

I pulled another jumbo pudding from my inventory to keep things from getting too chaotic. Aja and Madame Zamil seriously couldn't hold themselves back when it came to pudding... Actually, Madame Zamil went crazy for any food with eggs in it. Were lizardmen especially fond of eggs?

"Don't blame me if y'all overeat and feel terrible in the morning."

I highly doubted any of the women actually heard me.

Anyway, everyone was definitely fine and full of energy after dinner. I made a ton of food, but they managed to go through everything. It didn't surprise me how much the ogres ate, but the harpies were a different matter; despite their size, they could really pack it down.

And so we refilled our energy meters after working hard on day one.

The next day.

"Let's kick some butt today!" I declared.

"You sure look exhausted this morning, pal," said Shemel.

"Please, I know."

It felt like she was looking at me with disgust, but I couldn't afford to care. I felt great. Only 10 percent of my stamina and HP gauge had been cut down.

"Mm, let's do it," said Ira.

"Aye!" chirped Grande.

"Take care, everyone!" Pirna called.

"Master, please be careful," Ingrid urged.

"Good luck, Master," said Capri.

"..." said Aja.

Everyone's skin sure was nice and shiny, but anybody would look like that after taking a morning bath and eating good food! Yup! Hah, hah, hah.

"Is he gonna be okay?"

"This is how he always is."

Tozume seemed concerned, but Madame Zamil answered like a professional. She was right; I was totally fine. Totally. Within the hour I'd be back to 100 percent. Perfectly safe.

"Today's exploration is going to be a bit different from yesterday's dungeon crawl, right?" asked Grande.

"Correcto!" Ira said. "There should be a handful of small underground spaces all over the place."

"Yesterday's ruins were a large shelter for the wealthy. Does this mean we're looking at shelters for individuals?" I asked.

"That's possible," said Madame Zamil. "Or underground storage spaces for merchants and store owners."

Ira nodded. "Ah, that sounds realistic. As long as you were careful about temperature, that sort of thing'd be great for preserving products and keeping them safe from burglars."

"I see..."

Leaving Pirna and the harpies behind to tend to the fields, the rest of us casually walked across the Badlands. Grande, our earth grand dragon, had used magic to locate the underground spaces in the area, so we already knew where to look.

Shemel and her ogres had also investigated those spots, so we weren't getting lost anytime soon.

"Y'know, I can't help but feel like we'd cut down on time if I hurried up and made an airboard we could all ride," I said

"Mm, that's true," said Ira. "You have more than enough materials for it. Maybe you should do that tonight?"

"Not a bad idea. We could just make the prototype bigger and upsize the levitation magic tools so that it can support more weight. We can upsize the propulsion devices too, and once we add a magical wind wall, we'd be good to go."

As Ira and I discussed the design for the high-speed magic tool, we arrived at our destination. It didn't feel like we'd been traveling for long, but judging by the position of the sun, we'd been walking for a while.

"We've arrived," announced Grande.

"So it's below here?" I asked.

"Mm. This area has...collapsed a bit," she added. "There's dirt inside."

"Then I suppose I'll dig up this area. Man, that underground sonar of yours is super useful, Grande."

"Hee hee hee, is it not? Praise me more!"

"You're just the best," I told her.

Grande proudly puffed out her modest chest, and I gently rubbed her head. So far, we'd been entirely reliant on her. She honestly deserved all the praise in the world.

"All right, time to get diggin'!" I said.

"You got this, pal," said Bela.

"Good luck, Sir Kousuke," said Madame Zamil.

I pulled out my mithril shovel +9, stabbed it into the ground, and began eliminating dirt. Since this thing could eradicate a whole area of dirt in one swing, digging up an underground room was no effort at all.

"I can see the entrance."

"Seriously?! Talk about fast..."

It only took five swings of the shovel.

Ira used her magic to make sure there was no poisonous gas or other dangerous traps, and after confirming it was safe, Shemel and her girls charged in... And then they quickly re-emerged.

"This one is a no-go," she said.

"Since dirt got in, most of the stuff here is garbage," Tozume explained. "Nothing we were looking for, either."

"For real? Well, I might be able to repair some of it, so I'll collect the junk anyway."

But when I entered the underground room, I found that Shemel and the girls were totally right: nothing decent was left.

I ended up grabbing some junk, but... Well, hopefully repairing it would be worth it.

"Next stop!"

"Got it, Boss."

We went from underground room to underground room, opening them up and exploring their contents. Things were progressing well; we encountered no dangers. Sadly, each room was a total bust.

It was like rolling an underground room gacha system. It felt like our odds were terrible.

But just as I was starting to get kind of listless over our terrible luck, Shemel shouted out from the underground room she and the ogre girls had just headed into.

"Yooo! Looks like we hit the jackpot!"

Did we finally find what we were looking for?! Ira and I entered the room and were immediately thrilled with the sight before us.

"Look at all the books!" I gasped.

"Yes, this is incredible," said Ira. "This might've been the home of a scholar or something."

The shelves were lined tightly with books, making me think this might be a materials room or something. There was something resembling a table deeper within. Could this have been an underground study or research room?

I stuffed the books into my inventory and checked each of their names.

Adolist Scripture, Omitt Kingdom History Year 109 (Status Saved)
Adolist Scripture, Omitt Kingdom History Year 109 Copy (Status Saved)

"We've found it! An Adolist scripture! The original and a copy!"

"Thank goodness."

I would've liked Ira to have shot me a "Well done!" like that old meme, but oh well. There was no way she'd get it.

"Oooh, found the book you lot were lookin' for?" asked Shemel.

"Awesome shit!" crowed Bela.

"You went and made a huge base of operations for us, and we still ended up finding what we were looking for in two days," Tozume remarked.

She wasn't wrong. If I'd known we'd be this fast, I wouldn't have made a field. But honestly, none of this was a waste. The base was safe, provided shelter and water, and could also produce food, to some degree. It'd be useful for mining in locations near the rear base. None of this was for naught.

"Usually, we would have taken a great deal of time digging around looking for underground rooms," Madame Zamil pointed out. "We have Sir Kousuke and Lady Grande to thank for this."

"Mm, I am indeed very useful!" Grande placed her hands on her hips and puffed her chest out proudly. She was really fond of that pose, wasn't she? Well, she did look adorable, so it was fine.

"Let's hurry back to the rear base so I can analyze this," said Ira. "It would be really disappointing if this isn't the information we've been looking for."

"Man, it sure would be."

Imagine if the current anti-demi-human teachings of modern Adolism hadn't been developed after the fact, but was actually part of its original teachings? The Nostalgia-sect would suddenly find itself in dire straits.

I pulled the book out from my inventory, and, to my surprise, it was in fairly good condition. It must've been stored well, considering it'd been tucked away for at least three hundred years. This must've been the effects of "Status Saved."

"It has status saving magic cast on it," Ira said. "Show me."

"You got it."

Ira took the thick scripture out of my hand, and, after flipping through it for a bit, she checked the back, its interior, and the last page.

"This was copied thirty years before the fall of the Omitt Kingdom," she concluded. "This fits the era that the Saint of Truth was looking for."

"Then all that's left is its contents. Y'know, now that I look at the rest of the books, a lot of them are copies too. Maybe this room belonged to a professional copier? Like a storage or work space or something."

"Oooh, good one," said Bela. "Makes sense, considerin' how many books're in here."

"They're expensive, after all," Shemel added.

"Really?"

Three hundred years had passed since the fall of the Omitt Kingdom, but printing tech in this world hadn't progressed much, apparently.

Hrm, printing tech, eh? That would be way dangerous to spread around. Think I'll pass for the time being.

"Well, mission accomplished for now. I thought this would take longer, but we really wrapped things up, aye?"

"That's a good thing."

Finding this underground room was a genuine stroke of killer luck. In fact, it was so lucky that I couldn't help but suspect that maybe this was all planned by the being that tossed me into this world... But there was no way for me to confirm that one way or the other, and as long as things worked out in our favor, who was I to complain?

"If we've got what we're lookin' for, then there's no reason to be out here exploring anymore," Shemel said. "Are we good to cut things short?"

"Sounds good to me. Any objections?"

I cast my gaze toward Ira and Madame Zamil, who both nodded. Grande? Well, Grande was yawning with disinterest. She wasn't really there to look for scriptures so much as she was tagging along with me, so I guess her reaction made sense. It wasn't like she could eat scriptures, so why would she be interested in them?

"All right, then, folks. Let's head home."

Ira needed to start analyzing the text, and I decided to try making a giant airboard everyone could ride. I couldn't imagine it not proving useful.

We immediately returned to home base, where Ira proceeded to analyze the scripture. Meanwhile, I got working on that large airboard, and everyone else rested.

Creating a large airboard wasn't difficult in and of itself. I just needed to enlarge each of the key parts and make them stronger. The tricky part was tweaking the output of the levitation tools and propulsion devices, as well as the throttle. Oh, and I suppose sticking a sail on it.

To block the wind, I could make a glass... No, it would be

cheaper to just make masks and goggles for all the riders. Some large glass thing to protect against the wind would add weight to the vehicle. Once Ira had some free time, I'd ask her to make some magic tools that could generate a magical wind wall.

It all came down to the running cost. The propulsion devices were pretty fuel-efficient, but the levitation tools ate up quite a bit of magical power. And each corner of the board had a levitation magic tool...

Man, that's a long name. Let's go with "hover tool."

Each corner had a hover tool, so I'd have to see about making adjustments to try to lower the magic cost.

Could I charge the airboard base to a triangular shape and attach three hover tools? No... But what if I made the hover tools super large and made the entire contact area a source for levitation magic?

At the moment, the hover tools were supporting the board. The board itself was a square, so there was one set to each corner. What if instead of supporting it with these single points, we produced the levitation magic across a wider field? It was worth trying.

"You sure look like you're thinkin' hard," said Bela.

"Master always looks like that when he's making something," Capri told her.

"He almost always produces something absurd after making that face," added Madame Zamil.

The three of them were watching from a distance as I worked on the modified airboard. Actually, in Bela's case, "watching" was an understatement. It was more accurate to say she was staring with extreme curiosity and interest. She might've been thinking about how much she wanted to ride an airboard again.

If she crashed this thing a second time, I'd make her wear a tiger-print micro bikini. The mega-kinky kind that just barely hides the nips.

"Yikes!" Bela yelped, trembling in place. "I just got a mega cold chill down my spine."

Her adventurer instincts must have kicked in. Not a bad reaction at all. But she'd probably be okay as long as she didn't destroy any more prototypes. Probably.

As I carried on working, I could hear what sounded like combat noises coming from afar. Madame Zamil was gone, so she was probably sparring with someone.

One of the output tests resulted in a large propulsion device being launched at high speed toward the Black Forest, but apart from that, the process progressed smoothly. Look, I'd learned from previous failures and made sure to secure the board before testing output, okay? But it was far more powerful than I expected. It wasn't my fault. I just hope nobody got hit with a speeding propulsion device.

I did realize something, though. This was the perfect way of delivering an exploding magic jewel to a far-off location, wasn't it...?

If you weren't married to the idea of striking a specific spot and just wanted to annihilate a broad area from a distance, a twenty-shot rocket system could do unfathomable damage. More than just tens of thousands of soldiers, even.

Ha ha ha. It was time to leave this kind of dangerous talking in the back of my mind where it belonged. Wouldn't want to end up with a weapon of mass destruction in my hands. I mean, the gumption of someone to use a rocket launcher against soldiers armed with spears, swords, and horseback riders...

Hah, hah, hah, hah, hah! I'll develop it in secret...

"He's got a real nasty look on his face," Bela said.

"That's what he looks like when he's come up with a dangerous idea," said Pirna.

"Isn't that bad?"

"If it's actually dangerous, he won't ever reveal it to the world, so don't worry."

Pirna's powers of observation were really second to none. It made sense, considering she'd been watching me make guns and bombs since the very beginning.

Anyhow, for the airboard, I could use a workbench to make the parts, but I couldn't make the whole thing like that in one go. Why was that the case? Was it because I was still in the prototype phase? I could craft parts because those parts were already counted as "complete?"

I'd figured out quite a bit about my abilities over time, but there was still a lot I didn't get. I really wished this thing had a "help" feature.

I didn't manage to finish the modified airboard within the day, so I left that for tomorrow. With the sun setting, I decided to meet up with the others, have dinner, and talk with Ira about her progress.

"Long story short, this is exactly the scripture that the Nostalgia-sect hoped to find," she told me.

"Seriously?"

"Yes. I've only gotten through part of it, but so far there's been nothing in it about human superiority or making demi-humans into slaves. I'm not exactly well educated in the teachings of Adolism, but even I can tell that it's completely different from the infamous scripture about demi-human exclusion."

"Wow... That's wild."

Actually, didn't I have an ability that allowed me to automatically understand the languages of this world? What would happen if I looked at this scripture? With that in mind, I glanced over the book in front of Ira.

"Can you read it, Kousuke?"

"...Yup."

I could tell that the characters were completely different from the ones Ira and Sylphy wrote with, but the actual content of the book slipped into my mind with no problem. Wouldn't it be faster if I helped analyze this thing, then?

When I turned to look at Ira, she was glaring at me.

"It took me a lot of work to get this far, you know."

"...I feel really bad about that. Honestly."

"I think I deserve an apology."

"Seriously, I'm so sorry."

I'd assumed that dissecting old texts was the perfect job for Ira the mage and her killer brain. I never really took into account the fact that I could understand dragon tongue and a whole host of otherworldly languages.

I somehow managed to improve Ira's mood by promising to get her whatever food and dessert she wanted the next day. She was really willing to forgive me just like that, despite being made to work pointlessly for half a day... Ira was such a kindhearted person.

And so we decided that, tomorrow, we'd analyze and translate this scripture together. I was actually pretty curious about the teachings of Adolism, so it could be the perfect opportunity to learn.

"All right, I suppose I'll take a bath and get to bed early to prepare for tomorrow," I said.

"Mm, baths are important," said Ira. "Wash away the day's troubles."

Madame Zamil nodded her head deeply. "A wonderful way to describe it indeed," she said.

She was gently tapping her tail against the floor, her way of expressing when she was in a good mood. Madame Zamil was very fond of a good, hot bath and liked to take her time.

"Kousuke's first."

"I kinda feel bad about that," I said.

"It only makes sense that you'd be first!" Pirna insisted.

Shemel nodded in agreement. "Don't see no problems with the order."

To the women, the fact that they could sleep and even bathe in comfort out here was because of me, so they felt it only natural that I had the right to go in first.

Initially, I argued that I'd go in last and just wash up real quick with the remaining water, but the girls insisted they couldn't possibly enter ahead of me, and also, their actual objective, that they wouldn't be able to bathe with me that way. I ended up accepting my fate. I was in the minority here.

Still, it'd just be Ira or the harpies getting in with me, so it wasn't a big—

"Aye, don't mind us!"

"Yo, I'll wash your back or somethin'!"

"E-excuse us...."

"Wha—???"

I was just washing my hair when I heard a group of voices coming from behind me, and I instinctively turned around. My gaze was filled with Shemel and Bela's bare-naked red skin, and Tozume's blue skin... My word, they were massive. I'd be a fool to describe what exactly, but boy, were they *bouncy*.

"You're barely tryin' not to look," said Bela.

"Ain't you bored of seein' these already?" Shemel scoffed.

"That's that, this is this... Wait, no, that's not what I meant!" I yelped. "What are you girls doing?"

Bela and Shemel walked closer, ignoring my protests. Couldn't they at least cover up a little? Tozume, who was apparently the only one with a normal sense of shame, was hiding behind them.

"Now, now," Bela said. "Don't sweat the deets, Boss. Here, lemme wash your hair."

"Er, um, okay, sure. Thanks."

I couldn't possibly tell them to leave now that we were all naked together, so I decided to just let Bela wash my hair. Unfortunately, I had yet to craft shampoo, so we had to settle for soap.

"This soap sure smells nice."

"It's made from elven honey flowers," I told her.

These were flowers that you could extract honey from, also used in mead. I didn't actually know if they had a proper name or not, but everyone called them honey flowers, so who could say? They smelled delightful, so Sylphy and the other women were quite fond of this soap.

"La-di-da... La-di-da."

Bela hummed happily while caressing my scalp. I could feel the back of my head pressing against her bouncy boings. I tried to pay zero attention to them.

"All right, close your eyes!" she told me.

"Roger that."

SPLASH!

A bucket of warm water was dumped over my head, washing away the soap. It felt great.

"'Kay, I'll leave Tozume to wash your body."

"Me?!" the cyclops squeaked.

"Nah, I can do that myself," I assured her.

"I-I'll do it!"

Why did she sound so desperate? It was kind of scary, to be honest. These women were huge, and powerful to boot. I didn't want them to wind up using too much force and snapping me in half.

"...Why are you using your hands?" I croaked.

"If I use a towel I might push too hard, so..."

With that, Tozume began to glide her sud-covered hands down my back.

Ah, right. The towel might rip my skin off. Got it. Terrifying. In that case, it made sense that she'd just use her hands. Right? Right.

"Your shoulders, arms, and neck are so slender... And your hips are so tiny... Adorable..."

I could hear Tozume breathing heavily as she caressed my body all over. Suddenly, it felt like her touch had become strangely erotic.

"Hey, so uh, the woman washing me is kind of terrifying."

"I think I just learned all about Tozume's kinks and, uh, yeah. Not my thing."

"Now, now... It'll probably be fine."

Probably? *Probably?*

Also, what was all this about slender arms and stuff? I was pretty swole by now, what with all the exercise I'd gotten since I came here!

"I mean, compared to ogre men, you're pretty slender, Boss," Bela pointed out.

"And you're short," added Shemel.

"So, what, is it like how Ira and Pirna and the others look young to me?"

"Probs."

I looked like a little boy to a bunch of ogre women. Got it.

"...This is going to be okay, right?" I asked.

"If things get bad, I'll save you," said Shemel. "I'm sure she'll be back to normal soon."

"WHOA?!"

As Shemel was still speaking, I felt and heard Tozume slip backward. I bet if I turned around, I'd be met with one hell of a sight, but I decided not to—if she got embarrassed and slapped me, I might actually be insta-dead.

"Stop getting all freaked out over seeing a guy in the buff," Shemel scolded her. "You're not finished, right? Wash him properly."

"Uggh... S-sorry."

"Just be gentle, okay?"

I decided not to ask why she apologized. This was the true way of the warrior.

"Whew! Big baths rule."

"Just being able to stretch my legs out like this is amazin'."

"We are big, after all."

I could hear Shemel above me, and Bela and Tozume to my left and right.

After washing our bodies, the four of us got into the bath. For some reason, I ended up leaning against Shemel. Or I guess it was

more like she was holding me from behind. My head was sand-
wiched between two large, round, soft masses. It was something
else. They floated and bobbed and everything!

"I think it's about time someone explained this situation to
me, no?" I said.

Bela roared with laughter. "Ah ha ha ha, it kinda looks like
Shemel's boobs are talkin'!"

That's because I was hidden within her boobs!

"Let's just say we're checkin' to see how broadminded you are,"
Shemel said.

"What do you mean?"

"Most regular human men fear us, y'know?" said Bela.

"We wanted to see if you'd be willing to hang with us naked
without getting freaked out," Shemel explained.

"I mean, I was pretty scared for a second there," I admitted.

I couldn't see past the red boobs, but I certainly felt fear toward Tozume and her soap covered hands, especially while she
was breathing heavily. She was terrifying.

"She doesn't count," said Bela. "She scares us too."

"Ugh..."

Off to my left I could hear someone's cry of despair and then
the sounds of bubbles. It sounded like Tozume was sinking into
the bath in response to Bela's merciless words.

"Checking to see how broadminded I am, huh? That's a crude
way of putting it."

"Sure is."

"Yup."

So Shemel and the others now saw me as a potential partner, huh?

Sylphy, Ira, the harpies, Melty, Grande, and Elen. Shemel and the others were basically trying to join the circle of women who I was close to.

Sylphy and Melty were the ones who hired them as bodyguards for this mission, which meant they must already know about all of this. The groundwork had been laid without me even realizing it.

"Isn't this kind of a hassle?" I asked.

If they had Sylphy's approval and the cooperation of Ira and the others, the ogres should've been able to get on with this without beating around the bush. I was well aware of just how weak to pressure I was.

"Yeah, sure," Shemel replied. "But us ogres are careful when it comes to this sorta thing."

"Really?"

"Really. Our lives are basically on the line, and I don't just mean ours. I mean our kids, too."

Shemel began to explain why ogres were so careful when selecting partners.

"We eat a whole bunch, right?"

"Sure, yeah."

I nodded earnestly. Shemel and the others were big, and the amount of food they ate matched their size. I'd guess around five times more than me. And compared to small eaters like Ira and the harpies, probably ten times more.

"So, when we get pregnant, we gotta eat even more to make sure the baby inside us grows healthy. It goes without sayin' that we can't work when we're pregnant, so we're providing nothing to the food fund," Shemel went on.

"And once we have a kid, it carries on like that until we don't gotta take care of 'em. Obviously, when the kid is born we gotta eat right so we can give 'em milk, so we end up eating just as much as we did when we were pregnant. And even when the kid ain't bein' breastfed anymore, that just means they're startin' to eat a bunch too. In other words, in order for an ogre woman to have a child, we need to be kept fed by a husband who can manage that. Either that, or we gotta have quite a bit stored away.

"It'd be real bad if an ogre went and forcibly made a kid with someone, and then while she was pregnant, the guy ran out on her. It'd also be bad if the man couldn't provide, and it'd be bad if she went through everything she had stored away. We're ogres, aye? We'd end up dying of hunger, either with the baby still inside us or after we gave birth.

"That's why we need a hubby who won't abandon us when we're pregnant," she concluded. "Someone who'll look after us. We eat a lot."

"Now I get it..."

That's why they were so careful about picking a partner. It was probably similar for women of other races, but for ogres, it was much more serious. I could totally understand why they'd be so cautious.

"And in that sense, you're perfect, Boss," she said. "You're a helluva provider, and you ain't scared of us really, either. Purely in the sense of feeding us, or providing I guess, you could literally do it for as long as you wanted."

Were we to lose against the Holy Kingdom, I could take everyone to the Sorel Mountains or somewhere like the Black Forest, an area filled with monsters, build a base camp, and take care of everyone until we had the time to strike back. No problem.

"But I mean, we don't gotta rush nothin'," Shemel added. "We just want you to know that we're lookin' at you and we have approval from up top, that's all."

"Really?"

Usually, in situations like this, we'd end up gettin' busy on the spot. Or after getting out of the bath.

"Didn't you hear me?" said Shemel. "We're careful about this stuff. We're not gonna force you into nothin'."

"Though if you do fit the conditions, I might suddenly drag you into the thicket and take you to our village, aye," Bela added, terrifyingly.

"That's just you..." said Tozume. "And we just told him we weren't gonna force him into anything, so stop making things confusing."

I didn't want to be forced anywhere!

"Aw, c'mon," protested Bella. "That's what the Old Bag said!"

"And just how many years ago was that old lady of yours active...? Nobody's done that sorta thing for hundreds of years."

"...Huh, it's been like three to four hundred years, I'd say?"

"Man, races who live for a long time sure perceive things at a big scale, huh?"

If her "Old Bag" was active four hundred years ago, that would put her in the Edo period, back in Japan. A lot about sexuality would've changed in that much time. Hell, go back a hundred years or so in Japan and guys were still creeping into girls' rooms in the middle of the night.

"Well, anyway, that's the dealio," Shemel said. "I ain't gonna force you into anything anytime soon, but just think about it, 'kay?"

"So, you're saying I should prepare myself for that to happen eventually?"

"You won't have to if you're the one who gets proactive first, Boss," said Bela.

"I mean, that was part of the deal, so give up."

"The deal, huh?"

I surmised that this was probably part of a deal to make them my own private bodyguards. Sylphy and Melty probably wanted to make sure I had powerful bodyguards who could be with me at all times after the whole deal with Cuvi. I certainly had no complaints about the ogres' strength, and I also felt they were perfectly trustworthy and a good match for me.

"If you're all okay with it, then all right," I said, "I'll consider it... But I'd like for us to get to know each other a little better first, okay?"

The four of us soaked in the bath for a while. After we got out, we had some drinks together and chatted about how they became a party, where they came from, stuff like that. It was a peaceful, lovely time.

The day after.

Ira and I had been deciphering the Adolist scriptures from the Omitt Kingdom since the morning.

The actual translation process was fairly simple: I read the scripture out loud and Ira copied it down into a book of white paper.

Courtesy of my skill, the translations were perfect—not a mistake to be found. Not surprising, since I could read the text as if it were my own language.

"I worked so hard yesterday," Ira sighed, "and for what...?"

"I'm seriously super sorry about that."

The longer we translated, the more the light was beginning to vanish from her eyes. I really didn't like the terrifying look taking shape on her face.

I'll let you lay down in my lap, anything! Just forgive me!

As for the contents of the scripture, well, I wasn't sure how to describe it. The scripture was filled with passionate descriptions of the works of the creator, Adol, His words, and His teachings.

According to the scripture, Adol had come from the stars far away and landed on this planet, Leece, and made both it and Omicle into worlds where life could prosper.

Most of the creatures that currently lived on this planet were either brought here by Adol, or made by Him. A small chunk of life on this planet existed here before Adol changed it. Those life-forms were also loyal to Adol.

"Hm..."

"What's up?"

"Just something that's been on my mind for a while now..."

My head was buzzing with modern concepts: terraforming, genetic modification, bioengineering, and the development of intelligence in protozoan life. Could the being known as Adol actually be the kind of super-advanced off-worlder you'd normally find in a science fiction novel?

"So from your perspective, Adol would be less like a god," mused Ira, "and more a being possessing very advanced technology?"

"Yeah, basically," I said. "They used to say back in my old world that 'any sufficiently advanced technology is indistinguishable from magic'... I might be stretching it here, but it's kind of like how people who've only ever dealt with swords, spears, and bows see my guns and think they're some sort of magic. Only on a bigger scale than that."

"I think I understand what you're saying, but that way of thinking is heresy," Ira reminded me. "If you said anything like that to an extremist, you'd be interrogated and burned alive. You should probably keep that theory to yourself."

"Okay, that's terrifying."

We continued our translating until we got to the point where the text described the creation of demi-humans. According to the scripture, demi-humans were made by Adol as a way of exploring humanity's potential.

In other words, by performing genetic modification, combining DNA from humans with other different species' DNA, Adol created a bunch of different possibilities for humanity.

Was he a mad scientist? Apparently, the word "bioethics" wasn't in his dictionary.

"If I remember correctly," said Ira, "current Adolist teachings say that Adol turned sinners into demi-humans as a form of punishment."

"Right, right. I remember that too."

"But none of that is written here. In other words, this is proof of the modification that the Nostalgia-sect was looking for."

"It sure is. Let's keep looking for more."

A few hours passed as we continued translating the text. By the time noon arrived, we were pretty much done.

"If we include the smaller details, a lot has been modified," I said.

Ira nodded. "Mm. If nothing else, going by this scripture, Adolism doesn't denounce demi-humans. It is extremely likely that the teachings of Adolism in its current form were developed after the collapse of the Omitt Kingdom."

"The old Adolism even preaches that everyone should get along, humans and demi-humans alike, as beings created by the same god. It's actually pretty legit."

"Yes. It's possible that as things worsened between the Omitt Kingdom and the elves of the Black Forest, more and more modifications were made. And when the elves destroyed the Omitt Kingdom, those modifications came fast and heavy."

"That might explain why the original and its copy were tossed into an underground storage room. Who knows how the original text would've been taken at the time."

"Very possible. Perhaps the copyist couldn't bring themselves to destroy the original scripture."

"We didn't find any other scriptures, so maybe you're right. Perhaps they were a real historian."

We thought long and hard about the owner of the storage room. It could be as simple as them not being able to sell the text, so they tossed it into storage instead.

"And so that's that. The teachings of Adolism have almost definitely been modified."

"Huh," said Shemel. "Doesn't feel real, y'know?"

"When you think of Adolism, you think of the Holy Kingdom," added Tozume. "And when you think of the Holy Kingdom, you think of discrimination against demi-humans. And when you think about *that*, you think about Adolism. Hard to separate it all."

Bela nodded. "Even if you say real Adolism doesn't discriminate against demi-humans, I mean..."

"Just accepting it into our lives so soon isn't going to be possible," agreed Madame Zamil.

Their reactions made total sense. It'd been over two hundred years since the Holy Kingdom made Adolism its national religion, and over two hundred years since they acted on their anti-demi-human beliefs. The aggression that had built up between them in that time wouldn't just vanish out of nowhere.

"It wasn't God that saved us, nor was it the spirits," Pirna said as she and the other harpies munched on their lunch crepes. "It was you, Kousuke."

"Precisely," said Ingrid. "You're the one who's done it all."

"Everything and all!" Capri chimed in.

"..."

Even Aja, so endlessly quiet that I suspected she might be mute, nodded vehemently, eyes sparkling.

"All I can really say is that those humans sure believe in the most pointless things," huffed Grande, stuffing her cheeks full of her cream and fruit crepe.

She really seemed fed up by the whole thing. Perhaps in the dog-eat-dog world a dragon was used to, religion looked like a big waste of time.

The crepes on offer were the cream and fruit crepe Grande was eating and one filled with meat and vegetables. The sweet one ended up more popular by far. Maybe I should've gone with an 8:2 ratio.

"So we've accomplished our objective, then, yeah?" said Shemel. "Are we heading home?"

"Hm, we should be able to harvest some crops from the field tomorrow, so let's get what we can and leave for the rear base then," I replied. "As for who'll manage this place, we can just leave it to Arichburg as far as I'm concerned."

"...Are we riding in that thing again?"

I could see the blood drain from Shemel's face. She must've had an intense fear of heights.

"Well, yeah. It's just faster to fly."

After lunch, I was planning to finish the modified airboard. I figured we could use that to head back to the rear base tomorrow and then have Grande fly us back via gondola.

"I-is there any real reason to rush?" Shemel was sweating profusely. She clearly wanted to avoid this at all costs. "I mean, we finished up here way faster than we were expecting, right? So, um, I think it'd be a swell idea to take the airboard thing back. I mean, you gotta test it out and stuff, right?"

"You sure are gettin' desperate, Shemel," said Bela.

"Indeed," said Tozume.

"I understand not feeling worthy to have Lady Grande carry you, but..."

That wasn't it at all, Madame Zamil. It wasn't about respecting Grande—she was just terrified of flying.

"What'll we do?" I asked Ira.

"Shemel's making a lot of sense," she said. "Riding the airboard back from the rear base all the way to Arichburg would be a good test of its abilities. It's normally about two weeks of travel, so I'm pretty curious how many days it'll take the prototype to get back to Arichburg."

"It would be a good way to see how useful it actually is," I agreed. "We'll also get a better understanding of fuel consumption and cost."

"Mm. And if there's an emergency call from Arichburg, we can just have Grande carry us home."

"Good point. All right. Once we get back to the rear base, we'll use the golem communicator there to get in touch with

Sylphy in Arichburg. If nothing is amiss, we'll ride home on the airboard."

Ira nodded, and Shemel clenched her fist tightly in victory. Would it really be that bad to fly?

"Once we finish lunch, I'm gonna take a brief break, then get working on the modified airboard," I told everyone. "I whipped it up quickly, but I hit a wall trying to tweak the magic tools, making them bigger, and keeping it all efficient."

"Mm, I'll help," Ira said.

"Then I guess we'll, uh, take care of the field?" suggested Shemel.

"The harpies have wrapped that all up!" said Bela. "If we ain't got nothing to do, can't we just chill?"

She looked at me for approval, prompting me to look toward Madame Zamil.

"I do not see the problem with that. I'll be swinging my spear in the meantime."

"You sure are stoic, Madame Zamil," said Tozume. "I think I'm gonna watch Kousuke work on the airboard."

I got the impression cyclopes tended to like making stuff and fiddling with things. It seemed like Tozume was like that, anyhow.

"We'll be doing recon in the area and making sure there's nothing else in the batch of ruins," Pirna said.

"I shall sleep."

That was our Grande, compared to the workaholic harpies. But that wasn't quite fair; Grande had done tons of work on this trip. Besides, dragons did a lot of sleeping and eating, so this was perfectly normal behavior. It wouldn't be right for us to judge her actions based on what we thought was normal.

"All right then, folks. Just make sure to avoid any accidents or injuries this afternoon."

Everyone expressed their understanding in their own ways.

As for the sweet crepes, well... They were gone.

Fine, I'll bring out some more. Just so you know, the non-sweet ones are good too... Oh, the sweet ones are the best? Okay, sure. Fine.

Grande, Shemel, and I ended up enjoying the leftover crepes as a late-night snack later on.

After testing out a variety of options, I ended up making two modified airboards, each the size of a carriage. Considering the width of the roads and the size of parking spaces were all designed with carriages in mind, I wanted the airboards to fit in just as easily. We wouldn't all be able to ride in a single, carriage-sized airboard with eleven of us. If I tried to make one big enough for that, it'd be a giant vehicle, way larger than a carriage and probably as long as a bus. We'd need space for Grande and Madame Zamil's tails, not to mention how big Shemel and her girls were.

"I'd like to make them comfortable to ride in, considering we'll be on them for a while," I said.

"With the lack of rocking or shaking, they'll already be more comfortable than carriages," Ira pointed out. "If you make proper seats, I think you could even sleep in these."

"If they're not affected by the terrain, that also means they won't be affected by the rain, right?" Tozume said. "In that case, I think you should make it so we don't have to worry about getting wet."

That was a good point. The airboards didn't have to worry about wet terrain, so it'd make sense.

"I agree with that," I said. "What about safety? If we're totally visible from the outside, we might get attacked by bandits or hit with arrows, right?"

"Either way, we should have an elemental wall up at all times to keep out wind, rain, and sand," said Ira. "It should be possible to do that for the size of a single carriage. The problem is cost. Do we deal with the cost to build or the cost to run?"

According to Ira, it was ultimately about what sort of quality we went with for the device producing a wind wall. If we used a lot of mithril and made the production cost high, it'd be more effective, resulting in better fuel consumption. If we went cheap on the mithril, we could make a bunch of magic tools that could generate wind walls, but their effectiveness would drop and they'd use more fuel.

"In the end, if we're looking at hundreds or thousands of these going around, a cheap running cost would be for the best," she concluded.

"Wait, wait," I said. "Because we're using hover devices, we can kind of ignore weight, right? Then we could use wooden walls and iron plate armor to defend the passenger space. That would bring the total cost down, right? Maintenance would be way cheaper that way, too. If we made everything using magic tools, things'd be harder to maintain."

"If we are talking about ease of maintenance, then there's much to be said for the plethora of magic tools the airboard utilizes," said Ira. "It is always going to be tough to maintain one of these, so we might as well lean into it."

"I agree with Kousuke's idea," said Tozume. "Depending on the situation, people could find themselves camping outside. If that happens, it'd be easier to take shelter in the airboard if it had a canopy or was a closed space. Keeping wind magic active at all times would be a waste of magical energy. Shouldn't the magic wind wall primarily be used to prevent the passengers from being buffeted by wind? If we want to protect the passengers from wind, they could just wear masks."

"That's a valid point... Just because it's useful doesn't mean we have to rely on magic tools for everything," I agreed. "Let's leave those for solving specialized issues."

"Mm, okay," Ira nodded. "If we're going to make two, one of them should be enclosed and the other should have a canopy."

"Really? I guess that makes sense," I said. "We'll have two slightly different prototypes with different features we can test out."

Each airboard would have the same number of seats, the same control scheme, and its own propulsion system. The enclosed airboard would have one single large hover device, while the canopy airboard would keep the four smaller hover devices. As for the wind wall magic tool, I designed it with adjustable output for two modes: one that lowered air resistance to help with movement speed, and an emergency mode to protect the passengers from arrows and such. Knowing that you could use it for defensive purposes in a pickle would help make journeys feel safer.

Despite her size, Tozume was very good with her hands. She had a strong design sense, and a general idea of how to build a canopied or enclosed carriage, so she contributed a lot to the development of the airboards.

"You're amazing, Tozume," I told her. "Not only are you a talented adventurer, you could probably get by as an artisan."

"I'm nowhere close to the pros," she said. "But I can make most of the tools your average adventurer might need."

This level of quality was impressive for someone who wasn't a pro, in my opinion.

Taking into account contact brakes when designing the shape of the carriages, we settled on both designs being shaped like a large sled. In order to prevent the hover devices at the bottom being crushed by the airboard itself whenever it made contact with the ground, we added some height to the sled's legs. We also added side-brake-style ground brakes that could be controlled by the driver.

"It's done," I announced.

"Mm, sure is," said Ira.

"Who's going to drive these things and test them out?" asked Tozume. "You and Ira?"

"Sounds reasonable to me. Tozume, you can ride in either one."

"Then... I'll ride with you, Kousuke."

Ira and I hopped aboard the finished modified airboards and used the magic crystal to activate them both. I was riding in the enclosed, single hover device airboard, while Ira took the canopied model with multiple small hover devices.

"Let's drive safely!" I reminded her.

"Don't worry, I will."

I tilted both sticks outward and raised the altitude of the board slightly, then pushed them forward a little to get the airboard moving forward.

"Now that the whole thing's a bit heavier, it's a little slower to get moving," I remarked.

"Which also means that it will take time to stop," said Tozume behind me. "Braking early will be important."

"Yeah, otherwise you might find yourself in a huge accident," I said as I carefully raised the speed.

This time around, I attached foot pedals that could control a directional sail. Pressing down the right pedal would turn the vehicle right, the left pedal left. To some degree, you could use that method to turn. If you used that along with adjusting the output of the right and left propulsion devices, you could rotate if you wanted to.

The test drives went fine, and we found that, when both airboards were moving at just about the same speed, the large hover device model used less magical power.

"What are your thoughts?" I asked Ira.

"What do you think will happen if the four device airboard had to run with one of the magic tools malfunctioning?" she said.

Testing it out, I found that while the vehicle did shake and rock a lot, it could still run.

"I'd say it's a plus that even if one of the hover devices malfunctions, the four device airboard can still run," I said. "If the hover device on the other model kicks the bucket, that's all she wrote."

"That's a problem, but it's no different from normal carriages in that sense," Ira pointed out. "If a wheel gets damaged or broken, provided you don't have a spare, that's it."

"I don't think it's realistic for each airboard to come with spare hover devices," said Tozume.

"But if we're gonna put these things out en masse, we want to avoid a situation where the board breaks down and can't be repaired on site," I said. "I mean, I don't think it'll break easily to begin with, but... How is it in terms of resilience anyway?"

"It's not likely to break very easily," said Ira. "But these magic tools will be operational the entire time the airboard is running. We won't know what type of pressure they're under or how they'll break until we perform careful testing."

"So not something we're gonna solve in one day, eh?"

To find out how resilient the parts were, we'd just have to keep using them until they broke; make a whole lot of them and keep them continuously running.

"Oh, and about the build costs... In terms of what you build, we only have to consider the material cost," Tozume said. "But if artisans were to make these, making one large hover device would be simpler than producing four smaller ones. Am I wrong?"

Her input was eye-opening for me and Ira.

All I had to do was prepare the materials, put an order in on the crafting table, and once time was up, *DING!*, my order was good to go. But for an artisan, mage, or alchemist to make these hover devices, everything was different.

For example, in order to write the levitation spell into the mithril alloy that served as the core for the magic tool, they'd have to carve the same number of characters into the metal whether it was a small device or a large one.

In other words, in order to make one airboard usable, it'd take four times the time to finish a four device airboard.

I imagined it could take longer to carve the spell into a large hover device than it would a single small one, but there was no way that was the case if you were talking about four small devices.

"Maybe we should just develop the tech, then leave Melty and R&D to figure out the cost stuff," I said.

"Mm, agreed," said Ira. "Whether to focus on material cost or mass production is a decision too heavy for us. I'll write up a report about said issues as well as ease of maintenance. Oh, and I'll include Tozume's input, too."

"Awesome, you're the best."

I took the stance that we should leave those kinds of difficult things to people who understood them. A professional should deal with cost and usability issues. Not to mention, we'd only just built prototypes. We had no idea how reliable they were yet.

For now, it was important to just use these airboards and get whatever data we could.

The next day, after harvesting the crops, we split into two groups and boarded the modified airboards so we could make our way back to the rear base.

"Woo, we're going so fast, and there's no shaking or anything! Talk about comfy."

Shemel seemed pleased as punch riding on the airboard I was driving. She must have been happy to avoid flying through the sky.

"Not as fast as flight, but not bad at all," said Grande. She was seated all the way in back, looking outside the window.

From the outside, the modified airboard resembled a large floating sled. The enclosed version had glass windows so people could see outside.

Grande was all the way in the back because her tail kept getting in other people's way. It was a similar situation for Madame Zamil in the canopied airboard.

"Drivin' sure looks fun..."

I could hear Bela directly behind me.

Can you please stop whispering in my ear like that, you cheeky ogre?

"Do you want to drive?"

"Yussums!"

"Then once we get back to the rear base, you can drive it for a bit. But if you crash... He he he..."

I was going to make her wear either a micro bikini that just barely hid her nips or a frilly magical girl outfit. Hell, I could have her wear a pet-shaming sign, too, and make her walk around the rear base like that.

"It's mad terrifying that you won't elaborate," said Bela. "I've seriously got goosebumps."

"Wow, she's not lying!"

"Eeek! That tickles!"

Capri must've caressed her skin or something. Harpy feathers were like that.

There were five people in total riding on this airboard. Me, Shemel, Bela, Grande, and Capri. The passengers on board the canopied airboard Ira was driving were Pirna, Ingrid, Aja, Madame Zamil, and Tozume, for a total of six. We had fewer passengers on my airboard but more total weight.

Ogre bodies were big and heavy, while harpies were generally very light. Three harpies, for example, weighed less than a single ogre. I certainly didn't say that out loud— I valued my life, after all. In any world, bringing up weight with a woman was a stupid idea.

The journey from the excavation site to the rear base would normally be half a day's walk, but thanks to our modified airboards, it was a single hour of smooth travel.

And that wasn't even at top speed— the propulsion devices were only operating at half their max output.

As for why we didn't just book it, well, safety first, of course. It's not like we were in a hurry to begin with, and I'd tested out max speed already. I'm pretty sure I was going 200 kilometers an hour, easily. Honestly, considering air resistance was being cut to zero, I expected to be able to go faster using jet engine propulsion, so this told me that the propulsion devices still had room for improvement. They were just cylinders at this point, after all.

Would it be a good idea to work them into nozzle forms, maybe change the direction they were pointing or how wide they were? Now that I thought back on it, I was pretty sure jets had deflection nozzles. I decided to let R&D know the next time I commissioned something from them. Not that I was sure if my ideas would ever be put into use or not.

If we used it in combat, we could equip it with weapons... Maybe stick a chain gun on top? Just imagine a technical airboard that could encircle the Holy Kingdom's army faster than anyone on horseback, firing on them with a chain gun. It would be literal hell.

I decided I was going to make this dream a reality. I was merciless when it came to my enemies, after all.

Too one-sided? We were fighting for our right to exist. There wasn't anything better than it being one-sided in our favor. I didn't believe in murdering all of our enemies, but if it meant I could prevent casualties on our side, I'd do what I had to do. If the opposing force didn't want to die, then they could just surrender or simply choose not to participate in this war in the first place.

I could at least warn people before introducing something like that into combat. Even when it came to my enemies, I wasn't truly heartless. Heh.

"Now then, Ira's off to handle passing off the base we made in the Badlands to the folks here..."

"..."

The red ogre flashed me a sparkling gaze. Why did she love airboards so much? Did she just like vehicles?

"Look, just don't crash it, okay?"

"Of course, Boss!"

"Seriously. If you screw up again, you're gonna be heavily punished. I'm gonna traumatize you for life."

"Okay, now you're freakin' me out... I've got chills."

Seeing me say that with a straight face was enough to terrify her. Good. She should've been scared. If she crashed again, there would be no forgiveness. Her future would involve a mega tiny micro bikini or a frilly magical girl outfit, along with a plaque hanging from her neck describing her crimes. Then I'd drag her all around the rear base for show.

My seriousness must have gotten through to Bela, because she was extremely careful behind the controls. Excellent acceleration, perfect cornering, and she could even stop right on the designated spot.

"See, you can do it if you try!"

"Er, you think so, Boss?"

Bela turned to face me with a smile, and in that moment I saw her body accidentally push the right throttle all the way forward and the left throttle all the way back.

"Shit! You idiot!"

"Ah."

The airboard began to rotate at an insane speed.

"AAAAAH, AN ULTRA PIVOT?!"

Okay, so it didn't run on caterpillar tracks, but still. The problem we were facing was that the airboard Bela and I were on was spinning at a wild velocity.

"EEEEEEEK!"

"PUT THE THROTTLE BACK IN PLACE, YOU DOLT!"

"AYE!"

KACHINK!

Bela returned the throttles to their default position, cutting the propulsion devices and slowing the machine down.

"Whew, that sure was terrifying!" she said.

"You...bastard..."

"I ain't no bastard, boss," Bela replied with a dumb smirk that made me chop her on the head surprisingly hard.

"Augh!"

I was shocked she had the wherewithal to make that kind of sound.

"No more driving for you," I said. "I can't leave this thing in the hands of someone who'll bump it into full gear just because someone was talking to them."

"Aw, c'mon!"

No amount of sulking was going to get to me. There was no telling if she might smash into something if she got distracted.

"One more chance, please! I'll do anything for another chance, Boss!"

"You said 'anything,' right?"

"Ah... Yeah."

I could see the apprehension on Bela's face. I then went on to detail what would happen to her if she crashed, and even explained exactly what a leopard-print super micro bikini and frilly magical girl outfit were to further her fear.

"I'll drive super-dupes safely, promise!"

"I'm holding you to that. I'm surprised you're still so gung-ho about driving even after everything I said. What's so exciting about driving this thing?"

"Airboards are way cool, and driving them is super fun!" she replied, with sparkling eyes and clenched fists.

Her explanation was passionate, but none of it was getting through to me because she didn't have the vocabulary to back it up. The passion at least registered, though, and if she felt that strongly about it, I was fine with leaving this to her.

I ended up teaching Bela how to operate the airboard, one on one, and eventually Ira and Madame Zamil returned. They said everything had gone swimmingly, and Madame Zamil was holding some sort of gun. What was it?

"Welcome back. And, uh, what's that?"

"It is a new prototype magigun developed here at the rear base. We will be bringing it back to Arichburg along with its manual and so forth."

Ira held up a thick collection of materials—presumably development documents for the gun. I took the prototype from Madame Zamil.

"Huh..."

It was a frontloader. In form, it resembled the musket rifle from the materials I'd given them before. The big difference was that this magigun was developed by the artisans of this world from the ground up. A percussion-type gun...? I wasn't familiar. It had something resembling a firing hammer. The tip looked like a small piece of a magic crystal or something.

"There are also some materials from the rear base storage we're bringing to the front lines," Ira added.

"Roger that," I said. "So today let's grab the goods, do some maintenance on the airboards, and get some rest. We'll leave tomorrow."

"Mm, okay. I'll tell everyone else."

"Oh, before I forget. I made sure to hammer into Bela's head how to drive, so you won't have to do any of that tomorrow."

"Really?" said Ira. "In that case, I suppose I'll look over the necromancy tome while she drives."

"Don't blame me if you get motion sickness."

"Don't worry. I'll heal myself with magic."

There was magic for that? Man, nothing was off limits when it came to magic.

I left Ira and the others there and headed for the central area of the rear base so that I could grab the stuff we'd be taking to Arichburg. Madame Zamil accompanied me, her Shooting Star spear on her shoulders. I didn't think I needed security here, but there was no harm in letting her do as she pleased.

"Sorry for dragging you all over the place like this."

Madame Zamil quietly shook her head. "Please, this is my job,."

For this entire journey to locate Adolist scriptures, Madame Zamil guarded me along with Shemel and her girls. She did everything in her power to stay by my side and protect me, and when she couldn't, she made sure that Ira, Shemel, or Grande were with me.

Having noticed my gaze, Madame Zamil stared off into space before speaking.

"It was due to my own vanity that you were kidnapped by that accursed Cuvi," she said. "I refuse to allow myself to make the same mistake twice. I will not break the vow I made when I received Shooting Star. Not again."

"Cuvi..." I muttered. "What was his deal...?"

I still didn't understand the logic behind his actions. He spent years undercover in the Liberation Army, then kidnapped me at the end of it all. He could've assassinated Sylphy, Ira, Danan, or Sir Leonard if he'd wanted. Hell, it would've been simpler for him to kill me instead of kidnapping me in the half-assed way he did.

Instead, as soon as he handed me over to the castle in Merinesburg, I got out and escaped into the sewers.

If the enemy planned better, they should've been able to prevent my escape. Even if it wasn't Cuvi personally, he could've put a few big strong guys in charge of watching me. I would've been stuck in prison until Elen, Adolism's Saint of Truth, Eleonora, dropped by.

Apparently, as soon as Cuvi heard that I'd fled into the sewers, he split. What was his objective? If he had done his due diligence, would I have met Elen without meeting the slime girls? What would've happened if Cuvi had been there for that?

I didn't know. And if things did turn out that way, what did Cuvi have to gain? I had no clue what his motivations were. Cuvi was a demi-human, and he was so furry that there was no way he could hide among humans. What did he have to gain by working under the chains of modern Adolism? No matter how hard he worked, I couldn't see how he'd ever gain land, honor, or fortune.

And supposing he was a member of the Holy Kingdom, what sect did he even belong to? According to Elen, the guy who'd tossed me into jail without thinking anything of it was part of the main sect. But was Cuvi as well? And if he was, why didn't he seal the deal on my capture?

It was possible that the people of his sect just didn't take the words of a demi-human seriously. But then his boss should've been in a position to write up formal orders for Cuvi to make sure the job got done properly.

But again, all of this fell apart because the reality was that Cuvi was a demi-human. It didn't make sense that someone like him would work with the Holy Kingdom.

Could he have been a member of Elen's Nostalgia-sect...? No matter how hard I worked my brain, I couldn't reach anything resembling an answer. At the time I was kidnapped, I was so filled with rage, but now that I could think back on it with a clear head, I had no clue what Cuvi was trying to do. What was his objective?

Well, regardless of what it might've been, I'd make sure he paid for betraying me, Sylphy, and everyone else. I'd shave his whole goddamn body and put him out for all to see. For beast-folk, I bet that'd be a punishment worse than death.

"I have also put much thought into it but came to no conclusion," said Madame Zamil. "When did Cuvi betray us, and why?"

"We'll just have to ask him directly when we capture him. After we shave him, of course."

"Indeed, after we shave him."

The two of us grinned maniacally as we pictured it. Other people in the rear base recoiled awkwardly when they saw us pass. We kept on grinning evilly right up until the manager of the storage facility pointed it out to us.

C'mon, it was fun to imagine enacting punishment on the traitor!

CHAPTER 6

Massive Attack at the Badlands Base

227

A s SOON AS WE TOLD OVIS, the sheep demi-human who oversaw the rear base, that we were to leave tomorrow, he proclaimed that they would hold a farewell party. I didn't think that sort of grand event was necessary, but I was Sylphy's partner, and *she* was the head of the Liberation Army. Ira was the top mage in the organization, and the head of the R&D division as well, while Madame Zamil was like a commander entrusted with a decent chunk of its military.

Given Ovis's position, it would reflect badly on him if we left without being shown some genuine hospitality. Or at least that's how Madame Zamil explained it, so I decided to happily take Ovis up on his offer.

"It's an excuse to give us a breather. Just accept it."

"Ah, I get it."

I guess I'd ended up in a pretty powerful position after all this time. To think, I started off as a slave, with Sylphy trussing me up in a chained collar. Talk about being blessed.

"...Hm?"

As I looked up at the sky turning crimson, I noticed something odd in my line of sight.

"What's up?" asked Shemel. She followed my gaze, puzzled. If I was correct, she wouldn't be able to notice what was strange.

"Hey, Shemel? What color does the moon look to you?"

"The moon? If you're talking about Lanicle, it's the same color it always is."

"Is it now..."

In the sky of this world was a planet that looked about the size of my fist: Lanicle. The other planet, Omicle, was bigger than that. Lanicle usually resembled the moon, with a yellowish color, but today, it seemed red to me, almost like blood. But to Shemel, it looked the same as always.

"Remember that huge gizma attack back when we were in the Black Forest?" I asked.

"Yeah, I remember," said Shemel. "That was pretty fun... Wait, what's that got to do with now?"

"It's the same," I said. "This might be a sign of a coming attack. Sorry, but I need you to call Ira for me. Ovis, too, and any other important people here at the rear base. We might not have time, so hurry."

"Roger!"

Shemel moved fast. Was this because she trusted me even without any proof, or was it her gut instinct as a seasoned adventurer? Either way, I deeply appreciated the vote of confidence.

"But if we really are on the brink of a massive assault, who is it coming from...?"

Gizma were a possibility. A while back I blew up an entire fortress with powder, killing thousands of soldiers. Those bodies were devoured whole by the gizma, which meant I inadvertently fed them lots of nutrients. It was possible that those creatures then bred exponentially and were now on their way to attack us.

"The monster barrier's gotta hold, right?" I mused.

There was a large magic barrier cast over the rear base, powered by the bountiful magical energy pouring from the vein hollow. This wasn't a physical wall, of course, but a magical one that incrementally shot out magic waves that irritated monsters and kept them away.

If they were frenzied enough to not care about the barrier, or agitated for some reason, they could theoretically charge the barrier anyway.

"Either way, we need to prepare to counterattack."

The walls of the rear base were tall and thick. It was unlikely that gizma could break through them, but there was no guarantee they'd be the attackers. Since we had no clue what or who was coming, we had to prepare as much as possible.

"First... We should use everything we've got."

Golem ballistas were mounted at set increments along the base's walls, so I pulled ballista arrows (more like short spears) out of my inventory and put them against the castle walls. Once people started to gather, I'd have them set up at each ballista station. It'd be inefficient for me to run around and do it myself.

"And then... Just to be safe."

I pulled out a wooden box from my inventory, packed with hand grenades (the potato-masher kind with handles). If our attackers ended up being gizma, the goat's foot crossbows and golem ballistas would be more than enough to handle them. But if they happened to come in larger numbers than expected, it'd be good to have a weapon that did area damage.

That being said, while hand grenades were easy to use, there was always the danger of blowing yourself up... Those using them would have to be very, very careful.

"I think this should be more than enough, but..."

This would be enough to take care of the Holy Kingdom's proper military force, never mind just gizma. But I was still getting a bad feeling about things... I just didn't think that gizma would rush the base all at once.

"We'll just have to adapt, I guess... No matter what comes, as long as we have these walls, we'll have time to react," I whispered as if I were trying to convince myself.

I decided to check my own equipment.

I had a submachine gun, assault rifle, grenade launcher, light machine gun, a heavy machine gun, automatic grenade launcher, and an anti-tank rocket launcher. This would be more than enough firepower, surely. Plus I had ammo to spare. As usual, I was armed for ranged combat, but it didn't make sense for me to get up close and personal. This was my style.

"...And if things get real bad, I have my ace in the hole," I whispered, looking up at the blood-red moon.

Thanks to Shemel running all over the base, our expedition squad, along with the key figures from the base, quickly gathered together.

"Sorry to bother you all when you're busy preparing for the party, but I've gotta call it off."

"Wha—?!"

Not only Ovis, but the members of the party also raised their voices in surprise. I hadn't actually explained things to Shemel in full, so the others probably didn't know why I'd called everyone. I was deeply grateful for the fact that they hurriedly came together anyway.

"Let me explain," I said. "Is there anyone here who wasn't around back when the gizma attacked the elf village in the Black Forest?"

Grande, Tozume, and Bela all raised their hands. We hadn't met until after I left the Omitt Badlands. A few major figures at the rear base raised their hands, too. In other words, most people here had experienced that battle.

"All right, so lots of experienced folks here. That'll make things easy."

I explained that on the evening of the attack, the moon had appeared red to me and only me, and that today the same thing was happening. I also explained that the moon would appear normal to anyone else.

"...Now that you mention it, you said something about that back then," Ira murmured, remembering the details of the event. "The evening of the attack, me, Kousuke, and Sylphy were on the defense wall, waiting for the recon team to come back, when Kousuke suddenly asked if the moon was red. I remember now. Lanicle looked yellow to me and Sylphy, but only Kousuke saw it as red. He said it might be a sign of a massive assault."

"You have a good memory, Ira. In other words, although it only happened once, there's precedent. Things might not be the exact same as before, but that doesn't mean we shouldn't play it safe."

Bela quickly raised her hand. "So are a bunch of gizma gonna attack like before?" she asked.

That question meant she inherently believed what I said. I appreciated that.

"It's not impossible. Closer to the Kingdom of Merinard's borders, I blew up an entire Holy Kingdom military fortress filled with thousands of soldiers. The gizma likely disposed of those bodies, which means it's possible they've spawned exponentially."

"The fact you're not saying this with certainty means you have your doubts, yes?" asked Madame Zamil.

"Yeah. As you know, there's an anti-monster barrier set up here. Regardless of how much they've bred, would they really go out of their way to come here? I just don't think they would."

"Good point," she said. "Considering the barrier, it would be less strange if they went to the fortress on the territory border."

Ovis and the others agreed that, based on their experience of the frequency of gizma attacks out here, a gizma assault on the rear base was unlikely.

"But the fact that the moon looks red means something is coming," I said. "I'm pretty much certain of that."

In survival and crafting games with raid mechanics, the moon turning red was a pretty well-known signal to indicate the coming of a raid. Besides, we'd experienced something similar before here, and the fact that I was the only one who could see the strange moon was ample proof that we were on the verge of an attack.

It was undeniable that my skills were fashioned after survival and crafting games. I was willing to bet that me seeing a red moon as a raid warning was part of my skill set. I was naturally inclined to think that way.

"So, while it pains me after all the work you guys have done, we're gonna have to hold off on the farewell party so we can prepare immediately," I went on. "The raid could very well take place during the night, so could you tell the chefs to use their ingredients to make light stuff we can munch on during battle?"

"Understood," said Ovis. "I'll send the message across the base immediately."

"Our basic strategy will be to take formation on the wall and fight back with crossbows and ballistas. Outside of security officers, get anyone who can use a crossbow and prepare them to fight."

"Understood. I'll get the necessary personnel together."

Ovis and the head of security, a dog beast-person, quickly climbed down the wall. Ovis was super fast. I guess an herbivore beast-person was still a beast-person at the end of the day. He was clearly more physically gifted than a normal human.

"We'll get ready for combat," said Ira.

"Right," I said. "Ira, you can fight with magic, so you're good. Madame Zamil, Shemel, ladies—are you going to use crossbows?"

"I shall," replied Madame Zamil. "I know how to handle one."

"It'd be more effective for us to throw rocks than use a crossbow, methinks!" said Shemel. "Plus, Bela and Tozume have never used them before."

"We might break them by accident with our strength, y'know?" said Bela.

Tozume nodded. "People are gonna get really upset..."

"The head of security might be reduced to tears if you start breaking Liberation Army property, so stick to stones please."

Fortunately, I could get my hands on rocks and stuff any time I mined. I had plenty of big stones in my inventory, and I wasn't exaggerating about their size—they were as big as my fist. In the hands of Shemel and the ogres, they'd be deadly weapons.

"Are we on bombing duty?"

Pirna wore a big, excited smile. Did she enjoy blowing stuff up that much? Upon closer inspection, all four of the harpies looked pleased as punch. Was this their way of relieving stress?

"Yeah. I don't know if we'll end up sending you girls out or not, but let's prepare for it just in case."

I'd ask Ovis for some help to get the girls ready and equipped with bombs.

At my call, the party vibes that permeated the rear base quickly dispersed, and people prepared to counterattack the incoming threat.

Those who could wield crossbows collected goat's foot crossbows, equipped themselves with close-range weapons like swords, short spears, and axes, then spread out on the wall and began to monitor the situation.

Those with attack magic were equipped with staffs, and the members of the rear base R&D division pulled out prototype magiguns.

"It's fortunate we'll be able to test these in real combat."

"We've already fired them quite a few times, though."

Their pouches were stuffed with magic crystals and magicite, sources of magical energy, as well as cylindrical bullets. They were also waiting for the enemy to arrive. To them, this whole raid might well be nothing more than a weapons test.

"The projectors are working nicely."

"Mm, great visibility."

Powerful magical projectors were equipped at the top of the rear base's walls, illuminating huge chunks of the area around us. This was only possible because of the infinite magical energy coming from the vein hollow. Trying to do this anywhere else would burn through too much magical energy to be practical. I would've loved to make its energy consumption more effective so we could use them at other bases.

"Hm? What's that?" Tozume raised her voice from where she was keeping watch.

I looked where she was pointing, but I could see nothing in the darkness. Madame Zamil, Shemel, and the others were also tilting their heads.

"Something's there... People?"

Ira narrowed her large eye and focused in the direction Tozume pointed out. It was northeast or north-northeast, she said. People? Now? Here?

"Northeast, eh?" said Shemel. "Are they ghouls?"

"We took care of all the ghouls at the ruins, didn't we?" I said.

"Maybe more came climbing out of the ground?" Shemel suggested.

"All the ruins we didn't explore are still buried tight," said Tozume. "I doubt they'd be able to crawl their way out so easily..."

Tozume was right. They'd been buried for over two hundred years, so why would they suddenly crawl out now just to target us?"

"They're not ghouls," Ira whispered, her eyes locked on to the incoming figures. "They're zombies."

I'd expect nothing less from a mage of her caliber; she had successfully identified our enemies.

"Zombies...?" I repeated. "Aren't they moving kinda quickly?"

They weren't sprinting at us like ghouls, but they definitely looked like they were running. I really wished zombies would perform like zombies and just, y'know, slowly walk.

"Zombies typically move about that fast," explained Ira. "But our real problem is that we don't know why they spawned."

"Can they spawn naturally?"

"Not in those numbers," Ira replied, shaking her head.

She was right in that there were a lot of them out there. There were something like a hundred or more of them illuminated by the projector. Just how many were there?

Having paid close attention to our conversation Madame Zamil spoke into a small golem communicator to contact the officers in charge of the east, west, and south walls. "This is Zamil on the northern wall," she said. "Spotted an incoming mass to the northeast, north-northeast. Believed to be zombies. No clue why they've spawned. Could be a distraction. Guard your positions and be cautious against the undead."

"Understood," the officers replied in unison.

"A distraction?" I asked.

"Just a possibility," said Madame Zamil. "That annoying lich would use tactics like this, would he not?"

"Ah..."

An attack from the northeast. The undead. Considering those two facts, I'd realized who the mastermind was, though I didn't want to admit it.

"I'm fairly certain I tore him to shreds with mithril coated bullets," I said.

"We even took his Ring of the Dead," Ira added.

I literally filled him with bullets effective against the undead, and Ira grabbed the ring that he said he'd disappear without. He should've been gone. We both agreed on that.

"Was that ring the real thing?" asked Madame Zamil.

"It's definitely a magic tool related to necromancy," she replied. "I don't know if it's actually the Ring of the Dead, though."

"Right? There's no proof that he told us the complete truth. Especially since he's been around for over three hundred years."

Madame Zamil was implying that he might've had a plan in the event that someone took him down. And since there was no proof that the Ring of the Dead was the real deal, it was entirely possible that everything he'd told us was lies.

"...True," said Ira. "If he was a necromancer who became a lich, it's not out of the question for him to have prepared a vessel for his soul to go to, should his body be destroyed. In other words, it's entirely possible the lich has not been extinguished."

Especially considering we now had an unnatural number of undead closing in on us.

"Either way, if they're attacking, we have no choice but to blow 'em away, aye?" said Shemel.

"It'd be faster to take them all down than think about this tough stuff," Bela agreed. "Can I start throwin' stones yet?"

The two muscle-brained red ogres were playing with stone the size of their fists, anxious to start the fight.

"Wait for Madame Zamil's signal," I told them. "Also, just a warning, but you're gonna have to deal with some loud sounds if you stick close to me."

I released the safety on my assault rifle and packed in a clip of rounds. I knew I could take out zombies with regular bullets, but what about astral beings with no physical body? Back in the underground ruins, it was Madame Zamil, Grande, or Shemel and the girls who'd handled those things whenever they popped up, so I never got to test out my weapons.

"Hey, Kousuke?" Grande spoke up.

"What's up?"

"I could burn that mass of undead to ashes by myself, you know?"

"When the time comes, please do," I said. "You're our secret weapon, Grande. Y'know, in case of an emergency. Plus, this is a good chance for the folks in the rear base to get some proper combat experience."

"Hm, I see. Just make sure to give me the go ahead before things get too bad."

"Of course. I'll be counting on you."

Content with my answer, Grande flew to a house a little distance away from the wall and perched herself on its roof, apparently to avoid the sound of gunfire.

"Begin the attack!" Madame Zamil cried out, prompting me to raise my assault rifle.

All at once, the sounds of crossbows unloading filled our surroundings, a hail of large arrows cutting through the air and finding their marks in the zombies approaching the rear base.

"Looks like it's working," I said.

"If the vessel their soul occupies is destroyed, zombies can't maintain their existence, so they vanish," Ira explained. "Plus, these zombies are more fragile than normal."

"Why?"

"If you look closely you can tell— their bodies are fake. That's why you can't smell the usual rotten scent. They're likely made from the ashes of the dead or dirt that's absorbed blood."

"So, the store-brand version of a zombie, then."

On closer inspection, when a zombie got hit with an arrow in the arm or leg, it came crumbling apart. These things couldn't be all that strong... Could we even really call them zombies? They were more like evil mud dolls.

"But, uh, they're kinda coming back to life every time they get put down, aren't they?"

After getting hit by multiple arrows, the zombies were collapsing unceremoniously onto themselves. But after a few seconds, new zombies would emerge from the ground.

"Somewhere, there's a main body that's continuously creating zombies," said Ira. "Probably the lich."

"Power in numbers, huh?" I mused. "But can he really keep spawning zombies like this? Even if the bodies are made of dirt, his other resources have gotta be limited. The souls that go inside of them, or even the magic power required, no?"

I showered the approaching zombies in bullets, swapping out an empty clip with a new one as I questioned Ira.

"Of course," she said. "But in necromancy, there's a way to crush captured souls and turn them into magical energy."

"Oof, that sounds evil. So basically, they can use magic to kill their enemies, steal their souls, then crush them to generate magical power and steal more souls...?"

After reloading, I pulled the bolt, loading a bullet into the chamber.

"Correct. That's why necromancy was often used on the battlefields of yore. It was even called 'battlefield magic' back then."

"That sounds terrifying..."

Considering it was called "necromancy" in the present and feared as a taboo, something must've happened in the past to change that perception. Ira, Madame Zamil, Shemel, and the girls had all agreed that the lich, and necromancers in general, were not to be trusted.

"So, what's the plan?" I asked. "This kind of feels endless."

We had a limit on arrows, after all. They were being mass produced here, but that didn't mean we could just keep going forever.

"Don't worry," said Ira. "His resources will be depleted before we run out of arrows."

"What makes you so sure?"

"He's probably limited to the four thousand or so soldiers you killed at the fortress. Quite a bit of time has passed since they were killed, and he's unlikely to have collected even a third of those souls. After making that many zombies and producing more when they got put down, there's no way he won't burn through his resources."

"I see... In other words, he's mismanaging his resources, so he's gonna run dry fast."

"Mm-hmm. He has talent as a necromancer, but as a tactician he sucks. He lacks the fundamentals."

"SHUT UP! How dare you say that about me!"

Suddenly a loud voice shrieked at us from somewhere unseen. This hadn't been part of the plan, but apparently our trash-talking drew out the big boss. He had to be an idiot to come out of hiding when he could've just stayed quiet and kept up the attack.

"BWA HA HA! Genius necromancers never fail to prepare for any and all situations! You were fools to think you had gotten rid of me so easily!"

"Yo, I know you're proud of yourself and stuff, but this isn't that big a deal."

"It's mostly just annoying that you're still alive."

"But it's good for training."

"We're not gonna get any valuable drops, which makes it worse."

"Mad annoying."

"Talk about not reading the room."

"...No matter what you say, I shall kill you all where I stand, acquire fresh new souls, and gain control over the vein hollow! I shall turn my misfortune around!"

The voice was coming from a floating figure a few dozen meters away from the wall. He was kind of transparent, too. He must've abandoned his body after being filled with bullet holes and then burned by Ira, transforming into an astral monster.

"I think it's about time to exorcize you," I said.

I pointed the barrel of my gun at the dark figure, going fully automatic on his ass. The bullets tore through the air at over two times the speed of sound, colliding with the figure's body.

"GRAAAAAH!"

The bullets rained upon the figure, opening up fist-sized holes in his body, causing his humanoid form to collapse into mist. But soon, the black mist throughout the area gathered back together, causing his figure to reform.

"BWA HA HA HA! Not. Gonna. Happen! In my wraith form, physical attacks are meaningless!"

Arrows and large stones went flying his way, but they simply passed through his astral body. As he cackled maniacally, I pulled a new clip out of my inventory and reloaded my assault rifle.

"Huh? Are you stupid? I said physical attacks are meaningless! Are you incapable of learning?"

"Nah. Are you?"

I pointed the barrel at the astral lich and pulled the trigger. Just like before, the bullets flew through the air faster than the speed of sound and battered his body, passing right through.

Or so it seemed.

"GAAAH! IT HURTS?!"

This time, the astral lich cried out in pain. Of course he did. The clip I'd used was filled with mithril-coated bullets. If normal attacks didn't work, I'd just switch to silver or magic metal. The fundamentals.

"You got your ass handed to you the same exact way in the ruins!" scoffed Shemel. "Are you that stupid?"

"A real dumbass!" Bela crowed.

"Ladies, it's not his fault his head is literally empty," said Tozume.

I could feel the astral lich's shock at being spoken to like that by the ogre girls, of all people. Even over two hundred years ago, ogres were seen as muscleheads, huh?

"Still, it's gonna be a bit of a pain if my weapons are the only ones that do damage," I said.

I unloaded mithril coated bullets into him multiple times, and while it definitely hurt him in a big way, he showed no signs of dropping permanently dead. Considering fewer and fewer zombies were spawning, maybe he was using those souls to heal himself instead.

"At this distance, our weapons ain't gonna reach him..."

Generally speaking, Madame Zamil, Shemel, Bela, and Tozume were only equipped for close-range combat. Ira and I mained long-range weapons, but since the mithril-coated bullets weren't able to deal fatal damage to this guy, there was a limit to what I could do. It was possible that Ira's magic could end things, but she was busy guarding everyone here from his occasional magic attacks.

"Yah!"

"Whoa! That scared me!"

The harpies were doing bombing runs, but they weren't effective. I'd have to develop some aerial bombs coated in mithril when I got the chance later.

"Kousuke, do you require my assistance?" Grande asked as she landed next to me, having watched things unfold from the rear.

"Hm..."

While the lich used to be a human, he was a monster now. Would this be a good time to get Grande's help? It'd be bad if we gave this guy time to equip himself with any weird new knowledge.

"Sorry, Grande. Could you help me out?"

"But of course!"

Happy to be relied on, Grande began to smack the walls and floor with her heavy tail.

I was gonna be the one who had to fix the wall if she broke it, so I quietly hoped she wouldn't.

"Nngh?! That's the bizarre shrimp that ripped my underlings to shreds with her bare hands!"

"Who are you calling a shrimp?!" bellowed Grande. "I'll send you flying!"

The name calling was enough to send Grande into a fit of rage. She was usually so well-tempered, so it was a surprise to see her light up with just a single word. This lich guy had a real skill for targeted provocation.

"Bwa ha ha! It would appear you can fly with those tiny wings of yours, but I can make myself completely invisible! Don't think you'll get a lock on me so easily!"

"If that's the case, couldn't he have just snuck into the base and launched the zombie attack from there?" I muttered to Ira, who was preparing something other than defensive magic.

She gently shook her head.

"Kousuke, that thing could never pull off such a high-level strategy."

"...Good point."

Maybe he'd gotten dumber after becoming undead? Or maybe he was always stupid to begin with? Thinking back on it, he did say he was the first one killed in the shelter. Maybe the refugees took him out first because he was a totally useless leader during an emergency.

Grande, on the other hand, was so furious that all emotion had vanished from her face.

"You dare call my wings...tiny?"

That lich was a dead man...even though he was already dead.

"You are the first person to ever insult my wings."

"Huh...?"

The astral lich seemed to have caught on to the unsettling energy in the air, as he stopped cackling and began to watch Grande closely. Maybe he was able to see the surging magical energy within her or something."

"W-wait, young lady. Let's talk this—"

"KERBLAAAAAUGH!"

"EEEEEEK!"

Grande's silly cry was accompanied by a giant beam of light exploding out of her mouth, erasing the astral lich as he begged for mercy.

"He's gotta be dead now."

As usual, Grande's breath was less a blast of flames and more of a thick laser beam... It was so powerful that it seemed to have left no remains behind.

"I thought I was dead!" the lich proclaimed, invisible to the naked eye.

"He's a tough cookie. Where'd he go?"

"You trickster...! KERBLAAAAAAUGH!"

Reacting to the direction the voice came from, Grande fired her breath off again.

"BWA HA HA HA! You cannot harm me! Once I'm invisible, hitting me is impossible!"

"Grrr..."

Grande smacked her tail angrily against the top of the wall. Pieces were starting to fly all over the place, some of which hit me.

Please stop.

"I seem to have run out of pawns to use, so I'll pull back for today. But when next we meet, I'll have gathered even more souls! I will not give up until I have killed you all and obtained the hollow vein!"

"Well, Ovis?" I said.

"I really would like this taken care of... Please do something," he replied with an exhausted expression.

What could I do? If he turned completely invisible and ran off, there was nothing I could do to stop him. Even Grande couldn't pin down his precise location.

"Farewell, fools! I shall return to collect your souls!"

And so, the invisible former-lich taunted us and fled, leaving us no way to stop him. This was turning out to be a battle without any end in sight... We were gonna have to re-explore those ruins at this rate.

"Wh-what's happening?!"

Just as the thought crossed my mind, the former-lich's voice echoed out into the night. It seemed he'd failed to escape. He sounded like he was panicking, even.

"Wh-why can't I get away?! St-stop this!"

"Genius mages never fail to prepare for any and all situations," Ira whispered, holding up what looked like a magic crystal that gave off a terrifyingly powerful light.

Suddenly, black mist erupted from the ground in front of us, gathering around Ira's hand.

"AGGGH?! I-I'm being sucked in?! I-is this a soul seizing art?!"

"You're too weak," said Ira. "There will not be a next time for you."

Eventually, all of the black mist found its way into the magic crystal-like object in Ira's hand. The white light it gave off suddenly turned purple, making it look especially ominous.

"Ira, what just happened?" I asked.

"I used necromancy to seal the lich's soul inside of this crystal. Now he can't do anything anymore."

"Ah-hah! You did say you were going to read that tome to figure out how to deal with liches and stuff."

"Mm-hmm."

It didn't seem to me at the time like she'd been focused on reading that thing, but apparently she'd picked up some new techniques regardless. I should've expected as much from a genius mage like her. She was on a completely different level to that half-assed, self-proclaimed "genius" necromancer.

"Boss, is it just me, or is Ira one tough cookie?" muttered Bela.

"Anyone capable of becoming a court mage before she's turned ten is anything but normal," Shemel whispered back.

"Yeah, that makes sense."

I paid the ogres no mind as they whispered amongst themselves. I was busy lifting Ira into my arms and spinning around.

"You're just the best, Ira. So dependable!"

"Mm, praise me more."

With the smiling Ira still in my arms, I continued to spin atop the wall over and over again.

CHAPTER 7

Heading Home from the Scripture Hunt

THE NEXT DAY, after that zombie attack, we spent the whole day collecting the arrows that had been shot from crossbows and ballistas and fixing up the base's equipment. We were too exhausted to leave the day after that, so we decided to take the day off and hold our farewell party that night.

And so, the third morning after the attack, I stuffed my inventory full of the magic crystals and surplus goods manufactured at the rear base, then boarded the modified airboards with everyone else to head north past the Omitt Badlands.

In about three and a half hours, we passed the Badlands; in another three hours we passed Alpha Fortress on the border.

We glided along the side of the road, passing travelers and carriages and drawing all kinds of bewildered stares. By the time the sun was starting to set, we'd reached the town of Mazewood.

Driving at night was a scary prospect, so we decided to park the airboards at the Liberation Army's lot, build a temporary rest point in the corner, and stay there for the night. Given our current pace, it would take less than two more hours for us to get to Arichburg, but there was no reason to take risks.

"At the speed we've been going, if we'd left early in the morning, we could've gone from the rear base to Arichburg before nightfall," I said.

"Mm, sounds possible," Ira nodded. "Our magic crystal energy consumption rate is better than I expected. One should be more than enough for a one-way trip."

Magic crystals were blue crystals the size of a ping pong ball. It would only take two of them to fuel a round trip from the rear base to Arichburg and back via airboard.

"Let's check all the parts, just to be safe."

"Mm, sounds good."

Together, Ira and I set about conducting maintenance on the modified airboards.

Since their overall construction was simple, there were no issues with the propulsion devices. However, the mithril alloy magical circuits that transported magical energy from the crystal to the various devices had grown hot, causing degradation from constant magical flow. We needed to either increase the amount of mithril or widen the magic circuits.

As far as the hover devices were concerned, the large one had no issues, but the four smaller ones had gotten fairly hot. That didn't seem to be an immediate problem, but if these things were going to be used in the long term, the four hover devices probably wouldn't have a long life.

There was no friction or damage to be found on the controls. It was a surprisingly simple system, after all. Was there a way to further simplify things? It was forgivable for the controls themselves to be fairly complex. Foot pedals for the accelerator and brakes, a handle for left and right turns, a shift lever for moving forward and backward... Was any of this doable? If it was, then someone could drive with one hand while holding a gun in the other.

Or I could just equip the airboard with built-in weapons. I'd have to make it so that the airboard could move in all directions freely if I wanted to do that.

On a technological level, it didn't feel impossible. The vehicle could use foot pedals to control propulsion, and then movement could be controlled with two sticks, like in that one arcade robot game. If triggers were attached to the sticks, then boom, hover tank complete.

I liked the sound of it, but a technical airboard loaded with an onboard machine gun would be more than enough. Though, I could always build one on the side... No, I couldn't let myself go overboard.

Once we were done with maintenance, we had dinner at the cafeteria in the barracks, then chilled in the temp housing I built.

At this distance, individual golem communicators were effective, so I decided to get in touch with Sylphy. It rang several times before it connected.

"Kousuke? I'm guessing you must be close by."

"We're in Mazewood right now. We got our hands on an old scripture."

"Really? That is excellent. But why Mazewood? Couldn't you get back to Arichburg with Grande's help?"

"I took some time on-site to build new vehicles. We decided to use them to get home so we could give them a proper field test. Since we had to pick up and drop off some stuff today, we left late, but if we'd departed early in the morning, we would have reached Arichburg by the evening all the way from the rear base. Not a bad speed, right?"

"Ooh... Sounds like you have made something fascinating."

I'd been discussing the airboard with Sylphy for a bit when Grande crawled out from the pile of cushions in the corner of the room. Ira was nearby, sitting at a table and messing with that dangerous crystal she'd sealed the lich into, and the harpies were flying around outside even though it was dark out. Apparently, they'd gotten restless riding on the airboards all day.

"Is that Sylphy?" Grande asked.

"Grande, huh? How was the journey?"

"Hm, good question... It was quite satisfying. I got to spend the entire time with Kousuke, and he fed me lots of good food. Most importantly, we exchanged vows."

"Hey, hold—"

I couldn't believe she just said it outright.

"I see... I am happy for you," said Sylphy, ignoring me. **"It was worth having you go with him, then."**

"Indeed. Though Kousuke can be quite the wimp at times."

Look, that was only because the space Grande occupied in my heart was as more of a wise pet than a woman. It was hard to make that change so suddenly.

"I heard you acquired our objective. Was there any danger?"

"There were tons of ghouls in the ruins we first entered, but Madame Zamil, Shemel, and the others handled them," I assured her.

"Kousuke used his submachine gun thing to tear a lich to shreds," added Grande. "His weapons look strange, but they are certainly powerful."

"Ghouls and a lich, huh? I wasn't too concerned since Madame Zamil went with you, but it sounds like you had a rough time of it."

"You're telling me," I sighed. "Even after we beat the lich, he came back with an army of zombies to raid the rear base. It was a whole big thing. But we came out on top in the end, thanks to Grande and Ira."

"Mm, I was useful!" Grande chirped.

"It seems like you were all swept up into quite the predicament... I am glad everyone's okay. By the way, have you looked through the scripture yet?"

"Yup. It was written in the old language of the Omitt Kingdom, but thanks to my ability, I could read it fine. It's everything the Nostalgia-sect was hoping for. Ira copied down the passages I read aloud. I got a hold of a whole bunch of other books that I haven't looked through yet, too."

"I see, I'm glad. I'll be able to give the saint good news tomorrow."

I could tell over the communicator that Sylphy was relieved. If the contents of the scripture ended up being the same as what the current sect preached, it would be bad in a lot of ways. We were truly fortunate.

"We'll be leaving tomorrow morning, so we should get home before noon," I said. "You're gonna be blown away when you see the new vehicle Ira and I made."

The only issue was that these airboards weren't good for small, precise movements. Just moving a little and stopping perfectly was difficult. If they were used in town, I could see a lot of collisions happening. So what was the move here? I could add a mode that tightened the hover device's output to its absolute limit so it could brake quickly. But before even considering that issue, you'd have to work out how to deal with the blast of air caused by the propulsion tools. In a city, that would cause huge issues for everyone around it. I'd have to think of a system to reduce the aperture of the propulsion devices. If I shrank that down, the amount of air blowing out from it would be more manageable.

"I am looking forward to it," Sylphy replied. **"I plan on getting in touch with the saint via Lime and the others tomorrow afternoon, so please get here before then."**

"You got it. We'll be leaving early, so we'll be home early too. It'll probably take us less than two hours. Maybe even an hour."

"I see... Good to know. I shall see you tomorrow, then."

"Catch you soon!"

"Tomorrow it is!"

The rear base actually had its own long-range large golem communicator, but that was for Liberation Army use, so it wouldn't feel right to use it just for idle chat.

At the end of the day, perhaps it would be better for me to make my own powerful golem communicator...? No, that'd be pointless. The person broadcasting and the one on the receiving end would both need to output the same magic waves, so it wouldn't be that simple. Not impossible, though.

"Anyhow, tomorrow's the day," I said. "Let's get some early rest."

"Agreed," said Grande. "We should go to bed early."

She glanced in the direction of the entrance to our temporary housing, leading me to look over there as well.

"Eek..."

Pirna and Capri were excitedly looking at me.

In an attempt to locate an escape route, I looked out the window.

"Uh oh..."

Ingrid and Aja were outside the window waving their wings. Then suddenly, Ira was right next to me?! Grande was also holding my arm with her powerful clawed hands.

"No need to pretend to be scared."

"I know."

I knew things would end up this way from the beginning, of course. The moment they had me go out of the way to make temp housing, actually. Today was our last day out, after all.

"Bwa ha ha ha... Don't think I'm just going to keep taking this lying down!"

I had the ace in the hole that I'd acquired at the elf village. With this, I couldn't possibly lose. Today, they'd face Kousuke's Counterattack!

"I-impossible! How could this have happened?!"

"Don't forget. Medicines are my forte."

"You were a fool to think you could beat a dragon when it comes to stamina."

"Harpies are born knowing how to make harem colonies, Kousuke. You are much too naive."

"*GAAAAAH!*"

The next morning:

Today, my stamina is at about 50 percent. I repeat, 50 percent. It will take some time for me to recover, so please take good care of me. Especially Ira, Grande, and the harpies.

Was it just me, or had they sucked something out of me that they shouldn't have? Was I going to be okay? If I hadn't leveled up or gained skills and achievements, I might've died.

"Don't worry, we're being careful. It's totally safe."

"Ah, okay."

I left it at that. All we had on the docket for today was heading back to Arichburg via airboard. After that, I'd see Sylphy, drop off the goods we brought with us, along with the airboard, the prototype magigun, and the magic crystals, explain everything, and be present for the discussion with Elen... Actually, there was a lot on the docket.

B-but it was fine. As long as I ate properly, I'd recover my stamina just fine... As long as I wasn't running and flying around...

If it wasn't obvious, I was in the process of attempting to deceive myself.

I took a morning bath with everyone, finished breakfast, and got rid of the temp housing. The Liberation Army soldiers seeing this process for the first time were entirely flabbergasted. These soldiers must have enlisted after we took back the Kingdom of Merinard.

Sorry for all this, guys.

We said our goodbyes to the folks at the Mazewood Liberation Army barracks, then got moving on our airboards. There were lots of travelers between Mazewood and Arichburg, so we raised our altitudes and hovered above the field off to the side of the road.

Whenever we passed by merchant carriages, their bodyguards looked super on edge as soon as they saw us, but after less than two hours, we arrived back in Arichburg.

Did we have any troubles on the road? Mazewood and Arichburg were both on the Liberation Army's front lines, so needless to say, there were lots of soldiers on patrol, taking care of any monsters they came across. We weren't approached by any bandits either. The only kinds of incidents we came across were fellow travelers, merchants specifically, with busted wheels and the like.

When we arrived at the inspection line, I put the airboards back into my inventory, and, thanks to our positions in the Liberation Army, we passed right through. Nobody in line complained when we skipped ahead to enter Arichburg, and I was betting that was because of our flashy airboard.

Did I feel guilty about cutting? Nope. Our search for ancient scriptures was a Liberation Army mission of great importance. We needed to get everything to Sylphy ASAP, so I didn't feel bad at all.

Plus, if we stuck around after arriving so dramatically via airboard, we'd have been surrounded by merchants with questions. We didn't have time for that.

I sent Grande and the harpies to the lord's manor ahead of us once we entered Arichburg proper, since they could fly. They'd let Sylphy and the others know that we arrived. Grande was done accompanying me at this point, anyway. She said she was just going to hang around for a while, so she was probably going to bury herself in cushions in the living room of the manor.

Arichburg was absolutely thriving. It was the location of the Liberation Army's HQ, and where people, things, and money came together. Of course, the source of those goods was the fields of crops that I made, the gems and raw gemstones I mined and modified, the mithril and rare metals, and last but not least, the elven goods, like mead.

"It feels like this place is getting nicer day by day."

"Though poor Melty has been up to her neck in work," I said.

"Which is probably why there's been so much progress, to be honest."

The elven goods went for particularly high prices, apparently. I'd talked to Sir Leonard and Danan about it before, but elven mead was usually hundreds of times more expensive than regular ale. That was because, once the Kingdom of Merinard became a vassal state, it stopped getting elven products imported in, so elven mead became this rare, impossible-to-find drink. As such, it would've made sense for it to be tens of thousands of times more pricey than regular ale.

When I heard this, I couldn't help but tremble. The booze I leisurely drank every day was that expensive? Not that I wasn't still drinking it even now. We could mass produce it, after all.

Madame Zamil and I chatted away, greeting the various familiar soldiers who passed by. When we arrived outside of the manor, we were met by Pirna and the others, who led us to the meeting room inside.

"You're back? Excellent. That was fast."

Sylphy, Danan, and Melty were waiting for us in the meeting room. Sir Leonard wasn't present; he might've been out on patrol.

"Glad to be back," I said. "We managed to accomplish our mission of acquiring an Omitt-era Adolist scripture. This is the original, and these two are copies. This is the one me and Ira translated."

I placed the four volumes onto the meeting room table.

"Shemel and her girls did a great job serving as my bodyguards and helping to explore the ruins," I added. "And Grande was a gigantic help with pinpointing the locations of the underground ruins. Please reward them all accordingly."

"Do not worry," Melty replied with a smile. "You can leave it to me."

Would it really be okay...? It definitely would be. Melty could be a bit sketchy at times, but she knew how to value people. I'd confirm things with Shemel and the others later.

Why wasn't I reporting what happened with Shemel, Bela, and Tozume? I didn't have to. Those three would end up getting called in later to deliver their reports, so I'd just ignore it all for now.

"We found a bunch of other texts, but we figured it'd be best to leave those to the pros. If I help out, things should go pretty fast."

Just translating their titles and glossaries would make things easier on everyone.

"All right," said Sylphy. "As for the scripture, I'll also check its contents later. Can I leave the text analysis for the other books to you, Ira?"

"Mm, I'll handle them properly."

"You have my gratitude. Our call with the saint is scheduled for the afternoon, so feel free to do as you wish until then. Shemel, you girls are good for now. The guild will handle your rewards."

"Aye, aye!" Shemel replied. "If you need anything else, lemme know."

"Will do. I might be asking for your talents again soon. When that happens, I'll either do it directly or through the guild."

"Roger that. See ya later!"

"Catch you later, Kousuke!"

"See you."

With that, the three ogre adventurers went on their way. Considering how big they were, I immediately felt their absence and couldn't help but think that things had gotten a little lonelier without them around. They were easy to get along with, so I was hopeful we could continue working closely together in the future.

"So, how're things with the Holy Kingdom?" I asked.

"According to the saint, it's pretty much been decided that they'll strike at us and take back what they believe is their territory," Sylphy replied. "The Nostalgia-sect is calling for peace, but they're being completely overwhelmed by the main sect."

"I figured as much. There's no reason for the Holy Kingdom to lean toward peace."

We had taken back the southern region of the Kingdom of Merinard, but it was nowhere near as vast an area as the nation of the Holy Kingdom or the other vassal states they possessed.

Currently, the Holy Kingdom had a military comprising hundreds of thousands of troops... All of the Liberation Army's forces combined made for about five thousand soldiers, give or take. In terms of pure numbers, if they sent something like thirty thousand our way, we'd be doomed. Or at least, that's probably what they were thinking.

And normally, that would be the case. But with me around, that definitely wouldn't come to pass. I could mass-produce my trump card overnight if I had to.

"Also, the Nostalgia-sect's position in the Holy Kingdom has worsened," Sylphy added. "I suppose the main sect probably considers them a bunch of irregular sell-outs for denying their teachings and trying to get friendly with demi-humans."

"Aren't things moving a little too suddenly?"

"With the Saint of Truth out of the country, the main sect has made moves to expand their sphere of influence and power. Things have gotten so hostile that the Saint can't even go back right now."

"All of this happened so quickly..."

Did this mean that Elen was a target for assassination by the main sect now? Like when I got stabbed? Were we really in any position to have a leisurely chat about this? We had to hurry up and save her. What was my move here? Grande could carry me there, but what then? Would I rush in and kidnap her? How?

It didn't matter. I'd do what I had to do.

If I utilized my abilities, I could easily sneak into the castle and grab Elen. And if I managed that, I could use my airboard to outrun the knights.

Why wasn't I told about how bad things were getting? If I'd been informed earlier, I would've had more options available.

"Things turned out just as the Saint said they would," Sylphy sighed. She grabbed my cheeks with both hands, looking me square in the eyes. Her amber eyes stared deep into mine.

"The saint herself told me not to say anything," she said. "She felt that if you heard about her situation, you wouldn't have been able to stay still."

"Ugh..."

Elen totally had me read. I could see her laughing at me in my head.

"But what are we going to do?" I asked. "There's no way the Nostalgia-sect can flip the script on things with the current situation. The whole plan is a wash."

"Indeed. That's why we're going to talk things over today."

"Ugh... What are you thinking, Sylphy?"

"We have nothing to gain by abandoning the saint and the Nostalgia-sect. The enemy of our enemy is our friend, right? I believe we should make them our allies. Realistically speaking, the 'True Adolism' that the Nostalgia-sect preaches will prove to be an excellent weapon against the Holy Kingdom."

It was in the name, after all; the Holy Kingdom had a national religion, and if we went around proclaiming that the church's teachings were wrong, the skeleton that supported the framework, aka the country itself, would be shaken to its core. On top of that, the fact that the real Saint of Truth would be supporting this "True Adolism" would only bolster its legitimacy.

If we called in experts or researchers from a neutral third-party nation and had them vouch for the scripture and its contents, that'd be even better.

"We can still use the Saint and the Nostalgia-sect," Sylphy went on. "I believe that, despite the risks, it would be worth bringing them into the fold. We might also be able to count on them to mediate the humans within the Kingdom of Merinard who lean more toward the Holy Kingdom. We're already dealing with this now, but as we take back more territory, we're going to have to live alongside more and more humans who believe in Adolism. When that time comes, the Saint and the Nostalgia-sect will prove very useful."

She released her hands from my cheeks, and cast her gaze toward Melty and Danan. Melty nodded her head, while Danan furrowed his brows and let out a deep sigh; she agreed, but he didn't.

"Exiling or killing all the humans who believe in Adolism once we restore the Kingdom of Merinard isn't realistic," Melty said. "Not to mention there are those who've put down their roots here, and those who were born in this land as well."

"That's true, but..."

Danan understood the logic behind the choice but struggled with it on an emotional level. Sir Leonard wasn't there, but I imagined he probably felt the same way. The Holy Kingdom had killed his wife, after all.

"Anyway, that's where I currently stand," said Sylphy. "I know we don't all agree on this matter, but realistically we cannot keep fighting until one of us is annihilated."

"Kousuke could turn the Holy Kingdom into a barren waste-land of ash," interjected Ira, with a profoundly violent option.

"And if that happened, the nations of the world would come down upon us," Sylphy pointed out.

"Mm, I know. I just wanted to make a point. I do not believe that path would lead to anything good either," Ira said with a nod. "But if Kousuke chose to, that option is available to him. And he could probably do it on his own, if he wanted. That's why we all have to be careful. Overwhelming power can lead to self-destruction."

She stared at me with her single large eye, prompting me to nod firmly.

Up until now, I'd been fortunate enough to not be completely blinded by rage against the Holy Kingdom, but there was no tell-ing if that might happen down the road. Ira was saying that, if that did come to pass, I needed to control myself so I didn't take things too far.

"I got you," I told her. "I'll be careful. We'll be holding the meeting after lunch, right?"

"Correct," said Sylphy.

"Then I'm gonna hit up R&D and cool my head off a little. There's some stuff I gotta give them, too."

"Mm, I'll go with you," Ira said, walking up to my side and grabbing the sleeve of my shirt.

I could feel her intense resolve to keep me from doing anything stupid like running off to save Elen.

"...I'll see you later," I said to Sylphy.

"Yes. I shall put my all into making lunch," she replied with a smile before seeing us off.

I would do everything in my power to calm myself down before lunch, and focusing on work was the perfect way to do that.

I departed for R&D with Ira clinging to my shirt and Madame Zamil following silently behind. The entire walk, I couldn't stop thinking about how Elen could be in danger.

I wouldn't be able to relax until I got to speak to her directly. Now that I thought about it, though, the slime girls were on guard in Merinesburg. Elen getting assassinated would be bad for the Liberation Army, so wouldn't Sylphy have already ordered them to protect her? I should've asked when I had the chance, but I could always do so during lunch. It was time to focus on the matter in front of me and cool down for a bit.

As soon as I poked my head in at Arichburg's R&D division, the researchers and artisans thronged around me.

"Welcome back."

"We heard all about how you made some new vehicle!"

"We're almost out of magic crystals. Did you bring some from the rear base?"

"What about the prototype magigun...?"

"All right, calm down folks. Don't crowd me."

The ratio of female to male researchers in this division leaned heavily toward the former, and the lamia blacksmith in particular wore very revealing clothes, so I had to really focus on where I put my eyes.

I managed to push back the crowd enough to plop down the magic crystals and prototype magigun on the large table in the room. I also pulled out the Omitt Kingdom-era magic tools and the books we found in the ruins.

"YAHOO!"

One person grabbed the object they desired and dashed away to research it.

"This is..."

"Its structure is sound, but what is its power like?"

"It is certainly heavy."

Others began investigating the prototype magigun I brought back from the rear base.

"There are quite a few old books... Some at least three hundred years old. 'Old' might not even be the right word to describe them."

"There is much we can learn from studying the past. Who knows what new pieces of knowledge these texts might reveal."

Other researchers began racing their eyes through the books from the old kingdom.

"Damn, this thing is old!"

"The magic circuits are so wasteful. It's certainly made from lavish materials, though."

"Outside of its artistic and material value, it's basically a resource monster."

There were others insulting the old magic tools as well. These researchers sure were being harsh.

"Kousuke, Kousuke! I want to see that new vehicle!"

"As do I."

"All right, all right. Let's go to the testing grounds in the back."

With an alchemist, mage, carpenter, and blacksmith in tow, I headed to the testing grounds behind the R&D lab. It was a wide space used for test driving and test firing. I thought back on how I'd demolished numerous buildings to create this space; mansions that belonged to the wealthy class that fled after we took control of Arichburg. The Liberation Army was making great use of the furniture they left behind as well.

"This is the airboard we rode from the rear base all the way here," I said. "It floats via levitation magic tools, and the propulsion devices utilize wind magic to move the vehicle. With the current propulsion devices, at max speed, it moves faster than a horse. If you left the rear base in the morning, you'd arrive in Arichburg by sundown. Yeah, that fast. A one-way trip sucks about 80 percent of the power from a single magic crystal."

"Hm... So you have two airboards... Do they use different levitation magic tools?"

"I see one of them utilizes four smaller devices, and one uses a single large one."

"This tube...is this the wind magic tool?"

"The spell carved into it seems odd."

The R&D members immediately began inspecting the airboards. They figured out the whole propulsion device system shockingly fast.

"Ira, Ira! This spell on the wind magic tool! It's not complete, is it?"

"It's not. That's correct."

The alchemist called Ira over, and she set about explaining the modified wind magic that the propulsion devices used. She picked up a stick and used it to start writing some kind of calculation out on the ground.

"Kousuke's words gave me the hint I needed," she said.

"He can't use magic, right?"

"Mm. But he has knowledge and technical know-how that we do not." She glanced at me. "In fact, he might possess knowledge that could greatly enhance the magic we use today."

The alchemist and mage who were listening to her also turned their gazes my way. Actually, pretty much everyone was now looking at me.

Calm down, boys and girls. Staring at me isn't gonna suddenly make me produce new ideas for modifying magic, got it? Anyway, at this point isn't it a little late to be surprised that I have unique knowledge or crazy ideas? C'mon, folks.

"First, let's focus on the airboards, okay?" I said. "As you can all see, the propulsion devices are simple in construction, so I doubt we have to worry about them breaking down. That said, with a little rejiggering, I think we can make them produce thrust more efficiently. I'd love for you all to look into that. I think we should deal with each part one at a time."

They listened to my passionate requests, and it was decided that they'd focus on modifying the propulsion devices and the control system. The hover devices, they concluded, couldn't be modified any further, so instead they were going to look into how much time and how much it'd cost to make each version of the airboard.

"Actually, how exactly is this producing power in the first place?" one of the researchers asked.

"Normally, when wind magic produces wind, there's a counter-action to the output," I explained. "But there's actually a component to the wind magic spell that cancels out that counteraction. By removing that, we were able to make a new, modified wind magic that utilizes said counteraction."

"And you carved that spell into this tube to use the counteraction to create forward propulsion... How strong is it?"

"You should try it out for yourself. Just don't go full power. You'll end up dead."

"Dead, you say?!"

And so, the mages and alchemists, insistent on trying it out, ended up getting blown back one by one by Ira's modified wind magic. The artisans watching off to the side couldn't help but double over in laughter.

"Ba ha ha! You guys just went flying!"

"Now I get what you meant by 'dead.'"

"Ow, ow, *ow*... I didn't even put that much magical power into it."

"Same... On the flip side, doesn't this mean its magic consumption is really fantastic?"

"Yes," said Ira. "Both Kousuke and I theorized that the harpies and dragons are able to fly using this exact process."

"Kousuke's way of thinking is going to end up answering countless scientific questions we've had over the long years..." whispered one of the mages who had been thrown backward.

Ira trotted away, putting some distance between herself and the rest of us.

"I also created a brand-new spell from the magic that suppressed the counteraction," she announced. "Throw some rocks at me, you guys."

Ira pulled her mithril wand out of her pouch and held it up. The rest of us exchanged glances and then picked up some rocks and threw them at her. None of us wanted to hurt her, so we all held back and just kind of gently tossed them in her direction.

But suddenly, the rocks heading toward her all lost their velocity before reaching her and fell straight to the ground.

"Is this barrier magic?"

"It's similar, but a little different," said Ira. "Really try throwing some rocks at me. You can even shoot a crossbow if you'd like."

"I'll go and grab one."

A few of the artisans ran back to the research lab, while the rest of us started seriously throwing rocks at Ira. Yet again, all of them stopped just before reaching her, then dropped straight to the ground.

"Are you using the magic that cancels out the wind spell's counteraction to negate the momentum of the stones?" asked a researcher.

"Exactly."

"How would magic fare?"

"I surmise magic would be stopped as well."

Since Ira said as much, one of the mages lobbed a flame arrow at her. Just like she'd theorized, the arrow stopped in midair before hitting her, then vanished into nothingness. The arrows from the crossbows the artisans brought over, and the bullets from my handgun, shotgun, submachine gun, and rifle, all fared no better.

"What incredible defensive might..."

"It's still in the prototype phase. Activating this as a barrier consumes a lot of magical energy," Ira explained, putting her wand away and letting out a deep sigh. She was clearly exhausted.

"That might be because it's stopping the flow of the air, or maybe even particles invisible to the naked eye," I theorized. "Actually, if you used this on a living being, wouldn't they just die...?"

"No. The magical energy flowing inside a living creature acts as a kind of shield against magic coming from outside the body—although, things might be different with a truly overwhelming quantity of magical energy. You should still be able to stop an opponent coming at you with their fists or slashing at you with a weapon this way, though."

We decided to test this out and found that the weapons and fists were indeed stopped. It felt super bizarre, too. Everything just froze even though there was nothing physical to hit. If I was being honest, it was a deeply uncomfortable sensation.

"Y'know, I think there could be a lot of possibilities for this spell."

"Mm. On closer inspection, the spell's equation still has room for analysis and modification. In fact, it's utilized in other types of magic. I might be able to develop a completely new kind of magic from this."

Ira's large eye was practically sparkling. She sure did love magic. Or, perhaps more specifically, the pursuit of hitherto unknown knowledge. She did say something about being a pursuer of the truth before.

Most of the mages, alchemists, and artisans had moved on to either the airboard or the development of Ira's new magic by now, but I was still quite fascinated by the new prototype magigun.

Since everyone else's attention was elsewhere, I decided to take a look at the neglected magigun.

"Hrm, I see... This is really well thought out," I hummed as I looked over the prototype's manual. I was impressed. The craftsmen who'd designed it had based it on the bolt action rifle and front-loading musket I lent them for research, but they'd created it using this world's technology.

First of all, the feeder for the rounds was a front-loading system: you inserted the bullets from the barrel, then used a stick to push the round inward and load it. As such, the gun could obviously only fire a single shot at a time.

To load a common musket, one first had to load the gun with powder, then load the round so it pressed up against the hardened powder. But this magigun didn't require powder. Once the bullet was loaded, it was activated using a small-scale, magically generated explosion within the gun. The pressure produced then launched the bullet out of the barrel. They'd attempted a prototype magigun using wind magic instead, but its power was significantly weaker in comparison. They tried all kinds of different spells and ultimately concluded that explosion magic would create the most powerful weapon.

The gun itself was made of black steel. While heavy, it was extremely resistant to magic and could withstand the constant use of explosive magic. Since the metal was so resilient, it was a popular material among craftsmen who made quality equipment for defending against magic. Heavy infantrymen loved this stuff. It was more expensive than iron, but not nearly as pricey as the various magic metals. Since it didn't rust easily, it was a lot simpler to maintain than iron.

The designers had clearly studied the bolt action rifle I gave them; it even had proper clockwise barreling. The rounds themselves were acorn-shaped. The gun's bottom was hollow like a skirt. The explosive pressure would fill this empty bottom, dig into the rifling, and launch the bullet without letting any of that pressure go to waste.

From what I remembered, you were supposed to put something in the hollowed-out section. A wooden plug or a cork or something? Whichever it was, I could mention it to the designers later.

The screws on the base of the gun had been cut, and it had a breech made of magic steel, which was apparently the trigger for the explosive magic. If the breech broke for any reason, it could be easily swapped out for a replacement. Taking the breech off would also make the gun easier to clean.

As for the firing mechanism itself, you pulled the firing hammer back and pulled the trigger, setting off the explosion magic in the gun and firing the bullet loaded into the barrel. The magical energy that made all of this happen was supplied by the magicite set into the base that the firing hammer collided with. On a full charge, it could last for thirty shots.

If the soldier carrying the gun could charge it themselves, then as long as they had enough bullets and the gun didn't break, they could fire it as much as they wanted. And even if they couldn't, the magicite wasn't particularly bulky. If they carried around a handful of spares, they'd be able to get off quite a lot of shots. Hell, if they were in a rush, they could even use magic stones and magic crystals as alternatives.

Magic stones were disposable, but you could acquire them by defeating monsters. Magic crystals were also disposable but had much more power than a similarly sized piece of magicite; ten times as many shots, basically. The useful thing about magicite was that it could be recharged when it ran dry. Eco-friendly, you could say. According to the manual, the magigun was developed primarily with the use of magicite in mind.

As long as you had a mold and lead, you could even manufacture your own bullet noses in the outdoors—though the precision would drop slightly. And anyone who could wield even a little bit of magic could charge magicite. Theoretically, people could help resupply munitions on the front lines... Maybe? Lead wasn't exactly something you could just carry around with you, though. If we were going to do that, we might as well just make munitions en masse in the rear, then supply them to the front lines.

Would being able to produce bullets on the front lines in the case of an emergency be a source of comfort for soldiers? Was that the case for bowmen who could make arrows on their own? It wasn't hard to imagine folks making stone bullets using earth magic, and that was kind of terrifying.

Either way, as long as you had the facilities necessary to produce bullets, it'd be even easier to make them than arrows. This was a huge plus over using crossbows. In order to make crossbow arrows, first you had to make the arrowhead, then the arrow shaft, then connect the two, then attach the feather. It was a whole process.

Judging by the reports on mass production, the golem lathe and the lathe powered by thrust were really putting in the work, so mass production of guns and their various parts would be possible. The only problem would be the magic steel breeches. But if the plan for mass production of magic metals down in the rear base came to fruition, that wouldn't be an issue any more.

In terms of its firing capabilities, the magigun had a huge caliber. Something like 15 mm, maybe. And the firing range looked to be about 500 meters total.

Wait, really? That's about as effective as the bolt action rifle I gave them to study, isn't it?!

As for power, a single bullet could take down a gizma. Instant death for a human, probably. If it hit someone's limb, it'd be blown right off. We were talking 15 mm, after all. The largest caliber of weapon I'd crafted was the anti-materiel rifle, and that was 12.7mm.

A gun's power was heavily influenced by its caliber. But hey, my anti-materiel rifle was top class when it came to accuracy and velocity, so I was willing to bet its overall power and range would be higher than the magigun as well.

"Man, I didn't expect this at all... Was this a mistake?"

It was a weapon for killing. If it saw wide-scale use, there were going to be piles of enemy corpses on the battlefield. Plus, it was made exclusively with tech from this world. If the enemy got their hands on one of these and reverse engineered it, they'd be able to produce their own in the Holy Kingdom. Granted, they probably didn't have golem or hydro-powered lathes over there, so it wouldn't be that easy, but still.

There were lots of things that could use improvement, as far as I could tell. For example, its weight. The black steel used for its body was a heavy material to start with, but on top of that, the gun itself was built thick so that it wouldn't explode. It had to be over five kilograms. Carrying this thing around over your shoulders would be quite the burden... Actually, perhaps not? The humans and demi-humans of this world were stronger than the people back in my own world, so maybe this wouldn't be an issue...?

Actually, when I took a closer look at the manual, I noticed the developers had noted that due to how sturdy the gun was, it could be used as a close-range weapon too. I thought it'd be bad if the gun was bent out of shape, but the reason it was so thick was so that it could be used in close-quarters combat. In other words, this was intentional and not a design flaw.

Well, the fact it couldn't fire multiple rounds back-to-back was still something to look into. There was the matter of supply and also construction cost to handle as well. I doubted it would go into mass production and practical use very soon, but they certainly thought this thing through in terms of maintenance.

"I guess I'll actually give it a test fire."

What was that old phrase? "Seeing is believing?" I decided to try out the magigun for myself while the others surrounded the airboards, arguing over their specs, taking them apart and—

Wait.

"HOLD YOUR HORSES!" I yelled. "Who said you could dismantle the airboards?!"

"Don't worry, we'll put them back together again," said the dwarf blacksmith who was taking apart my airboard.

"It's just the tip," added the cat demi-human alchemist taking a spanner to the other one.

"Don't sweat the deets! Ooh, are you going to test fire the magigun?"

"I was quite fascinated by that weapon as well. Let us proceed!"

The blacksmith and alchemist pulled out some busted armor, logs, and old materials from storage, and placed them down as targets.

"I swear, if you guys don't put those back together properly, I'm going to use you to experiment with the mecha idea I've been thinking up..."

The researchers taking apart the airboards suddenly started to tremble.

He he he, I'll make you fly like little birdies... And if I fail, you'll come plummeting to the ground!

With that matter settled, I focused on the firing test at hand. The targets were approximately 50 meters away, with wooden plaques around them bearing several poorly drawn circles. The targets in question were the following: a log equipped with busted metal armor, a log without armor, and a large clay doll shaped like a human. The doll was created using earth magic and made to be about as sturdy as an actual human body.

"All right, let's start with the armored target."

"Aye!"

I was used to long-range firing.

I switched my sniping skill off, since it raised the power of my shots by 40 percent. Testing with it on would drastically alter the results.

I gripped the magigun and lined up its iron sights with the chest of the armor, then fired.

ZOBOOM!

The explosive sound of the shot ripped through the air, and the bullet created a massive hole in the center of the armor and the log and exploded out of the back. The recoil was a lot milder than I'd expected, considering how heavy the gun was.

"...This thing is crazy powerful," I said.

"Way more than I'd anticipated," agreed the stunned cat demi-human alchemist.

The dwarf alchemist looked equally blown away. "What's the point of armor against this?"

It was strong enough to render your average armor useless.

Next, I tried shooting the clay doll. A huge hole was blown open in its chest. When a bullet made contact with its neck, the head went flying, and the same went for the limbs. This was an awful sight to behold.

It was accurate within about two centimeters when firing from fifty meters away. How, you ask? Because the first shot blew a giant hole through the center of the target, and all the other shots fired after the fact fell inside that one hole.

I had the dwarf smith try their hand at firing the gun, too, and they had about the same results I did.

"The fact that even I can fire with such accuracy is something else..."

"With just a little bit of training, anyone can take out enemies with one shot from far away."

Just to try it out, we had Ira put up a standard magic barrier in front of an armored log, then shot at it. The end result was that the bullet pierced the barrier with no issue, went through the armor, and then through the log as well.

"...Is it just me, or is this thing too dangerous?" I said.

"I certainly have no complaints with its abilities as a weapon," said the dwarf. "However, in our current situation I believe we can overwhelm the Holy Kingdom with our crossbows alone. I personally recommend these should only be put in the hands of a small few, so that we can take out their mage squad when the time comes."

"We'll have to report all of this to Sylphy and Danan... But hey, prototype be damned, I'd say this is a nearly finished product."

Of course, there would inevitably be issues that wouldn't surface until we got these into circulation. For example, the trigger and the area around the firing hammer seemed a bit delicate; I got the feeling they might break if not handled carefully. These would be things to improve on as we went along.

"If we're going to use these on the front lines, how much stuff is each soldier going to have to carry with them?" asked the dwarf blacksmith.

"Bullets, first of all," I replied. "One fully charged piece of magicite will get them thirty shots, so that's the bare minimum they should have on them. If possible, sixty would be ideal. An extra piece of magicite would be good, too, just in case."

"And tools for maintenance," added the alchemist. "Having each soldier carry a spare breech is a good idea."

"Isn't that the core part of the weapon?" said the dwarf. "It'd be bad if they lost it on the battlefield. We could just have soldiers retreat to the rear if their breech gets messed up."

"Hm, that might be true as well," agreed the dwarf. "In that case, tools for cleaning the body of the gun itself, and tools for removing the breech. Sixty rounds for the gun. Compared to the weight of arrows a soldier has to carry, this is rather light. We could have them carry more."

"That'll all depend on the supply situation," I pointed out. "Depending on how things go, you might be right. Realistically, they'll have food, water, and potions on their person, so that's a lot to coordinate with their other equipment. If they want to carry a sword for close-range combat, that's also going to add more weight."

Since we'd gotten a fairly good grasp on the gun's abilities through testing, we started talking over the logistics of using it on the battlefield for real. We put bullets in a leather pouch to test its weight. A single bullet weighed about thirty-two grams, so thirty shots came out to about one kilogram, sixty shots were two. Quite a bit of weight, but if we could make a pouch specifically for carrying bullets, sixty would be the sweet spot. If the situation called for it, we could just give the soldiers more pouches.

"For now, let's make about fifty of these, put together a test unit of thirty soldiers, and have them test the guns out. Does that sound good?" asked the dwarf blacksmith. "It would be dangerous to suddenly introduce these into real combat without doing proper testing."

"That sounds about right to me," I agreed.

"Then I shall whip up a report," said the cat alchemist.

I nodded. This seemed to close the book on the prototype magigun research for now. It was hard to imagine the Holy Kingdom could have any idea we were developing such a dangerous weapon. When the time for live combat arrived, it was going to be extremely one-sided.

I couldn't help but feel a little bad for the enemy soldiers doomed to fall on the battlefield, but I wasn't about to stop now. All I could do was wholeheartedly recommend they surrender beforehand.

I managed to kill time until lunch in a rather peaceful way, developing all kinds of new things to distract myself from feeling uneasy. But as soon as I stepped away from R&D, I started thinking of Elen, and I could feel the doubt creeping back in at the corners of my mind. Was she okay? Was she in danger? There was no guarantee I'd be able to do anything for her if I was with her right now, but knowing how dangerous her current situation was, I couldn't possibly stay calm.

"Kousuke, you look worried," said Ira, walking beside me.

"To be honest, I am," I replied. "You might've heard this already, Ira, but someone once tried to assassinate Elen with a dagger coated in basilisk poison. She only survived the attack because I happened to be there to protect her and take the hit. I just can't stop imagining what would happen if something like that went down again."

I'd only survived that encounter because of a series of lucky coincidences stacking on top of one another; my being a Fabled Visitor, Elen (a true saint) immediately using a healing miracle on me, and the power of her miracles being enhanced because I was stabbed inside of a holy place.

If Elen had been the one stabbed, she probably wouldn't have survived... No, I wouldn't have let her die right in front of my eyes. I would've used an antidote or a life potion to try and save her.

In that sense, maybe our encounter really was fated. No matter how the dice rolled, perhaps we were always going to meet and become close to one another? Yet again I could feel the interference of some supernatural power at hand... When I first came to this world, if I had been dropped into the Badlands instead of the woods, what would've become of me? If I hadn't been able to start a fire and battle those lizard brains, if Sylphy hadn't found me?

Would I still have met her? Or would I have met Ira and Melty instead? I bet I would have ended up in the elf village one way or the other.

Just what awaited me going forward...? No, it didn't matter if someone or something was meddling with my fate. I would simply do the best I could, no matter what. Whatever any higher power had in store for me, I would do everything I possibly could to achieve what I wanted for myself and the people around me. God saves those who save themselves, right?

"I know my worrying isn't going to fix anything... Merinesburg is just too far away. And even if I did run off to try to save her, if I ended up dead or caught by the Holy Kingdom, that would just make everything even worse."

"Mm," Ira replied briefly. I'm sure she had other things she wanted to say, but she was holding herself back.

I can't imagine she enjoyed hearing me go on about someone I was attached to who she'd never even seen or spoken to. Plus, even though Elen was a member of the Nostalgia-sect, she was still a saint of Adolism, our enemy. Ira couldn't have been pleased about any of this.

"Hey, I'm sorry..."

"You do not need to apologize. I would be stunned if you could abandon the Saint. It's because you're so compassionate and sweet that I love you."

"Really...? Thanks."

"Mm,"

Ira wrapped her hand around my finger. Her small, small hand...

We returned to the lord's manor like this, finding Sylphy, Melty, and Grande all waiting for us in the cafeteria. Apparently we were the only others who'd be eating with them.

"Danan and Madame Zamil won't be joining us?" I asked.

"Danan is eating elsewhere," said Sylphy, emerging from the kitchen with pot in hand. "Zamil said she didn't think it right to partake in my cooking."

"You are kind of a princess, after all!" said Melty.

"'Kind of'?" Sylphy delivered a light chop to Melty's head "I'm a full-on princess, thank you very much."

Their relationship truly was quite mysterious, especially on Melty's side; she really knew when and where to turn the work switch on and off.

"So, did you get a chance to relax?" asked Sylphy.

"Yeah, I guess so," I replied. "On the way back here, I ended up overthinking things again, though."

"Oh, Kousuke... But that's who you are. Do not worry. I have Lime and the others guarding her."

"You do...? Then... Yeah, that's a relief."

I knew firsthand how strong the slime girls really were. In a serious battle with them, even I couldn't win. Melty could take down a grand dragon like Grande, and even she didn't think she could beat all three of them on her own. If they were guarding Elen, then she'd be genuinely safe.

While we indulged in the chicken-adjacent sandwich and soup that Sylphy made, I explained what happened during our scripture hunt and the whole deal with the airboards. I told her about the prototype magigun stuff as well.

"Sounds like every day was a busy one," she said. "Things were dull back here. Nothing but routine work, I guess you could say."

"I personally think it's a good thing that nothing happened," said Melty, smiling as she stuffed salad in her mouth. Or, should I say, elegantly munched on some salad.

"Indeed. Peace is a priceless commodity for you guys."

"...I suppose that's true," said Sylphy.

Someday soon, we'd be facing the Holy Kingdom on the battlefield. When that day came, death and carnage would become just another part of our day-to-day lives... Although I doubted whether I personally would be going anywhere that'd put me in the direct path of any blood splatter.

A part of me was relieved, but another part of me couldn't have cared less. I was still the one handing out weapons to people and seeing them off to the battlefield. It was there that tons of our enemies would be killed, and we'd probably see casualties on our side as well.

"Are you still having doubts?" Sylphy asked me.

"A little," I admitted. "But I've pretty much made peace with it."

In fact, I'd already made my peace with accompanying Sylphy to the depths of Hell itself. If I was gonna do this, I'd go all the way. I'd thrust myself straight into it. I had the feeling that when it was time to write the history books, they'd describe me as the worst mass murderer in the history of the world, but I didn't give a damn.

"Kousuke, you see this dinner knife?" said Melty. "It is meant to be used when eating. It is not a weapon to be sent to the front lines. Do you understand?"

"I get what you're saying, but I personally think I'm a bit more dangerous than that," I protested.

"That's true," said Sylphy. "You're like an axe... Or a mithril mining axe, I suppose."

"Hee hee, true," Melty giggled. "I would say you're about that violent. And if you underestimate a mining axe, you'll find your weapon and armor smashed to bits."

Grande hummed thoughtfully. "Mm, I am not so sure, humans. I would say he's much more dangerous than that."

"Grande is right," said Ira. "If we left Kousuke to his own devices, he could reduce the entire Holy Kingdom army to ashes on his own."

"Don't you think that's a bit much?" Melty said, as if Ira was joking. But Ira simply shook her head silently.

"No, not at all. I'm not joking."

"You mean like when he blew up that fortress, right? A plan like that?" Sylphy asked, but Ira once again shook her head.

"If Kousuke truly wanted to annihilate the Holy Kingdom," Ira said, staring straight at my face, "then, without question, he could do it from very far away, entirely safely, while their army of hundreds of thousands were still at their camp. There wouldn't be anything left of them."

I was fairly certain I'd never told Ira about the magic jewel bombs, or the rocket cannons using the new propulsion system we designed, but she'd been by my side for a long time now. She could put two and two together.

"If you're asking whether I could actually do that or not, I probably could," I conceded. "But I don't plan on it. We could beat the Holy Kingdom that way, but if I did that all on my own, it'd be a problem in more ways than one."

If we were gonna go down that path, I'd have to make magic jewel bombs, test them, make explosive devices to make sure they'd actually activate, and develop rockets to make sure they'd get to where they needed to be when they exploded. If we fired a magic jewel loaded rocket and blew ourselves away, what would be the point?

"When did your abilities get so ridiculous...?"

"They've always been like this. I'm a walking military weapon."

I've produced mass quantities of weapons and food here, created powerful long-range weapons that should've never existed in this world, and I was probably on the verge of developing a weapon that could suppress a large area from afar. If I was in the shoes of the king of the Holy Kingdom, I'd be sacrificing anything and everything to either bring me in, or kill me.

"...When you put it like that, we really can't afford to send you to the front lines," said Sylphy.

"I figured you'd say that. But if we're gonna take full advantage of my skills, I should be as close to the front lines as possible."

My abilities were all about structure creation, destruction, and crafting. They were much more useful closer to the front lines.

"So you'd better not just stuff me away in the rear. You gotta take me to the front lines."

Sylphy and Melty shared a silent glance and sighed. I wasn't going to budge on this. In a way, I was prolonging this war, so I needed to at least see the battlefield with my own two eyes and breathe its air myself. I needed to feel it on my own skin. This was my responsibility.

"We can discuss that at length in the evening," said Sylphy. "In bed, perhaps."

"Agreed," said Melty. "Let us go with that."

"Ooh, that sounds like fun," said Grande. "Do not leave me out."

"...I'm not budging on this," I insisted.

These women thought they could change my mind with their talents in bed, huh? My steel will could not be bent that easily. No bending here.

So please calm down! Let's handle this peacefully, okay? Also, Grande! Whose side are you on?! I'm gonna be in a ton of trouble if I can't get them to forget about this by nightfall. Elen's my only hope! Lady Saint, please! I'm begging you!

CHAPTER 8

A Sudden Change in the Holy Kingdom

AFTER WE FINISHED LUNCH, Sylphy, Ira, Melty, and I made our way to the communications room on the second floor. This place used to be where valuables were stored in the manor, but when we occupied this place, it was already empty... As such, it made for the perfect place for something as important and secretive as the large golem communicator.

"Your Highness."

Danan had been talking with a member of the Liberation Army before we arrived; he greeted Sylphy when we entered the room.

"Did I keep you waiting?" asked Sylphy.

"No, not at all," said Danan. "I only just got here myself."

"I see. Well done, everyone."

"Yes, ma'am!"

The soldiers in the room all greeted Sylphy accordingly. They were stationed there in case we received any emergency calls. They weren't just waiting around, either; they seemed to be doing some kind of paperwork. As for what exactly that entailed, I had no idea. It probably had something to do with the room's secrecy.

"We're going to be using the other room," Sylphy told them.

"Yes, ma'am."

With that, Sylphy exited into the back room, so we followed. That was where the large golem communicator was.

Sylphy operated the machine with experienced hands and began to call for the other side. It wasn't long before the call connected and we heard a voice from the other side.

"Heyooo! This is Lime from Merinesburg!"

The voice I could hear could only be described as "physically light and chill." Somehow. Even if she hadn't given her name, it would have been clear as day that this was Lime.

"Lime, eh? It is me, Sylphy."

"Your Highness! Doin' swell?"

"I am, actually. Kousuke is with me today."

"Really?"

"Heya, Lime. It's me. You been doing good?"

"Yuppers! I'm always super-duper good."

I could hear Lime's cheerful voice from beyond the communicator, along with some audible slapping noises that were probably coming from her hopping up and down excitedly. She must've been really happy.

"Lime, today's our scheduled day to get in touch with the saint," Sylphy reminded her. "Is she in the royal district?"

"Yup! She's waiting."

"Perfect. Can you connect us?"

"Okie dokie! Also, can I talk to Kousuke after?"

"Of course."

"Yay! Okay, connecting you now!"

After a moment, another voice came through over the call.

"Can you hear me? This is Eleonora speaking."

"Yes, you are coming in loud and clear. This is Sylphyel. We have good news for you today."

"What do you mean?"

I could sense her tilting her head inquisitively on the other side.

"Well, we discovered an Adolist scripture in the ruins of the Omitt Kingdom. We have examined its contents, and we found that they support the claims of your Nostalgia-sect. We have an original version of this scripture, and a copy as well."

"Is that so...? That is good news. Unfortunately, I do not bring such positive tidings."

"Go on."

"The home country has begun summoning soldiers. This nation is their objective. They plan on crushing our revolution."

"I see... I suppose I should be surprised it took this long."

Sylphy placed a hand on her chin and thought in silence. It was true that quite some time had passed since we arrived in Arichburg. We had already taken care of the Holy Kingdom's soldiers to the south of the city, so this felt like kind of a slow response... But the Holy Kingdom was a large nation. The larger a country got, the more time it would take to make any kind of decision.

"I see you are neither surprised nor panicked. Are you not afraid?"

"We assumed this was coming eventually, and we prepared for it. That is all."

Sylphy turned her gaze toward me.

It was indeed true that we were prepared for them to send the full might of their army at us. It wouldn't be possible to hand out bolt action rifles and maguns to everyone in our army, but the crossbows and golem ballistas were being mass-produced. Our magic metal production plan was bearing fruit, and we were already prepared to mass produce magic crystals.

Not to mention harpy bombs, which were highly effective against large military forces, and which I'd been quietly producing en masse on my own. Our airborne recon and bombing units were all being strengthened. Oh, and by the way, the only harpies I had relationships with were the ones who had evacuated into the Black Forest. Whenever I went to check in on their training exercises, though, the harpies had suspicious looks in their eyes... Dealing with that many harpies at once would probably kill me.

"Either way, you have our gratitude for the information," Sylphy said. "How are things over there? I cannot imagine the Nostalgia-sect is in a good state."

"Yes, well, you are right," Elen replied. **"The Nostalgia-sect in the homeland has been cornered. One by one, they're being brought in for interrogation and held captive... They're being moved to the territory in the Kingdom of Merinard."**

"So they've begun putting pressure on you guys," I said. "Seems like they don't care about appearances anymore. But if that's the case, will the scriptures—"

"Wait, is that you, Kousuke? Are you there?"

"Yo, I am."

"It has been quite some time since I last heard your voice. I have heard you're getting along well with the elven princess, the cyclops girl, the many harpies, and the sheep demi-human woman as well. You seem to be having quite a good time after leaving me behind, you savage beast."

"It's all true, so I can't deny that... But I want you to know I haven't hidden how much I care about you. With things so dangerous in the Holy Kingdom, have you been safe?"

"For now. Given who I am, I can tell when someone has it out for me."

"Really? Considering how you almost got stabbed that one time, I find that questionable."

"They got lucky. Are you trying to make a fool of me? Do not make me tear it off."

"Tear what off?!"

It had been quite some time since the two of us shared a back and forth like this, and before I even realized it, the three women in the room were giving me a look.

"I know you told us so already," said Sylphy, "but you two really are quite close."

"You seem very relaxed with one another," remarked Ira.

Melty laughed. "Hee hee, you're sooo close..."

Okay, okay! Calm down, folks! Let's focus on the problem at hand, okay?

I cleared my throat pointedly. "Ahem! Um, so what's the plan going forward? I'm guessing our number one priority is getting this scripture and the copy to Elen, right?"

"Do not think I didn't see you change the subject," said Sylphy. "But fine. And yes, you are right. I am not sure how meaningful that will be right now, but it would be better for her to have them than not."

"But of course. We need that text if we are to crush the main sect's claims and end these unfair interrogations and arrests."

"Hm, I see. Then how are we going to get these to her?" said Sylphy.

"Our best bet is to hand them over to trustworthy people who can transport them for us," said Melty. "Of course, if they travel via carriage, they will have to take the long way around the Sorel Mountains..."

Melty turned her gaze toward me.

"If we want to move fast and without being seen, Grande is the way to go," she said. "It'd take about two weeks by carriage, right?"

The airboard would be faster, but it stood out like crazy on the road. In that case, having Grande fly over the mountains would be much more covert. But if she was going, I had to go too. Grande wasn't a member of our army; she was cooperating because of our private relationship.

"That's true, but... We can't just send you alone," Sylphy said.

"Want me to break my horns off again?" Melty suggested.

"Don't even joke...." I groaned.

"Mm. Never again," Sylphy agreed. "I am not kidding when I say you could die."

None of us was going to let that happen. It was true that Grande's blood could heal her, but cutting off one's horns in and of itself was extremely dangerous. I wished she wouldn't calmly bring up the option.

"Then what are we going to do?" said Melty. "Do we have any other choice but to send Kousuke alone?"

"What if we sent a member of the Liberation Army as his bodyguard?" said Sylphy.

After observing in silence for most of the conversation, Danan finally spoke up. "Your Highness, we can of course do that, but there's a chance that they would only slow him down, depending on the circumstances."

He wasn't wrong, either. Having been kidnapped once before, I hadn't really interacted with human soldiers much, so very few of them understood my skills.

"But wouldn't it be too dangerous to send him alone?"

"I shall make sure it is not."

"You ask us to put our faith in you, Lady Eleonora?"

"Do you not trust me? We are as one, now. Or at least, I believed that to be the case."

Sylphy closed her eyes in thought in response to the voice on the other side. I also began to think.

First and foremost, not trusting Elen at this point was a nonstarter for me. I had no intention of doubting her. If she said there would be no danger, then I trusted she'd make the necessary moves to guarantee it.

There was no other choice but to send me. We couldn't afford to lose these texts, so utilizing my inventory system was obviously the safest way to go.

Since we found the scripture, we had to get it to Elen. This was an unchanging fact.

And if we wanted Grande to take it to her, it was only right that I went. I already had issues with treating Grande as a vehicle at our beck and call, but given our current situation, I'd get on my knees and beg her if I had to.

As for other options, well, could we have the harpies carry it over the mountains? That would be difficult for them on their own. Wyverns called that territory home, and their flight abilities were on another level. It would be too dangerous.

"Our only choice is to ask Grande and for me to go with her," I concluded.

"But... Well..."

"You don't need to worry about me. Unlike before, I've got all the equipment necessary to protect myself. I'm pretty sure I can take care of most things that come my way."

"..."

Sylphy shot me a pained look. Ira and Melty wore similar expressions.

"Then, should I prepare for his arrival?"

"Please give us time," said Sylphy. "This is a big decision. I'd like for us to meet over communicator tomorrow at the same time. Is that all right?"

"I shall await your decision. Just know that we do not have much time. Once the army gets moving, it will prove difficult to stop them."

"I understand. Just give us one day."

"You shall have it. Might I speak to Kousuke for a moment?"

Sylphy sighed. "...Yes, you may. We'll leave you two be."

"You have my gratitude."

As soon as she was finished speaking to Elen, Sylphy turned around and began pulling at my cheek before leaving the room entirely.

"Bwah!"

Ira rammed her head into my solar plexus, and Melty grabbed and pulled at the other cheek before leaving. As for Danan, well, Danan left quietly and immediately.

Soon, I was the only person left in the communications room.

"Ah, um, so I know I asked earlier, but are you really doing okay? Nothing—"

"I'm not okay."

I could hear her displeased voice from beyond the communicator.

"I'm terribly lonely. I've been wanting to hear your voice for so, so long. You big dummy..."

"Augh!"

Elen's overwhelmingly cute words made me feel all kinds of things, including a strong sense of guilt. Ugh, she was on the same level of cuteness as Sylphy when she acted like an innocent girl.

"I'm seriously sorry," I told her. "There was a lot to handle here, and the golem communicator is usually monitored by the Liberation Army, so it didn't feel right to use it for personal matters... Plus, I'd have to align things with your schedule and the slime girls' too, right?"

"Urgh... It is fine. I know we will be able to see each other soon, so I shall be patient. I am a saint, after all. If nothing else, I can persevere."

Apparently, in Elen's mind, it was a done deal that I would be heading over there. To be fair, I felt the same way, too. Regardless of how we decided to get the scripture to Merinesburg, I was going to have to go.

"I will be waiting for you."

"And I'll make sure not to disappoint."

And so, the two of us chatted for a bit.

"In that case... I hope to meet you in the coming days. Please do not disappoint me."

"Don't worry, I'm pretty sure I'll end up there. I'm looking forward to seeing you, too."

"...You do not appear to be lying, so I shall forgive you for now. I am quite excited as well... See you soon."

"Yeah," I replied sadly to Elen before cutting the comm—

"Don't end the call yet!"

"Hey, don't you dare end the call."

"We'd like to talk to you too, you know?"

"*Oooh*, right. My bad."

I could hear the slime girls on the other end of the communicator, so I hurriedly stopped my hands from ending the call. I'd forgotten that Lime asked to talk to me earlier.

"You can be quite cold-blooded, Kousuke," said Poizo.

"He was so busy with the Saint that he completely forgot about us," said Lime. **"That's our Kousuke."**

"Look, I'm sorry," I apologized earnestly, since they were totally right.

"But, eh, we heard it all, so we have no questions about what to do next," Lime teased.

"That conversation with the saint sure was lovey-dovey," said Bess.

"Super hot!" added Poizo.

"Ah, jeez..."

Of course they heard us talking, since we were using Lime as a throughline. I totally forgot! But hey, nothing we said was particularly embarrassing, right?

"We're also looking forward to seeing you!" said Lime.

"Y-yes, I suppose we are, to a degree?" Bess hummed. **"You'll be staying with us when you drop by, right?"**

"Since this isn't an official visit by the Liberation Army, you certainly can't stay with the Saint!" Poizo pointed out.

Indeed, our Liberation Army hadn't been recognized as an enemy nation by the Holy Kingdom. They viewed us as a rebel force, and the countries around us took the same stance. We were not yet a nation.

If Elen were to use her authority to approach us in an official capacity, her Nostalgia-sect's position in the Empire would immediately worsen. It'd be a poor move. It was possible she'd even be accused of treason.

"Yeah, I'm guessing I'll stay with you ladies. Elen might come up with some reason to keep me with her, though, so I can't say for absolute sure."

"**Gotcha!**" said Lime. "**Can't wait.**"

"**I-I suppose,**" Bess agreed grudgingly. "**Well, we'll welcome you, I guess.**"

"**C'mon, Bess, be honest with yourself!**" said Poizo. "**I know I'm excited to see him!**"

Talking to them like this reminded me of the time I spent in the sewers—a surprisingly relaxing time, in fact. Walking through the sewer system, gathering what limited materials I could to make stuff with, training with Lime and the others and getting laid out flat... Okay, I'd rather not remember that last part.

"**We'll check to see how strong you've become when you get here!**" chirped Lime.

"Nah, I think I'll pass on that. I'm not the sort to engage in direct combat."

"**But getting strong, just in case, never hurt anyone!**"

"I get what you're saying, but..."

"**Then each time we beat you, we'll squeeze you good.**"

"Squeeze what?! That's scarier than the alternative!"

This wasn't some sort of joke. The slime girls together were more terrifying than even all the harpies at once. I'd wither up and die!

"A-anyway, I'll probably be heading there in a few days, so I'll be counting on all of y'all."

"**Leave it to us!**"

"We'll take good care of you."

"You had better bring gifts."

Damn you, Poizo!

But what would make them happy? Maybe some food or something? They were big eaters.

"All right, I'll prepare something for you all. See you soon, okay?"

"'Kaaaay!"

"We'll be waiting."

"See you later."

With that, I finally ended the call on the golem communicator. I let out a sigh and opened the thick door of the room, stepping outside. After greeting the soldiers working there, I returned to the meeting room where Sylphy, Ira, Melty, and Danan were sitting and talking, along with Madame Zamil and Pirna.

They sat around a large map of the Kingdom of Merinard, spread out over the table. It seemed like they were looking into ways to get the goods to Merinesburg without using me or Grande.

"How's it hanging?"

"I don't know why, but for some reason the way you phrased that was deeply unsettling for me. Never say it again."

"Sorry, sorry. But realistically, putting aside the issue of whether Grande will agree, if we want to get the scriptures there ASAP, using me is the only choice."

Everyone went silent. I'm sure they must have all talked things over while I was conversing with Elen and the slimes, but as far as I could tell, nobody had come up with a good alternative.

"Let me at least accompany him," Madame Zamil suggested, but Ira shook her head.

"Impossible," she said. "You would be spotted immediately. Melty could disguise herself by cutting her horns off and wearing a hood, but she should not ever do that again. There is no guarantee she will survive."

No matter how Madame Zamil disguised herself, anyone would be able to tell at first glance that she was a demi-human. Ira would be noticed as soon as someone saw her face, and Sylphy wasn't gonna pass either, unless she cut off her ears. And in the first place, sending the top players in the Liberation Army was pure nonsense. Melty might've done it once, but cutting her horns off was extremely dangerous and reckless. I wouldn't allow it to happen a second time.

If we were willing to let someone take a risk like that, we might as well just have me deal with the danger myself.

"Our most effective choice is for me to take Grande there. It's the least dangerous option, too."

"That's... But!" Sylphy's voice was unsteady.

"And quite frankly, as long as I don't instantly die on the spot, I'll be fine," I added. "When I have all my tools and materials on me, it's pretty much impossible to keep me tied down."

Ropes and handcuffs were pretty much meaningless to me. As long as I wasn't quickly knocked out and blindfolded like before, I could get out of most situations. And quite frankly, after what happened, I developed a means against blindfolding. If I'd forced my eyes open the whole time, I could've put the blindfold into my inventory. After that, all they could really do was physically destroy my eyes. Magic wouldn't work on me either.

"If they tried to capture me, unless the person guarding me was crazy strong like Sylphy, Melty, Danan, or Sir Leonard, they'd never be able to keep me imprisoned. Don't worry. And more importantly, this is it, right? This is for all the marbles."

If we abandoned the Nostalgia-sect now, all that'd be left was a full-on bloody battle with the Holy Kingdom, with enormous casualties on both sides. We could win a war, but beating them too harshly could come back to bite us in the ass. Ultimately, we were going to have to pursue peace with them. To that end, I wanted to make sure we secured the Nostalgia-sect as allies, so they could act as our connection to the Adolists of the Holy Kingdom. We could not abandon the Nostalgia-sect.

"Sylphy, we have no choice," Ira said. "Plus, we could never stop Kousuke."

"Grr..."

"That's true... Sylphy, we should just do what we can on our end, no?" said Melty. "If there's movement in the homeland, then we need to prepare."

Ira and Melty delivered the final blows. Sylphy could do nothing but sigh.

I was happy that she was so concerned, but there was no moving me on this.

"There's plenty for us to do," Sylphy conceded. "Getting supplies where they need to be, acquiring weapons and arrows, drawing up a plan for the battlefield, recon, personnel, intelligence... Danan."

"Yes!"

"Work with Melty to conscript new troops. We'll be taking a counter-attack approach to the enemy forces. Don't just focus on training crossbow soldiers. We need engineers, too."

"Understood."

Thanks to the inclusion of powerful long-range crossbows, powerfully destructive hand grenades, and the airborne bombs wielded by the harpies, the Liberation Army's battle tactics had undergone a drastic evolution.

From what I'd heard, as a form of positional defense, they'd stop the enemy's forward progression, use the crossbows and golem ballistas to hit back, and then send the harpies to aerially bomb areas where the enemy was densely gathered. When the enemy's mage squad tried to break through our position, bolt action rifles and maguns would take them down.

Of course, there would inevitably be foot soldiers using swords for close-quarters combat, so all of our bowmen would be equipped for those encounters. The ideal was that they'd be taken down before they could reach our position, but nothing ever went that perfectly in this world or any other.

I would've loved to make and deploy a land mine generator ahead of our defensive positions, but the anti-personnel land mines I'd made before were still sitting in my inventory. I'd have to use them eventually.

Were they inhumane? Maybe, but in this world, there were no laws against using or producing anti-personnel landmines, so it wasn't my problem to deal with!

"At the earliest, we'll have you fly out tomorrow," said Sylphy. "Kousuke, please go tell Grande."

"Roger that. I'll head over now."

I set off to meet up with Grande to negotiate the terms of all of this. It really felt like I'd been relying on her nonstop lately. I was going to have to reward her properly for all of this... What was she going to request of me, though?

Regardless of what it might be, I had to answer her properly. We were really using Grande at this point, so she needed something of equal value.

None of this meant anything unless I could *find* her, though. She should either be buried in cushions in the living room of the manor or have gone to her bedroom here, since this was our first time back in a while. It was time to pull up my sleeves and look for her.

"WHAT IS THE MATTER, KOUSUKE?"

Since Grande wasn't in her bedroom or the living room in the manor, I ended up hitting up her place outside of town, but...

"What exactly is all of this?"

"Huh?"

Seemingly incapable of comprehending my question, Grande tilted her head. Except nothing about this was normal or comprehensible.

"Is something wrong, Sir Rider?"

"Is there some kind of problem?"

"Er, you guys..."

To try and explain things, well... A bunch of lizardmen folk were doting on Grande and taking care of her. It all seemed a bit crazy, and I couldn't wrap my head around it. They were treating her like royalty or some kind of object of worship.

"The problem is with us...?!"

"That is unthinkable! What can we do to improve ourselves?!"

"Wait, wait, wait! I'm totally lost here. In the first place, why the heck are you guys taking care of Grande? Start from zero and explain things to me!"

I pushed back her adorers and asked them for an explanation, prompting them to passionately explain who they were and what they were doing there.

"In other words, you're dragon followers."

"Correct! Those of us commonly referred to as lizardmen worship dragons! There are none who do not revere their glory!" replied the lizardman—er, lizardwoman, in this case? "Lizardman woman" was the correct terminology, but whatever.

The rest of the lizardmen voiced their agreement.

"And as the man recognized as her rider, we must pay proper respect to you as well," added a second one.

"This is only the obvious treatment for the man recognized by our mistress herself," agreed another. "According to Lady Grande, she's allowed Princess Sylphyel to ride her as well."

"I knew Lady Sylphyel was something special... She made a rider her mate and is even allowed to ride Lady Grande herself. She is truly deserving of being our leader."

The lizardmen nodded amongst themselves, their eyes sparkling.

Now that I thought about it, Madame Zamil often referred to Grande as "Lady Grande," and she always seemed to be extra polite with her, the same as when she spoke to Sylphy. Madame Zamil was usually polite, so I'd never thought much of it until now.

"Okay, so that explains why you're living the dragon celeb life, huh?" I said to Grande.

"I do not hate being doted upon, Kousuke."

Grande smiled widely as she ate a fruit that her followers had peeled for her. This was their object of worship, eh? To think, she tagged along with us because Melty bopped her and made her cry.

"Anyway, I get it." I turned back to the lizardman. "I've gotta talk to her in private, so could you guys leave us alone?"

"Understood," said the female lizardman who'd explained things to me before. "We shall be in the small cottage over there, so once you have finished your discussion, please call for us. It would appear you have little knowledge of our faith, Sir Rider, so I'd like to give you a simple explanation of it, if possible."

"R-right."

Quite frankly, I didn't want to hear it. It seemed like a pain. But now that I was involved, I probably ought to learn more about it. I resigned myself to listening later.

After watching the lizardmen leave, I turned toward Grande.

"It hurts me to ask this, but I need your help again."

"Hm? You wish to fly? I do not mind, especially since it is a request from my dearest Kousuke."

"God, that hurts worse somehow... Not that this makes up for it, but I'd be more than willing to hear out any requests you might have."

"Mm, wonderful. I shall answer one of your requests, and you shall answer one of mine. An eminently fair trade."

Grande wore a pleased smile on her face as she reclined on an oddly fancy couch that the lizardmen must have prepared for her.

"That being said, you and I are a couple, are we not?" she said. "There is no reason to think so hard about this, as far as

I am concerned. There need not be an exchange every time a wife lends a husband her power. Or at least there should not be."

"You might be right, but I'd rather not forget to be grateful and wind up taking your help for granted," I told her. "That'd be wrong. It's because of our relationship that I want to make sure we respect each other."

Grande nodded her head happily.

"Mm, you truly are a wonderful mate. So, what do you need from me?"

"I'd like you to take me over the Sorel Mountains to Merinesburg. I'm going to be there for a few days, taking care of some things."

"Hm, I do not mind, but is that not enemy territory for you?" Grande replied, tilting her head.

Gosh she was cute. But that wasn't the point.

I gave her a brief summary of our current situation.

"In other words," said Grande, "you have an insider over there, and you need to bring them something that will help everyone deal with your enemies?"

"That's it," I said. "And it's the sort of place where demi-humans can't just walk around in the open, so it's gotta be a human that goes. Plus, I've had direct contact with the insider there, so if we want to send someone who can get the goods there for sure, who can respond to any situation that comes up, I'm the best choice."

"I see... Understood. I shall take you over the mountains, no problem. I have seen that massive human settlement from above before. We shall arrive in less than two quarters."

"If we leave after lunch, we'll get there around the time it gets dark…"

"Correct. Personally, I think we should leave a little earlier."

"Good idea. It's not as though we have to head there after getting in touch with them. We can probably leave before noon or even earlier in the morning."

"Mm. We can simply discuss things tonight at the manor."

"Right. I'll be counting on you, Grande."

"But of course. I do not hate the sensation of you riding on my back."

I gently caressed Grande's head, and she smiled and narrowed her eyes like a cat. She really was like an adorable pet. She fell asleep like that after I petted her for a while, so I left her on her fancy sofa and walked toward the cottage where her followers were waiting.

"Welcome!"

The cottage was surprisingly fancy, and quite open. In the back was an altar bearing a chunk of Grande's scale. There was a furnace in the corner of the room, making it all feel like something of a gathering hall. It definitely didn't feel like a place of worship.

"We have been waiting for you. Please, take a seat."

The lizardmen bowed their heads to me and directed me to sit in a very nice chair, so I did as they asked.

"Sorry, but could you keep this brief?" I asked. "There's a lot I need to get done."

"Absolutely. We know all too well that as the Rider and Lady Grande's mate, there is much you must see to."

The shaman-esque lizardman that appeared to be their leader nodded in response to my request. They had quite the unique necklace of feathers and all kinds of trinkets on them. *Extremely* shaman-esque.

"Since ages of old, we lizardmen have worshiped the dragons. This was born of a great respect for those with strength. And dragons are both strong and wise. At times, they bared their fangs at us, at other times they lent us their strength. And on very rare occasions, they allowed others to ride them and become their partners. Though this was long thought to be nothing but legends and fairytales."

"Huh... The grand dragon elders also had a vague recollection of that stuff," I said.

"The elders, you say?! Have you perchance been to the holy land of the dragons...?"

"I've got no clue if it was a holy land, but I have been to the grand dragon nest deep within the Black Forest. I met Grande's parents and relatives and stuff."

"Oooh. This is remarkable. You truly are the second coming of the legend..."

Starting with the shaman lizardman in front of me, they all put their hands together and began to pray toward me. I really wished they'd stop.

"To be entirely transparent, I am from the Dragonis Mountain Nation to the west. I heard rumors of a dragon in the Kingdom of Merinard who lives alongside humanity, so I was sent here by our Church."

"The Dragonis Mountain Nation…"

"Yes. It is a kingdom of those who worship dragons and live alongside them. The blood of dragons flows within the royal family there."

"Could they be related to the dragon who fell in love with the human girl?" I asked. "The same one the elders mentioned…?"

The shaman nodded, rubbing their chin. "That is the story that has been passed down. If the grand dragon elders are aware of it, then it must be the truth."

Apparently, it was common for dragon horns, wings, fangs, and claws to appear on members of the royal family—just like Grande, actually.

"Our nation possesses flying dragon soldiers and dragon knights," the lizardman shaman went on, "and while it might not be a large country, it is said that our military might is equivalent to the largest nations of the world. Even the Holy Kingdom, with their anti-demi-human beliefs, can't afford to treat us lightly."

"Seriously?"

"Yes. Which brings us back to you, Sir Rider… No, Lady Grande's mate and partner. You are a member of the Liberation Army, and I sincerely believe our nation would spare no expense to lend you their support."

"Wait, for real?"

"To us, Grande in her human form, living aside humanity, is the living demonstration of our beliefs. And you, her partner, having been to the holy land and back, are a saint. To refuse to support your Liberation Army would go against our beliefs.

"And on top of that, thanks to the Holy Kingdom's beliefs, our nations have never exactly seen eye to eye," the lizardman shaman added, shaking their head. "I believe our nation has already sent an urgent messenger. There will be official contact from them in the near future."

"Wh-whoa."

Was it really okay to get this kind of backing from another nation this way...? No, this had to do with religion, so... The lizardman shaman was clearly a passionate believer, so if the rest of them were similar, it was possible.

"I'll pass on the information to the higher-ups of our organization," I assured them. "They'll probably be getting in touch with you guys shortly, so be ready for that."

"Understood. In the meantime, would you like to hear more about our faith?"

"Sorry. I can't explain the details, but I really am mega busy right now. Once things calm down a bit, I promise to come and ask you for more details. But for today, I need to get going."

"I see... That is unfortunate, but I understand. I look forward to your return."

"I promise I'll make it happen."

This would have massive repercussions for not just me and Grande, but the Liberation Army at large. It was clear even to me that the shaman wasn't just making things up, which meant I needed to approach this with a certain level of seriousness.

"Then I'll see you later."

"Indeed. Until we meet again."

The lizardman shaman made a complex sign with their hands, then bowed, and the other followers did the same.

So now we had an outside nation getting involved thanks to Grande's presence... Just what sort of impact would this have on our fight?

AFTERWORD

THANK YOU SO MUCH for picking up Volume 5 of *Survival in Another World With My Mistress*!

How have you all been doing? It's currently the middle of winter where I live, and it's crazy cold. I'm talking below freezing temperature, obviously. So, so cold.

Now then, I suppose I'll talk about some of the table setting details that didn't come to light in this volume. Specifically, about overlords.

So overlords are unique beings that randomly occur within demi-human races. An overlord is born with a much stronger body, overwhelming magical potential, and a life span equal to or greater than that of an elf or a cyclops.

The reason behind their existence is currently unknown, but it would seem as though they appear most frequently at the turning of an era, or in periods when demi-humans are struggling the most.

Additionally, on occasion, beings called "heroes" are born among the humans, and much like overlords, they possess powerful bodies and magical potential at birth. Conversely, heroes appear during eras when humanity finds itself struggling, so researchers believe that both overlords and heroes are beings born from the same concept.

Long ago, an overlord used their tremendous power to raise the ranks of demi-humans and nearly annihilate humanity. The overlord was called the Demon King.

In the end, a hero appeared among the humans as a sort of counter-balance, and defeated the Demon King.

A long period of time followed, bringing us to the present, where humans and demi-humans are both considered one race called "humanoids." Compared to many years ago, they live alongside each other relatively peacefully. That said, the teachings of modern Adolism threaten that peace in a big way.

The fact that Melty, an overlord, was born during this period was perhaps inevitable. The problem is, who made that decision?

And that brings me to the end of my overlord explanation, though I was careful to leave some mysteries unresolved. Next I'll talk about the stars of this volume, the ogres—crap, I've got no more pages! I won't be able to write about them now! I guess I'll have to save this for the next volume!

So with that, it's time to depart.

To "I" of GC Novels, Yappen who draws all the amazing illustrations, everyone involved with the publishing of this volume, and all the readers who picked up this book: you have my sincerest gratitude. Thank you very much.

I'll see you in the next volume!